SIDEWINDERS:
CUTTHROAT CANYON

SIDEWINDERS:
CUTTHROAT CANYON

William W. Johnstone
with *J. A. Johnstone*

PINNACLE BOOKS
Kensington Publishing Corp.
www.kensingtonbooks.com

PINNACLE BOOKS are published by

Kensington Publishing Corp.
119 West 40th Street
New York, NY 10018

PUBLISHER'S NOTE
Following the death of William W. Johnstone, the Johnstone family is
working with a carefully selected writer to organize and complete Mr.
Johnstone's outlines and many unfinished manuscripts to create addi-
tional novels in all of his series like The Last Gunfighter, Mountain
Man, and Eagles, among others. The novel was inspired by Mr. Johnstone's superb storytelling.

All Kensington titles, imprints, and distributed lines are available at
special quantity discounts for bulk purchases for sales promotions, pre-
miums, fund-raising, educational, or institutional use. Special book ex-
cerpts or customized printings can also be created to fit specific needs.
For details, write or phone the office of the Kensington special sales
manager: Kensington Publishing Corp., 119 West 40th Street, New York,
NY 10018, attn: Special Sales Department; Phone: 1-800-221-2647.

ISBN-13: 978-0-7860-1999-1
ISBN-10: 0-7860-1999-9

First Printing: June 2009

10 9 8 7 6 5 4 3 2 1

Printed in the United States of America

The wise man avoids trouble,
so as to grow old with grace and dignity.
—Sir Harry Fulton

Nobody ever accused us of bein' smart.
—Scratch Morton

CHAPTER 1

Scratch Morton dug an elbow into Bo Creel's ribs, nodded toward the building they were passing, and said, "That's new since the last time we were here, ain't it?"

As Bo looked at the building, a nearly naked woman leaned out a second-story window and called to them, "Hey, boys, come on inside and pay me a visit."

Bo ticked a finger against the brim of his black, flat-crowned hat, said politely, "Ma'am," then used his other hand to grasp his trail partner's arm and drag him on past the whorehouse's entrance.

"You'd have to pay, all right, like the lady said," he told Scratch, "and we're a mite low on funds right now."

"Well, then, let's find a saloon and a poker game," Scratch suggested. "There should be plenty of both in El Paso."

Bo didn't doubt that. The border town was famous for its vices. That was the main reason Scratch had insisted on stopping here. They had been on the trail for a long time, and Scratch had a powerful hankering for whiskey and women, not necessarily in that order. They had come home to Texas, and Scratch was of a mind to celebrate.

For most of the past two score years, the two drifters had been somewhere else other than the state where they were born. Of course, Texas hadn't been a state when Bo Creel and Scratch Morton entered the world. It was still part of Mexico then. They had been youngsters when the revolution came along, and after that they'd been citizens of the Republic of Texas for a while.

By the time Texas entered the Union in 1845, Bo and Scratch had pulled up stakes and gone on the drift, due to Scratch's fiddle-footed nature and Bo's desire to put the tragedy of losing his wife and family to sickness behind him. They had been back to the Lone Star state a few times since then, but mostly they'd been elsewhere, seeing what was on the other side of the next hill.

The long years showed in their tanned, weathered faces, as well as in Scratch's shock of silver hair and the strands of gray shot through Bo's dark brown hair, but not in their rangy, muscular bodies that still moved with the easy grace of younger men.

As befitting his deeply held belief that he was God's gift to women, Scratch was something of a dandy, sporting a big, cream-colored Stetson, a fringed buckskin jacket over a white shirt, and tan whipcord pants tucked into high-topped brown boots. The elaborately tooled leather gunbelt strapped around his hips supported a pair of holstered Remington revolvers with long barrels and ivory grips. People had accused him in the past of looking like a Wild West Show cowboy, and he took that as a compliment.

Bo, on the other hand, had been mistaken for a preacher more than once with his sober black suit and vest and hat. His gunbelt and holster were as plain as could be, and so was the lone .45 he carried. Not many preachers, though, had strong, long-fingered hands that could handle a gun and a deck of cards with equal deftness.

Having lived through the chaos of the Runaway Scrape and the Battle of San Jacinto, Bo and Scratch both claimed to want nothing but peace and quiet. Somehow, though, those things had a habit of avoiding them. It seemed that despite their best efforts, wherever they went, trouble soon followed.

Bo was determined that things would be different here in El Paso, since they were back on Texas soil. They would replenish their funds, have a few good meals, sleep under a roof instead of the stars, stock up on supplies, then ride on to wherever the trail took them next.

It was a good plan, but it required money. Bo set his eye on the Birdcage Saloon in the next block as a likely source of those funds.

He recalled the Birdcage from previous visits to the border town. It was run by a big German named August Strittmayer who insisted that all the games of chance there be conducted in an honest fashion. Bo was sure some of the professional gamblers who played at the Birdcage skirted the edge of honesty from time to time, but by and large, Strittmayer's influence kept the games clean.

"You can have a beer at the bar in Strittmayer's place while I see if there's an empty chair at any of the tables," he suggested to Scratch.

"Now you're talkin'," Scratch agreed with a grin. "The scenery's plumb nice in there, too."

Bo knew what Scratch was referring to. On a raised platform on one side of the room sat the big cage that gave the place its name. Instead of a bird perching on the swing that hung inside the cage, one of the saloon girls was always there, in the next thing to her birthday suit. The girls took turns rocking back and forth on that swing. They might not sing like birds, but their plumage was mighty nice.

When Bo and Scratch pushed through the batwings and went inside, they saw that the saloon was doing its usual brisk business. Thirsty cowboys filled most of the places at the bar and occupied all but a few of the tables. A group of men gathered around the birdcage in the corner, calling out lewd comments to the girl on the swing.

Strittmayer had laid down the law where those girls were concerned: The saloon's bouncers would deal quickly and harshly with any man who so much as set foot inside the cage. He couldn't stop the comments, though, and the girls who worked the cage soon learned to ignore them and continue to wear a placid smile.

The air was full of the usual saloon smells—whiskey, tobacco, sweat, and piss—and the usual sounds—loud talk, raucous laughter, tinny piano music, the click of a roulette wheel, the whisper of cards being shuffled and dealt. Bo nodded toward the bar and told Scratch, "Go grab a beer."

"I can handle that job," Scratch said.

Bo spotted a dealer he knew at one of the baize-covered tables where poker games were going on. The man wore the elaborate waistcoat and frilly shirt of a professional tinhorn. Close acquaintances knew him as Three-Toed Johnny because of an accident with an ax while splitting some firewood one frosty morning. He was an honest dealer, at least most of the time. Bo hadn't seen him for a couple of years. The last place they had run into each other was Wichita.

The hand was over as Bo came up to the table, and Johnny was raking in the pot. No surprise there. One of the players said in a tone of disgust, "I'm busted. Guess I'm out." He scraped back his chair and stood up.

Johnny stopped him and held out a chip. "No man leaves my table without enough money for a drink, my friend," he said.

The man hesitated, then said, "Thanks," and took the chip. He headed for the bar to cash it in and get that drink.

Bo said, "Some people say that's what got Bill Hickok killed. He busted Jack McCall at cards, then tossed him a mercy chip like that the day before McCall came back into the Number Ten and shot him."

Three-Toed Johnny looked up and grinned. "Bo Creel! I didn't see you come in."

Bo sort of doubted that. Johnny didn't miss much.

"It's good to see you again, amigo," the gambler went on.

Bo gestured toward the empty chair. "You have room for another player?"

"Most assuredly. Sit down."

"Wait just a damned minute," a man on the other side of the table said. He was dressed in an expensive suit, but the big Stetson pushed back on his head, the seamed face of a man who spent most of his life outdoors, and the calluses on his hands all told Bo that he was a cattleman. The suit and the big ring on one of his fingers said he was probably a pretty successful one. So did the arrogant tone of his voice.

"Is there a problem, Mr. Churchill?" Johnny asked. Bo could tell that the gambler was keeping his own voice deceptively mild.

By using the hombre's name, Johnny had also identified him for Bo. The upset man was Little Ed Churchill, the owner of one of the largest ranches in West Texas. Little Ed wasn't little at all, but his pa Big Ed had been even bigger, Bo recalled, hence the name.

"This fella's a friend of yours," Churchill said as he jerked a hand toward Bo. "You said as much yourself just now."

"And that's a problem because . . . ?"

"How do the rest of us know that you and him aren't about to run some sort of tomfoolery on us?"

Johnny's eyes hardened. "You mean you're afraid we'll cheat you?" he asked, and his soft tone was really deceptive now. Bo knew how angry Johnny was.

Bo wasn't too happy about being called a cheater himself.

"I've seen you play, Fontana," Churchill said. "You win a lot."

"It's my job to win. But I do it by honest means."

So Johnny was using the last name Fontana now, Bo thought. Johnny had had half a dozen different last names at least. Bo wasn't sure Johnny even remembered what name he'd been born with.

"To tell you the truth," Johnny went on, "I don't need to cheat to beat you, Churchill. All I have to do is take advantage of your natural recklessness."

One of the other players rested both hands on the table, in plain sight, and said, "I don't like the way this conversation is going. I came here for a friendly game, gentlemen, not a display of bravado. And certainly not for gunplay."

"Shut the hell up, Davidson," Churchill snapped.

The man called Davidson paled and sat up straighter. He was in his thirties, well dressed, with tightly curled brown hair and a mustache that curled up on the tips. As Davidson moved forward a little in his chair, Bo caught a glimpse of a gun holstered in a shoulder rig under the man's left arm. Despite his town suit, Davidson looked tough enough to use the iron if he had to.

"I can go find another game," Bo suggested. He didn't want to sit in on this particular one badly enough to cause a shootout. "I just thought I'd say hello to an old friend."

"There's no need for that, Bo," Johnny said. He gave Churchill a flat, level stare and went on. "Bo Creel is an honest man, and so am I. If you doubt either of those things, Churchill, maybe it's you who had better find another game."

"I won't be stampeded, damn it." Churchill nodded toward the empty chair. "Sit down, Creel. But remember that I'll be watching you." He looked at Johnny. "Both of you."

"It's going to be a distinct pleasure taking your money," Johnny drawled.

"Shut up and deal the cards."

Johnny shut up and dealt.

CHAPTER 2

Bo wasn't sure what would have happened if he or Johnny had won the first hand after he sat down. Little Ed Churchill might have been more convinced than ever that he was being cheated.

The man called Davidson was the one who raked in that pot, however. In fact, judging by the way what had been a fairly small pile of chips in front of Davidson when Bo sat down began to grow after that, the man's luck appeared to have changed for the better.

Davidson won three out of the next five hands, with Bo taking one and Johnny the other. Bo understood now what Johnny meant about Churchill being reckless. The man was a plunger when he had a decent hand and a poor bluffer when he didn't. Bo wasn't surprised that Churchill lost a considerable amount of money in a short period of time.

The cattleman's face was red to start with, and it flushed even more as he continued to lose. Bo felt trouble building. If not for the fact that he and Scratch needed money, he would have just as soon gotten up from the table and walked away.

Scratch ambled over from the bar and stood there watching the game with a mug of beer in his hand. Churchill glanced at him and glared.

"What two-bit melodrama did you come from?"

Scratch's easy grin didn't hide the flash of anger in his eyes that Bo noted. "I'll let that remark pass, friend," the silver-haired Texan said. "I can see you've got troubles of your own."

"What the hell do you mean by that?"

"Well, from what I've seen so far of your poker playin', my hundred-and-four-year-old grandma could likely whip you at cards."

Churchill slapped his pasteboards facedown on the table and started to stand up. "Why, you grinning son of a—"

"Gentlemen, gentlemen!" The booming, Teutonic tones of August Strittmayer filled the air as the saloon's proprietor loomed over the table. "All the games in the Birdcage are friendly, *nicht wahr*?"

"Don't talk that damned Dutchy talk at me," Churchill snapped. He settled back down in his chair, though. Strittmayer was an imposing figure, two yards tall and a yard wide in brown tweed, with a bald head and big, knobby fists.

"Trouble here, Johnny?" Strittmayer asked.

"Not really," Johnny answered with a casual shrug. "Mr. Churchill is a bit of a poor loser, that's all."

"No one leaves the Birdcage unhappy," Strittmayer declared. "Why don't you come over to the bar and have a drink with me before you go, Herr Churchill? I have some splendid twenty-year-old brandy that I would be pleased to share with you."

"Who said I was going anywhere? I'm staying right here, damn it, until I win back my money!"

"I'm afraid we don't have that much time," Strittmayer said.

Johnny added, "Yeah, we'd all grow old and die before then."

For a smart man, Johnny never had learned how to control his mouth, Bo thought. Churchill paled at the insult. He glared at Strittmayer and demanded, "Are you throwing me out, you damned Dutchman?"

Strittmayer looked sorrowful. "Although I regret to say it, yes, I am, Herr Churchill."

"Do you know who I am?"

That was a stupid question, given the fact that Strittmayer had just called the cattleman by name. But Churchill was too angry to be thinking straight, Bo decided.

"Most certainly I do."

"You'll lose a hell of a lot of business if I tell my ranch hands to stay away from this place."

"Then I suppose I shall have to make up that business some other way," Strittmayer said.

Churchill got to his feet. "You'll be sorry about this," he said. "And you can keep your damned twenty-year-old brandy. In fact, you can take the bottle and shove it right up your—"

Strittmayer's hamlike hand closed around Churchill's arm and propelled the rancher toward the door. "I think you have said enough, *nicht wahr*? Good evening, Herr Churchill."

The whole saloon had gone silent now. Everybody in the Birdcage watched as Strittmayer marched Churchill to the door. Even the girl in the cage wasn't swinging back and forth anymore.

Churchill cursed loudly at the humiliation as Strittmayer forced him through the batwings. When the rancher had stalked off, Strittmayer stepped back inside, dusted his hands off as if they had gotten dirty, and beamed around at the crowd. "No more trouble, *ja*? The next round of drinks, it is on the house!"

Cheers rang out from the customers as most of them bellied up to the bar for that free drink. Bo had a feeling that the bartenders would be reaching for special bottles full of booze they had watered down especially for such occasional demonstrations of generosity on Strittmayer's part.

"Sorry about that, gents," Three-Toed Johnny Fontana told the other cardplayers at the table. "Poker should be a game of more subtle pleasures."

"I don't know," Davidson said with a smile. "I enjoyed watching that blowhard get thrown out of the place. A man like that gets a little money and power and thinks he owns everything and everybody."

Bo nodded toward the big, affable German who had gone back to the bar and asked Johnny, "Can Churchill really make trouble for Strittmayer?"

Johnny shrugged. "That depends on how badly his pride is wounded. August does enough business so that it won't hurt him much if Churchill orders his men to stay away from the place."

"What if he tries something a little more drastic than that?"

"You mean like coming back here with a bunch of those hardcases who ride for him and trying to wreck the place?" Johnny shook his head. "That seems like a little bit much for a dispute over a few hands of poker."

For once, Johnny's ability to judge other men, which was so important in his profession, seemed to be letting him down a mite, Bo thought. He had seen something bordering on madness in Little Ed Churchill's eyes as he was forced out of the saloon. As Davidson had said, some men got that way when most people didn't dare to stand up to them. It enraged them whenever they ran into an hombre who didn't have any back up in his nature.

But maybe Churchill would show some sense and go back to his ranch to sleep off that rage. Bo hoped that would turn out to be the case. When Johnny said, "Shall we resume the game?" Bo nodded.

Davidson's luck was still the best of anyone's around the table, but Bo won a few hands and was careful to cut his losses in the ones he couldn't win. He had increased their stake enough so that he and Scratch could afford a couple of hotel rooms and some supplies. He was about to call it a night when he heard a lot of hoofbeats in the street outside.

"Strittmayer!" a harsh voice bellowed as the horses came to a stop. "I told you you'd be sorry, you damned Dutchman!"

Bo dropped his cards and started to his feet, but Scratch grabbed his shoulder and forced him back down. "Everybody hit the dirt!" Scratch shouted, his deep voice filling the room.

Even as Scratch called out the warning, the glass in the two big front windows exploded inward as a volley of shots shattered them. The saloon girls screamed and men yelled curses as more shots blasted from the street. Muzzle flashes lit up the night like a lightning storm.

As Bo dived out of his chair he rammed a shoulder into Davidson, knocking the man to the floor out of the line of fire. Bo palmed out his Colt as Scratch overturned the poker table to give them some cover. Scratch crouched behind the table with Bo and drew his long-barreled Remingtons. Everybody in the saloon had either hit the floor or leaped over the bar to hide behind the thick hardwood, so the two of them had a clear field to return the fire of Little Ed Churchill and his men.

Churchill must have gathered up a dozen or more of his ranch hands in some of El Paso's other saloons and gambling dens and brothels and led them back here to Strittmayer's place. Bo didn't know if the cattlemen had spun some wild yarn for his men about how he'd been cheated at cards and then run out of the Birdcage or if Churchill had simply ordered his men to attack. A lot of cowboys rode for the brand above all, and if the boss man said sic'em, they skinned their irons and got to work, no questions asked.

Either way, lead now filled the air inside the Birdcage. The mirrors behind the bar shattered, and bottles of liquor arranged along the backbar exploded in sprays of booze and glass as bullets struck them.

Davidson crawled along the floor and got behind the same table where Bo and Scratch had taken cover. He pulled his gun from the shoulder holster Bo had seen earlier and started firing toward the street. He glanced over at Bo and Scratch and said, "I knew Churchill was a little loco, but I didn't think he was crazy enough to come back and lay siege to the place."

From behind the bar, Strittmayer called, "Everyone stay down, *ja*?" The next moment, several shotguns poked over the bar. Each of the weapons let go with a double load of buckshot. That barrage blew out what little glass remained in the windows and ripped into the cowboys in the street. Men and horses went down, screaming in pain.

Anger flooded through Bo. Not only was Churchill trying to kill everybody in the saloon, but now he had led some of his own men to their deaths, all because Churchill was a stubborn, prideful bastard who couldn't admit that he wasn't a very good poker player. What a damned waste, Bo thought.

He could only hope that some of that buckshot had found Churchill as well, so that maybe this fight could come to an end.

That didn't prove to be the case. With an incoherent, furious shout, the rancher leaped his horse onto the boardwalk and then viciously spurred the animal on into the saloon. The horse was terrified, anybody could see that, but Churchill forced the wild-eyed beast on. Men rolled and jumped desperately to avoid the slashing, steel-shod hooves.

Three-Toed Johnny leaped up from somewhere and shouted, "Stop it! For God's sake, stop it!" He had a derringer in his hand that Bo knew had come from a concealed sheath up the gambler's sleeve. Johnny swung it up toward Churchill, but the cattleman was faster. He had a six-gun in his right hand, and as he brought it down with a chopping motion, powder smoke geysered from the muzzle. The slug punched into Johnny's body and threw him backward.

Bo and Scratch fired at the same time, but Churchill was already jerking his horse around. Their bullets whistled harmlessly past his head. Churchill sent his horse crashing into the overturned table. Bo and Scratch threw themselves to the side to get out of the way, but the table rammed into Davidson and knocked him down. His gun flew out of his hand.

"Now I'll get you, you damned four-flusher!" Churchill yelled as he brought his revolver to bear on the helpless Davidson, who lay sprawled on the floor under the rearing horse.

Bo and Scratch fired again, and this time they didn't miss. Their bullets tore through Churchill's body on an upward-angling path, causing him to lean so far back that he toppled out of the saddle. Suddenly riderless, the panic-stricken horse whirled around a couple of times, and then leaped out through the one of the already broken front windows.

The shooting from outside had stopped. Churchill's men were all either dead or had lit a shuck out of El Paso. The survivors probably wouldn't stop at Churchill's ranch either. After this brutal attack on the saloon, the men who had lived through it would take off for the tall and uncut and keep going, so that the law would be less likely to catch up to them. With Churchill dead, his wealth and influence couldn't protect them anymore.

A pale and visibly shaken August Strittmayer emerged from behind the bar clutching a reloaded shotgun. "They are all gone, *ja*?" he asked.

"Looks like it," Bo replied. He heard a lot of shouting from outside. The city marshal and some of his deputies were coming toward the Birdcage on the run, he assumed. The sounds of a small-scale war breaking out had been enough to attract the law.

Bo didn't pay any attention to that at the moment, but hurried to the side of Three-Toed Johnny instead. As Bo dropped to a knee, the gambler's eyelids fluttered open. His vest was soaked with blood over the place where Churchill's bullet had ventilated him.

"I think I'm . . . shot, Bo," Johnny gasped out as his eyes tried futilely to focus.

"I'm afraid so, Johnny," Bo agreed.

"Pretty . . . bad . . . huh?"

"Bad enough."

"Well . . . hell . . . we all draw . . . a bad hand . . . sooner or later." Johnny's head rolled from side to side. His eyes still wouldn't lock in on anything. "Ch-Churchill?"

Scratch had knelt on the gambler's other side. "Dead as he can be, pard," Scratch said.

"Good . . . At least I'm . . . not the only one . . . to fold—"

His eyes widened and grew still at last, and the air came out of him in a rattling sigh. Bo waited a moment, then shook his head and reached out to close those staring eyes as they began to grow glassy.

Strittmayer said in a hollow voice, "I never thought . . . I never dreamed that . . . that Churchill would . . . would do such a *verdammt* thing! To come back with his men and open fire on innocent people! The man was insane!"

Bo and Scratch got to their feet and started

reloading their guns. "I don't reckon he was loco," Scratch said. "Just poison-mean and too used to gettin' his own way."

That was when several men with shotguns slapped the batwings aside and rushed into the saloon, leveling the Greeners at the two drifters as a gent with a soup-strainer mustache yelled, "Drop them guns, you ring-tailed hellions!"

CHAPTER 3

The man with the mustache turned out to be Jake Hamlin, the local marshal. The other shotgunners were his deputies, of course. They had seen half a dozen cowboys and a couple of horses shot to pieces in the street and had no idea what had prompted this bloody massacre, but the busted windows of the Birdcage told them that the fatal shots must have come from inside the saloon. So they had charged in and thrown down on the first two gun-toting gents they had spotted, in this case Bo and Scratch.

It took a good half hour for Strittmayer, Davidson, and the other witnesses in the saloon to convince the lawman that Little Ed Churchill had been responsible for the hell that had broken loose. Churchill had been an important man in West Texas, and now he lay dead on the sawdust-littered floor of the saloon. To Jake Hamlin's mind, that meant somebody was guilty of murder, and who better for that role than a couple of no-account drifters?

"Creel and Morton, eh?" the marshal mused

when he found out their names. "I think I got paper on you two back in my office."

"We're not wanted in Texas," Bo said.

"And any reward dodgers you got on us from other places, well, those charges are bogus," Scratch added. "We're law-abidin' hombres."

"If you put those two fellows in jail, you will be the laughingstock of El Paso, Marshal!" Strittmayer bellowed. "I will see to this myself. Why, for Gott's sake, they saved the life of Herr Davidson here!"

Hamlin frowned. "What the hell'd you say? Here, here?"

"No, Herr here!" Strittmayer said, pointing at Davidson.

Hamlin snarled and sputtered and finally said, "Oh, shut up and lemme think!" After a few moments of visibly painful concentration, he turned to Bo and Scratch and went on. "All right, I reckon you two acted in self-defense. But there'll have to be an inquest to make it official, so don't even think about slopin' outta town until then."

"We were planning to be here for a day or two anyway," Bo said.

"Yeah, well, just remember what I told you!" Hamlin turned back to Strittmayer. "Anybody else killed?"

"Just poor Johnny there," Strittmayer replied as he waved a hand at the fallen gambler. "Several people were wounded, and my beautiful saloon, *ach!* It is shot to pieces!"

"Well, you can talk to Little Ed's lawyer about the estate payin' for the damages, but I wouldn't hold my breath waitin' for it if I was you," Hamlin advised. He looked around the room and raised his voice. "This saloon's closed for the night! Everybody out! Go home!"

Davidson said to Bo and Scratch, "Do you fellas have a place to stay here in town?"

Bo shook his head, and Scratch said, "Not yet. We'd just rode in and stabled our horses. This was the first place we stopped."

"Come on over to the Camino Real with me then," Davidson suggested. "That's where I'm staying. We'll see about getting you some rooms and a good hot meal."

"You don't have to do that," Bo said.

"I think I do. Churchill would have killed me, sure as hell, if not for you two."

Bo and Scratch couldn't argue with that, so after saying good night to Strittmayer, who promised to see to it that Johnny Fontana got a proper burial, they headed for the Camino Real Hotel with Davidson.

The Camino Real was El Paso's best hotel, and its rooms didn't come cheap. The fact that Davidson was staying there confirmed that he had plenty of money. As the three men walked along the street, he said, "We were never actually introduced. I'm Porter Davidson."

"Bo Creel," Bo said as he gripped the hand that Davidson put out. "This fancy-dressed drink of water with me is Scratch Morton. But I reckon you already know that since we told our names to the marshal."

"Pleased to meet you, Mr. Davidson," Scratch said as he shook hands with the man. "Too bad there had to be so much gunplay first."

"Yes, it ruined what had been a fairly pleasant

evening. But maybe we can make something out of it yet."

Davidson spoke to the clerk at the desk in the hotel lobby, and maybe slipped him a greenback, too. Bo wasn't sure about that. But either way, within minutes the clerk was sliding a pair of keys across the desk to them. Even though the clerk had said originally that the hotel was full up, at Davidson's urging he had somehow found a couple of vacant rooms on the third floor.

"Is the dining room still open?" Davidson asked.

"I believe it's just about to close," the clerk said.

"Would you go out to the kitchen and let the cook know that we'll need two dinners? Whatever's left will be fine, as long as it's hot."

"Yes, sir."

As they went into the empty dining room and sat down at one of the tables, Scratch commented, "You seem to be the big skookum he-wolf around these parts, Mr. Davidson."

"Not really," Davidson said with a laugh. "I guess it doesn't take long for word to get around, though, when you own a gold mine."

Scratch lifted his eyebrows.

Bo wasn't particularly surprised, though. Davidson hadn't struck him as a cattleman, and on the frontier a rich man who didn't run cows was usually mixed up with either the railroad or mining.

"I didn't know there were any gold mines around here," he commented. "There are a few down in the Big Bend, but they're not what I'd call bonanzas."

"The mine's not in Texas," Davidson said.

"New Mexico Territory?"

"No. It's across the border in Mexico, in the mountains. A place called *Cañon del Despiadado.*"

Bo and Scratch looked at each other, then back at Davidson. "Cutthroat Canyon," Bo translated.

"That's right."

"Does it live up to its name?" Scratch asked.

Davidson chuckled. "No, most of the time it's a pretty peaceful place." His face grew more serious. "The trouble happens between there and here."

Bo said, "You have trouble, do you?"

"Yes, as a matter of fact. That's one reason I wanted to talk more to you two fellows. That and my gratitude for what you did for me, of course. I'm hoping I can persuade you to do even more. I'd like to hire you both."

Before the discussion could continue, the white-aproned cook came out of the kitchen carrying a couple of plates of food. "The waiters have all gone home already," he explained as he set the plates in front of Bo and Scratch. They contained thick steaks, baked potatoes, and biscuits and gravy. "That's all we got left."

"Looks mighty fine to me," Scratch said with a smile. "We're much obliged, mister."

"Got half a pot of coffee back in the kitchen, too, if you'd like some."

"Bring it on," Bo said.

For the next few minutes, they were too busy eating to ask Davidson what he had meant about hiring them. The mine owner sat there with an amused smile on his face as he watched them putting away the food.

"You fellows look like you've been on short rations for a while," he commented.

"We had to stretch our provisions the last few days on the trail," Bo admitted. "I figured we could shoot a jackrabbit or something while we were on our way across the southern part of New Mexico Territory, but game was pretty scarce."

"It's been mighty dry over that way," Scratch put in. "Reckon most of the critters 'cept for the rattlesnakes have gone off lookin' for someplace that's more hospitable. And I've never cared much for eatin' snake, although I've known some hombres who think it's good."

"Well, you won't go hungry if you work for me," Davidson said. "There's a nice little valley right outside the canyon where the Mexicans from a nearby village have their farms. We buy our food from them. And there's a cantina in the village with some pretty girls who work there, too, if you're interested in such things."

"Interested in tequila and señoritas?" Scratch said. "I hope to smile we are!"

Davidson leaned forward and clasped his hands together on the table. "I think we should discuss wages then."

"Let's talk about the job first," Bo said. "Just what is it that you'd be hiring us to do?"

"That's a fair enough question. Like I said, there's been trouble between El Paso and the mine. I bring the ore here by wagon. There's no way to refine it in the canyon, and this is the closest railroad stop so that I can ship it out. There's been talk of building a spur line down there into the mountains, but the railroad and the Mexican government have to work out all the details first. It's liable to be a long, drawn-out process. In the meantime, I've got ore sitting there that I can't get out because of bandits."

Bo nodded. "I reckoned that was what we were getting to. Your ore shipments have been held up?"

"Several times. I've lost shipments, and men who worked for me have been killed."

Scratch's voice was dry as he drawled, "You ain't makin' the job sound all that appealin', Mr. Davidson."

"We've ridden shotgun on gold wagons before," Bo said. "It's a good way to get killed."

Davidson shook his head. "I'm not asking you to ride shotgun. I thought that if the two of you trailed the wagons at a short distance, when the bandits attack you'd be able to jump them and take them by surprise."

Bo took a sip of coffee and slowly nodded. "That might work. Once anyway. After that, the hombres who are after your gold would be watching for us."

"Once might be enough to scare them off," Davidson said. "They've had their own way so far, like Churchill, and nobody's been able to stop them. I want to put the fear of God into them. Maybe even wipe them out."

"Bo and me, we're pretty tough," Scratch said, "but even so, I don't reckon the two of us would be any match for a whole gang of *bandidos*."

"I don't expect the two of you to take care of them by yourselves. I have several other men who'll be riding back across the border with me. That's why I came to El Paso, to recruit some good men who can take care of this problem. From what I saw of your abilities in the Birdcage, the two of you will fit right in with the other men I've hired." Davidson looked back and forth between them. "Well, what do you think? Will you take the job? Remember, we haven't even talked about wages yet, but I'm sure we'd be able to reach an agreement on that matter. I believe in paying for the best."

"Give us a minute to ponder on it," Bo said.

"Of course," Davidson replied with a nod. "I need to speak to the hotel clerk anyway. I'll wait for you out in the lobby."

He stood up and walked out of the dining room. Bo and Scratch looked at each other over the remains of their supper, and Scratch said, "What do you think?"

"I don't much cotton to being lumped in with a bunch of hired guns," Bo said. "You know that's what Davidson's talking about."

"Yeah, but he seems like a pretty good fella, and he's got a right to get his gold up here without havin' it stolen. Not to mention the hombres who work for him bein' killed like that. Such things don't sit well with me."

"I know, you never have liked outlaws. Neither do I."

Scratch grinned. "And I'd be lyin' if I said I didn't have a hankerin' to visit Old Mexico again. I ain't as young as I used to be, and the heat down there feels good on these bones o' mine."

"Not to mention the señoritas."

The grin on Scratch's rugged face widened. "They feel pretty good on these bones o' mine, too."

Slowly, Bo nodded. "Well, since we don't have anywhere else we have to be . . ."

"As per usual."

"I don't suppose it would hurt anything if we rode down there with Davidson and had a look around. If we don't like the lay of the land, we can always pull out. Wouldn't be anything stopping us."

"That's right." Scratch drank the last of his coffee. "Be good to spend some time in Mañana-land again."

They found Davidson in the lobby. With an eager expression on his face, the man asked, "Have you made up your minds?"

"We'll ride down there with you," Bo said. "Whether or not we stay depends on what we find there."

"Fair enough," Davidson said with an emphatic nod. He shook hands with them again and added, "I think everything will work out just fine once we get to Cutthroat Canyon."

CHAPTER 4

Davidson wanted to leave at first light, but since the inquest into the deaths of Little Ed Churchill, his men who had been killed in the attack on the Birdcage, and Three-Toed Johnny Fontana would be held in the morning, Bo and Scratch had to wait for that. If it had been necessary, they would have said to hell with Marshal Jake Hamlin's order and ridden out anyway, but Davidson thought it over and told them to cooperate with the marshal.

"I don't want to get on the wrong side of the law," he said.

He also told Bo and Scratch not to worry about supplies. He would provide everything they needed for the trip to the Cutthroat Canyon mine, which was a two-day ride south of El Paso.

The inquest was held at the county courthouse and was well attended, since Churchill had had plenty of friends and enemies both. The cattleman's lawyers showed up and indignantly demanded justice for their client, claimed that Bo and Scratch had foully murdered Churchill with no provocation. None of the men who had been with Little Ed testified to back up that claim, however. It seemed that none of those who had been involved in the battle could be found.

On the other hand, August Strittmayer, Porter Davidson, and numerous other citizens of El Paso who had been inside the Birdcage when the shooting started took the stand and told the coroner's jury exactly what had happened. Once the testimony was concluded, it didn't take the jury long to return with a verdict stating that Bo Creel and Scratch Morton had been justified in their actions when they shot Churchill, and Strittmayer and his bartenders had been acting in self-defense when they cut loose with those Greeners. Everyone involved was free to go.

"I'll see you at the livery stable in ten minutes," Davidson told them as they paused on the steps outside the courthouse. "I want to get back to the mine as soon as I can. Those bandits have never bothered the mine itself, only the ore shipments, but you never know what they might be brave enough to do."

Strittmayer lumbered down the steps as Davidson departed. The big German shook hands with Bo and Scratch and said, "You cannot wait for Johnny's funeral?"

Bo shook his head. "I'm afraid not. We gave Davidson our word that we'd ride down to that mine of his with him. You know anything about that hombre, August?"

"Not really," Strittmayer said with a shrug. "He has been bringing ore shipments here to El Paso for the past six months or so, about every two weeks. His mine must be a good one, *ja*?"

"He ever cause any trouble?"

"Oh, *nein, nein*. He is a very friendly fellow and knows a great deal about mining. I know something of that myself, and we have had several good discussions. I like him."

"So do I," Scratch said. "I hope we can give him a hand with his problems."

Strittmayer's head inclined in a solemn nod. "*Ja,* the robbers who steal his ore. I have heard about them. You two should be careful. There is much danger below the border."

"There's a heap of danger everywhere we go," Scratch said with a laugh. "It seems like that anyway."

Bo pressed a coin into Strittmayer's hand. "Put some flowers on Johnny's grave for us. He was a good hombre. Deserved to go out better."

Strittmayer shrugged again. "He died in a saloon. I think he would have preferred that to a bed in some rented room in a boardinghouse."

"You're probably right about that," Bo agreed. "Just see to the flowers and we'll be obliged, August."

"*Ja*. It will be done."

They had spent several minutes of the time Davidson had given them in talking to the saloon keeper, so Bo wasn't surprised when they got to the livery stable and found Davidson already there, along with half a dozen other men.

Scratch nudged Bo with an elbow and said under his breath, "Look yonder. It's Jim Skinner."

"I see him," Bo said.

Jim Skinner stood slightly apart from the other men with Davidson. He was a couple of inches taller than Bo and Scratch, without an extra ounce of flesh anywhere on his body. You could sharpen a knife on his cheekbones. Lank dark hair fell to his shoulders. He wore two gunbelts that crossed each other and held a pair of holstered .45s. A Winchester was tucked under his left arm.

Bo happened to know that Skinner also carried a knife in a sheath that hung down his back from a rawhide thong around his neck. Bo knew that because he had seen Skinner use that knife to cut a man's face half off in a saloon up in Wyoming one time during an argument. Skinner had taken the poor son of a bitch by surprise with the blade.

"Hell, I didn't know he'd be one of the hombres Davidson hired," Scratch said as they approached. "I ain't so sure now about workin' for the fella."

"We gave our word that we'd ride down there to the mine at least," Bo reminded him. "You know any of those other hombres?"

"Can't say as I do. They all look like they still got the bark on, though."

That was true. Even though none of the other men were quite as sinister-looking as Jim Skinner, all of them had the hard-eyed faces of gents who were used to trouble. Of course, most people might say the same of him and Scratch, Bo reminded himself.

"There you are," Davidson said as they came up. "Are you ready to ride?"

"Soon as we throw our saddles on our horses," Bo said.

"While you're doing that, I'll introduce you to the other men. Unless you already know some of them?"

"I know Creel and Morton," Skinner said in a gravelly voice. He turned his head and spat. "Didn't know they was the other two gents you said you hired."

Davidson frowned as he looked back and forth between Bo and Scratch and Skinner. "Is there bad blood between you men?"

"Our trails have crossed a time or two," Skinner said.

"That doesn't answer the question."

"There's no bad blood," Bo said. "But Skinner's got quite a reputation as a gunman."

"That's not necessarily a bad thing, is it?" Davidson asked. "I need men who can handle themselves when there's trouble."

"And no man I ever killed died with a hole in his back neither," Skinner added.

Scratch bristled. "You ain't callin' us backshooters, are you, Skinner?"

"Nope. I'm just sayin' that happen I decide to take your measure, old man, you can count on me comin' at you from the front."

Davidson held up his hands. "All right, that's enough. I'm paying you men to fight bandits, not each other."

"We'll steer clear of Skinner," Bo said, "and he can steer clear of us."

Skinner jerked his head in a nod. "Sounds good to me."

"That's settled then," Davidson said. "Get saddled up. We've already wasted enough of the day."

While Bo and Scratch got their mounts ready to ride, Davidson introduced the other five men, as he'd said that he would. The big, tow-headed Swede was named Hansen. Jackman and Tragg could have been brothers with their swarthy faces and thick black mustaches, but they weren't related. "That we know of," Jackman added. The slender, baby-faced kid whose cold eyes belied his innocent appearance was called Douglas, with no indication of whether that was his first or last name. The final man was Lancaster, and when he said hello to Bo and Scratch, Bo heard a trace of a British accent in his voice. Remittance man, more than likely, who had been in the States for a good long time.

Bo cinched the saddle snug on his rangy lineback dun and said to Davidson, "With a group this big trailing your gold wagons, it'll be hard to keep those *bandidos* from spotting us."

"I thought maybe you could split up so that you wouldn't be as noticeable, then converge on the wagons if there's trouble."

Bo thought it over for a second and then nodded. "That might work," he allowed.

"But only once, like Bo told you last night," Scratch added as he led his big, handsome bay out of the barn.

"I'm hoping that once will be enough," Davidson said.

The nine men swung up in their saddles. They had a couple of packhorses loaded with bags of supplies and a pair of long crates, one on each horse. Douglas and Hansen led the pack animals as the group started out of El Paso. They rode to the long wooden bridge that spanned the lazily twisting Rio Grande. Horseshoes rang on the planks as the riders crossed the border into the Mexican town of Juarez.

Dogs barked at them and children ran after them

as they followed the dusty streets through Juarez, but the men paid no attention to those distractions. Soon enough the settlement was left behind, and the riders headed due south across the flat, semiarid terrain toward the greenish-gray mountains that rose in the distance. The mountains were farther away than they looked, which explained the two days it would take the men to reach them.

Despite the fact that summer was still more than a month off, the temperature rose steadily as the sun climbed higher in the sky. Bo took off his frock coat after a while, and Scratch removed his buckskin jacket. Sweat trickled down Bo's back.

"It'll be cooler in the mountains," Davidson said with a smile as he pulled a bandanna from his pocket to wipe moisture from his face. He had changed into gray trousers and a white shirt and flat-crowned black hat, and he wore a holstered six-gun like the rest of the men. Bo recalled the way Davidson had shucked his iron from that shoulder rig during the battle of the Birdcage the night before, and figured the mine owner was plenty tough despite being something of a dude.

"Did you study engineering, Mr. Davidson?" he asked.

"Yes, I did, as a matter of fact, along with geology. That's a good background for a mining man, don't you think?"

"Always helps to know what you're doing, no matter what it is."

"What's your specialty, Mr. Creel?"

Scratch laughed. "We both been studyin' on how

to stay out of trouble for more'n forty years now. Haven't quite got the knack of it yet, though."

"Surely you've done something besides just . . . drift."

"A little of everything," Bo said. "Drove freight wagons and stagecoaches, scouted for the army, even toted a badge a time or two—"

"But didn't like it much," Scratch put in.

"No, we're not really cut out to be lawmen," Bo agreed with a faint smile. "We've done our share of cowboying. Chopped firewood and sold it one winter in Deadwood. Mostly, though, we just amble around from one place to another."

Skinner moved his horse up so that he was riding even with them. With a sneer, he said, "Don't try to make out like you're better'n the rest of us, Creel. You two have hired out your guns plenty of times, just like me and these other boys. What about that range war up in Montana you were mixed up in?"

"Is that true?" Davidson asked. "You were part of a range war?"

Bo shrugged. "The fella who owned one of the ranches did us a mighty big favor once. We were just paying him back, I guess you could say. Anyway, he was up against some mighty big odds. He would've been wiped out if somebody hadn't given him a hand."

"That was quite a ruckus, all right," Scratch said.

"Last I heard," Skinner said, "you two had a murder charge out against you up there."

Davidson frowned. "I heard what you told the marshal last night. Is it true you're wanted for murder?"

"Those charges were dropped," Bo said as he

gave Skinner a hard glance. "And the only reason they were filed in the first place is because one of the gents who ambushed us had a crooked judge for a friend."

"But you *did* kill him—the man who ambushed you, I mean?"

"Darned right we did," Scratch said. He slapped his thigh. "I got an old bullet wound in my leg that aches when the weather's right to prove that the ornery son of a gun had it comin', too."

"Don't try to stir up trouble," Davidson told Skinner.

"Not tryin' to stir up anything," the skull-faced gunman said. "I just don't want these two old buzzards thinkin' that they're any better than the rest of us. They're goin' down to that mine of yours for the same reason as the rest of us—to kill Mex bandits for pay."

Bo was tempted to tell Scratch that they were riding away right now. He'd already had a bellyful of Jim Skinner, and the trip had barely started. The idea of spending even a week around Skinner was distasteful.

But they had given their word to Davidson, and Bo liked the mine owner. If they could help Davidson get those ore shipments to El Paso, Bo supposed he could put up with Skinner—at least for a little while.

He hoped this job wouldn't last too long, though.

Jackman, Tragg, and Hansen started talking about some whores they had been with back in El Paso, and that shut Skinner up. Douglas and Lancaster were both pretty close-mouthed, Bo noted. But at least Skinner left Bo and Scratch alone following the brief clash, for the most part riding a short distance away from the others.

They stopped from time to time to rest the horses, and at midday they paused longer to make a sparse lunch on biscuits and jerky from the bags of supplies. While they were eating, Scratch nodded toward the crates and asked Davidson what was in them.

"Just some mining equipment," Davidson replied. "That's another reason I went to El Paso, to pick up that gear."

This was a dry, thirsty land, but the men had brought along plenty of full canteens. The water they had would last them until they reached the mountains, barring some sort of bad luck. And once they arrived at their destination, there would be streams to provide cool, clear water that came from springs higher up.

"Have you ever been down here before?" Davidson asked Bo and Scratch late that afternoon.

"Quite a few times," Bo replied. "Not in recent years, though."

Scratch said, "Last time we rode through these parts, a fella still had to worry about the Yaqui and the Apaches. Never could tell when you'd run smack-dab into a raidin' party. From what I hear tell, though, most of the Injuns have pulled back even farther into the mountains since Major Jones and the Frontier Battalion of the Rangers made it too tough on 'em every time they crossed the border. The Rurales chase 'em down here, too."

"Yes, well, the Rurales aren't the most efficient law enforcement group in the world," Davidson said.

"Between their corruption and their incompetence, they haven't been able to do a thing about the bandit problem in this area. I found that out when I lodged a complaint with the Mexican government about my ore shipments being robbed." He shrugged. "I'll give them a little credit, though. The Indians haven't bothered us. As you said, Mr. Morton, they seem to have retreated."

"Mr. Morton was my pa. Call me Scratch."

"Same here," Bo said. "I'm just Bo."

"Very well."

Davidson didn't tell them to call him Porter, though, Bo noticed.

They made camp that night next to a dry wash. Davidson thought they ought to camp inside the wash, so that they could build a fire without it being seen, but Bo shook his head.

"I've known flash floods to come along and fill up one of these arroyos quicker than I can tell you about it," he said.

"Flash floods?" Davidson repeated. "Out here in the middle of this arid landscape?"

"All it takes is a good storm up in the mountains," Scratch said. "That's why they sometimes call 'em gullywashers."

Skinner snorted. "I would've told you the same thing, Boss, if these two old mossyhorns hadn't jumped in first."

"You're mighty free with that mouth of yours, Skinner," Scratch snapped. "And I'm gettin' a mite tired of bein' called names."

Skinner's angular jaw jutted out defiantly. "I can think of worse things to call you, old man."

"Settle down," Davidson said, his voice sharp. "Don't make me regret hiring you—any of you."

Scratch built up a ring of rocks so that he could kindle a tiny fire inside it without the flames being seen by any enemies lurking in the night. That was enough to boil their coffee and fry some bacon. Davidson promised the men that their next supper would be a better one, since they would have reached the canyon by then.

After they had eaten, the men settled on shifts for standing guard. The ones who would be sleeping first spread their bedrolls on the ground and circled them with ropes to keep snakes from crawling up and trying to share their blankets. Despite the heat of the day, the thin, dry air would cool off rapidly as night settled down.

Bo and Scratch had deliberately volunteered for separate shifts on guard duty. They didn't trust the other men completely—they didn't trust Jim Skinner at all—and thought it would be best if at least one of them was awake most of the night.

Bo rolled up in his blankets first and dropped off to sleep immediately, a skill he and Scratch had both learned more than forty years earlier when they were both members of Sam Houston's army during the Texas Revolution. He didn't know how long he had been asleep when he came awake instantly at a light touch on his shoulder.

"Roll out, pard," Scratch whispered. "We got trouble comin'."

CHAPTER 5

Bo pushed his blankets aside and reached for his coiled gunbelt and holstered Colt, which he had placed beside him before he went to sleep. As he got up from the ground, he strapped the gunbelt around his hips and then quickly thonged down the holster.

"What is it?" he asked, keeping his voice as quiet as Scratch's.

"Ain't sure, but I heard some horses out there in the darkness. Just a hoofbeat or two, and then a little whinny that stopped short, like somebody'd clamped a hand over the critter's nose. That's all, but it was enough to tell me that somebody's skulkin' around out yonder."

Bo agreed. The lurkers might be Indians or bandits or maybe even some innocent vaqueros who were just passing through the area—although that last possibility wasn't very likely.

"Who's on guard with you?" Bo asked.

"That Britisher, Lancaster."

"Did you tell him what you heard?"

"Nope. Figured I'd roust you out first."

"Go tell him about it now, while I wake up David-son and the others."

"Be careful around Skinner," Scratch warned. "A hydrophobia skunk like him is liable to lash out and bite anybody who gets too close."

Bo nodded. He had already thought the same thing about Skinner.

He went over to Davidson's bedroll first and knelt beside the mine owner. "Mr. Davidson," Bo said quietly.

Davidson rolled over fast and sat up with a gun in his hand. Bo saw the light from the half-moon in the sky overhead glint on the barrel. "Easy," he said. "It's just me, Bo Creel."

"Bo," Davidson said as he lowered the revolver. "Sorry. I guess I was dreaming. I thought there was some sort of danger out there—"

"Dreams sometimes come true. Scratch heard something suspicious a minute ago. He and Lan-caster are checking it out."

Davidson pushed his blankets aside and stood up, still gripping the gun. "Wake everyone else," he said in a brisk voice. "We need to be ready in case—"

Before he could go on, a man yelled and a gun sud-denly blasted in the darkness, followed instantly by the slamming reports of two more shots. Bo saw the muzzle flashes from the corner of his eye, and knew they came from the general area where Scratch had gone. Fearing for his trail partner's life, he broke into a run as behind him Davidson shouted for the rest of the men to get up.

Whoever had snuck up on the camp wasn't the

only danger, Bo knew. In the dark like this, and roused out of sleep, if the men Davidson had hired started firing blindly, they'd be just as likely to shoot each other as anybody else.

Not to mention the fact that a snake-blooded varmint like Jim Skinner might not-so-accidentally take a few potshots at somebody he didn't like— such as Bo and Scratch. If he killed them, he could always claim that he had mistakenly thought they were Apaches or bandits or whoever the attackers turned out to be.

That thought flashed through Bo's head as he ran toward Scratch, but he didn't have time to do anything about it. More Colt flame bloomed in the night like crimson flowers as shots roared out.

Bo spotted a couple of struggling figures, and from the moonlight reflecting on the silvery hair of one of them, he knew it was Scratch. The other man still wore his hat. It was a high-crowned sombrero, telling Bo that the lurkers were Mexican bandits. He stepped up behind the hombre wrestling with Scratch and brought his Colt crunching down on the man's head. The sombrero absorbed some of the blow's force, but it was still powerful enough to unhinge the bandit's legs and drop him to his knees. Scratch laid him out from there with a roundhouse right.

"Thanks, pard," he told Bo as he bent to pick up the Remingtons he must have dropped when the bandit attacked him. "They come up out of the arroyo and jumped Lancaster before I could warn him."

"Is he all right?"

"Don't know." Scratch wheeled in that direction. "Let's go see."

They started toward the spot where Lancaster had been posted, crouching as bullets whined overhead. Some of the shots came from the lip of the arroyo, while others originated in the camp. The battle lines had been drawn pretty quickly.

And Bo and Scratch found themselves trapped between the two forces.

"Get down!" Bo said as a bullet tugged at his sleeve. "Those slugs are coming too close for comfort!"

Both of the Texans hit the dirt and crawled behind some good-sized rocks that offered at least a little cover. From there they could fire at the bandits who had crept up to the camp along the arroyo. They aimed at the muzzle flashes, because they couldn't see anything else in the darkness.

After a few minutes, someone yelled in Spanish over the thundering gunshots. Bo caught enough to the words to recognize them as an order to fall back.

"They're lighting a shuck," he told Scratch as he paused with his thumb on the hammer of his Colt. Sure enough, the shots from the arroyo began to dwindle, and then stopped completely a moment later. A ragged rataplan of swift hoofbeats drifted through the night.

Bo turned his head and called toward the camp, "Hold your fire! They're pulling out!"

Davidson added to the order, shouting, "Hold your fire! Hold your fire!"

An eerie, echoing silence fell over the landscape as the shooting stopped. After a moment, Davidson broke it by asking, "Are they gone?"

"I think so," Bo replied. "Better lie low for a few

more minutes, though, just to be sure. Scratch and I will check out the arroyo."

"We will?" Scratch said.

"We're the closest to it," Bo pointed out.

"Yeah, I reckon," Scratch agreed with a sigh.

After reloading their guns, they darted out from behind the rocks. The arroyo was only a few yards away. They covered that ground quickly and slid down the sloping bank to the sandy floor of the arroyo. There was enough moonlight for them to see as they made their way along the jagged gash in the earth.

"The varmints are gone, all right," Scratch said after he and Bo had searched for a few minutes.

"They figured to take us by surprise and wipe us out before we knew what was going on," Bo said. "They hadn't counted on those keen ears of yours, partner."

He lifted his voice and called to the rest of the men, "All clear down here!" The words were barely out of his mouth when a shot blasted up above.

"Now what the hell?" Scratch muttered as he and Bo charged up the slope, climbing out of the arroyo as fast as they could.

They found Davidson and a couple of the other men standing around a dark shape on the ground. Bo recognized it as the man he had knocked out with his pistol, the one who had been struggling with Scratch.

"What happened?" he asked as he and Scratch came up to the others.

"This bandit was still alive," Davidson said. "I thought he was dead, but he tried to get me with a knife as I walked by. I had to shoot him."

"Good thing you were quick about it, Boss," Jackman said as he picked up a long, heavy-bladed knife from the ground beside the dead man. "Bastard would've gutted you with this if he'd gotten the chance."

"It's a shame you had to kill him," Bo said. "I'm the one who knocked him out. I was hoping we could ask him some questions, maybe find out who's behind the trouble you've been having down here, Mr. Davidson."

The mine owner grunted. "It doesn't matter what their names are. They're all just damned Mexican bandits, like this one. And you could've gotten me killed by not finishing him off when you had the chance."

Bo heard the anger in Davidson's voice, and knew the fear the man felt at the realization of how close he had come to dying probably prompted it. Not seeing any point in aggravating the situation, Bo just said, "Sorry," and let it go at that as he knelt beside the corpse.

The wide-brimmed sombrero hid the bandit's face. Bo pulled it aside and studied the dead man's features in the moonlight. He was surprised to see how young and unlined they were.

Scratch saw the same thing. He said, "Hell, he ain't much more'n a kid."

"That's right," Bo said. He put the dead bandit's age around twenty.

"He was plenty old enough to use a gun and a knife," Skinner pointed out. "Little greaser got what was comin' to him."

Davidson said, "We'll bury him in the morning before we ride on."

Skinner spat. "Waste of time. Throw him in the arroyo. The *zopilotes* will take care of him."

"I won't leave any man for the buzzards," Davidson snapped. "Not even a bandit."

"I'm glad to hear you say that," Bo said.

"Do what you want," Skinner said. "Just don't expect me to help dig the grave. The only effort I'll go to for scum like that is pullin' a trigger."

He stalked back to the camp and started straightening up his bedroll.

"Clearly, they spotted us and followed us," Davidson mused. "I guess they thought this would be a good chance to get rid of me. If I was gone, they could take over the mine."

Bo frowned in thought and ran a thumbnail along his jawline. "Operating a mine seems like more work than a bunch of *bandidos* would want to do," he said. "It strikes me that they'd be more likely to want you and your workers to dig out the gold, then steal it from you."

"Maybe. Whatever their motive, it didn't work."

"Was anybody else hurt?"

Lancaster spoke up. "I've got a bullet crease on my arm where the first shot hit me. Nothing serious, but it hurts like the bloody devil. I was able to return the man's fire and downed him. That's what started the whole fray."

"I didn't see any other bodies layin' around," Scratch said.

"Neither did I," Bo agreed. "The bandits must've taken everybody who was wounded or killed with them except for this one fella, and they couldn't get to him. From the looks of it, he and the hombre who jumped Lancaster were trying to sneak all the way into camp before the shooting started. Might have made it if Scratch hadn't heard their horses."

Davidson grinned and clapped a hand on Scratch's shoulder. "Good job, my friend. You probably saved all of us from a very unpleasant death."

"Can't think of a death that'd be all that pleasant," Scratch commented. "No, wait a minute, I reckon I can, if a fella was to—"

"That's enough talk about dying," Bo said. "Let's get some sleep instead. We've still got a long ride in front of us tomorrow."

CHAPTER 6

Bo and Scratch dug the grave for the dead bandit the next morning, starting while the sky was still gray with the approach of dawn. Hansen helped them, and so, to their surprise, did the cold-eyed kid called Douglas. Bo gave up one of his blankets to wrap the body before they lowered it into the ground.

Hansen explained that his father had been a Lutheran minister. He volunteered to say a prayer before they filled in the hole. It was in Swedish, but Bo didn't figure that really mattered. El Señor Dios could probably speak all sorts of lingos.

"If we're done here, we need to get started," Davidson said as Scratch tamped down the last shovelful of earth. Skinner, Lancaster, Jackman, and Tragg had all mounted their horses already. Lancaster's bullet-creased arm had a rag tied around it as a makeshift bandage.

Scratch tied the shovel back onto one of the pack-horses where they had gotten it, and the rest of the group swung up into their saddles. They took the horses down a caved-in bank and along the wash for fifty yards or so before finding a place on the other side where they could climb out easily.

Bo checked the ground in the arroyo as they crossed it. He saw several dark splotches on the ground and on the rocky banks that were probably bloodstains. The bandits had suffered other casualties during the brief battle the night before besides the young man Davidson had killed. It was impossible to tell, though, just how serious the other injuries had been.

Bo still regretted not being able to ask questions of the bandit he had knocked out, but there was nothing that could be done about that now. He put the matter out of his head and concentrated instead on keeping a close eye on the landscape around them, just in case the bandits tried to ambush them again.

That wasn't going to be easy, considering how flat and open so much of the terrain was. In broad daylight, no one could approach them without being seen. There wouldn't really be a good spot for another ambush until they reached the mountains.

"You may not have any more trouble," Bo mused as he and Scratch rode alongside Davidson that morning.

"What makes you think that?" the mine owner asked.

"The bandits know now that you're bringing in reinforcements. They've seen us, swapped shots with us, and might just decide that it'll be too risky to hit those gold shipments in the future."

Davidson laughed. "I'd like to think that's true,

Bo, but you don't know how determined those bastards are. They know I'm bringing high-grade ore out of the mine. I can't imagine them just turning their backs on it."

"Well, I reckon we'll see."

"Yes, we will. And I bet it won't take long to discover that they're still out to ruin me."

That was sort of an odd way to put it, Bo thought. Stealing gold shipments wasn't exactly the same thing as trying to ruin Davidson, although that might be the end result if the robberies continued.

The ride that day was long and hot and tiring, but they didn't run into any more trouble. Gradually, they drew closer to the mountains. Even after it seemed as if the gray-green peaks were close enough to reach out and touch, hours went by before the riders actually reached the foothills. Once they began climbing, the air was a little cooler, and that was a welcome relief.

By late afternoon the mountains towered above them. Pine trees covered the slopes, and the valleys between the mountains were lush with grass. The riders passed occasional farms with garden patches and small herds of sheep and oxen.

No one was moving around, though, and Bo wondered if the Mexican farmers had retreated inside the adobe huts with their families. Despite the beauty to be found in many places south of the border, Mexico had a history of being a violent, unstable land where the common people had plenty of reason to be leery of Indians, bandits, revolutionaries, and the government alike. No wonder they hid when they saw a group of hard-faced gringo strangers coming.

Davidson led them through a pass and into another valley. This was a long, flat area between two mountain ridges. A stream meandered along the middle of the valley, and cultivated fields bordered it. About halfway along the valley's length, buildings clustered to form the village Davidson had mentioned. Most were humble adobe huts, but Bo could see a good-sized church with a square bell tower that had a cross mounted on top of it. There were some frame buildings as well, constructed of rough-hewn planks sawn from pine trees brought down from the mountains. It looked like a nice place, nothing fancy about it, but still a good home for the people who lived in the valley.

At the far end of the valley, the mountains came together to form a steep, rugged wall. The only breach in that wall appeared to be a canyon about a hundred yards wide. Davidson pointed to it.

"Cutthroat Canyon, gentlemen. The mine is about half a mile up it."

"Is that a box canyon," Bo asked, "or is there another way out?"

"It extends another mile or so into the mountains and then comes to a dead end," Davidson explained. "At least, as far as horses and wagons are concerned it does. A man could probably climb out, but then he'd just find himself in the middle of those mountains with nowhere else to go."

The sun had dropped down nearly behind the peaks to the west. Even so, some of its rays still slanted into the valley, and Scratch pointed toward the church and said, "Sun's reflectin' off something in that bell tower, Bo."

"It's the bell, of course," Davidson said. "A big brass thing, a hundred years old or more. The old Spanish padres brought it here when they established the mission many years ago. Or so I've been told."

That was a reasonable explanation, Bo thought—but he had seen the reflection, too, and it hadn't really looked to him like the sun shining on brass. He had seen glints like that before—too many times, in fact—and they had nearly always come from rifle barrels.

"Maybe we'd better circle around that village," he suggested. "Those bandits could have set a trap for us there."

"I doubt that," Davidson said. "Like I told you, they've always left us alone around here. They've only struck out on the trail between here and El Paso. Besides, it's the shortest way to the canyon."

Bo shrugged. "You're the boss." He looked over at Scratch, and the glance they exchanged carried a clear message. The Texans would be riding wary as they passed through the village.

It appeared that Davidson was right, though. No shots rang out as the riders entered the settlement. In fact, it was oddly quiet. No dogs barked, and no children ran out of the huts to follow the men along the road. Bo might have thought that the inhabitants had abandoned the village if not for the cook smoke that rose from several crude chimneys.

Scratch noticed it, too. "Where is everybody?" he asked quietly.

"It's late," Davidson answered before Bo could say anything. "These people work hard. They're all in their houses resting after a day in the fields."

"I suppose," Bo said.

They saw their first sign of life as they neared the church. A brown-robed priest came out of the sanctuary, saw the men on horseback, and stopped short. As they passed by, the padre crossed himself and backed through the open door of the church.

"What was that about?" Bo asked with a frown.

"You mean Father Luis?" Davidson said. "He's a very devout man. I imagine he was about to ask us inside to pray with him, but I guess he changed his mind when he realized that we've been riding a long way and probably want to get back to the mine as soon as possible."

That explanation made sense, too, Bo thought— but for some reason, uneasiness still lurked inside him. Back in El Paso, Davidson had struck him as being honest, open, and friendly, and so far the man hadn't done anything to make that opinion change.

And yet, Bo wasn't feeling so sure now about taking this job. Maybe it was because Davidson had hired Jim Skinner. Was that just a lapse in judgment on Davidson's part, or did he really not care that he had a vicious, low-down snake like Skinner working for him?

He and Scratch hadn't made any promises other than telling Davidson they would ride down here with him and have a look at the situation, Bo reminded himself. They could ride away any time they chose, and if Davidson tried to pay them for helping out against the bandits the night before, well, they could always refuse the money. They wouldn't want to be beholden to the man if they weren't going to work for him.

They left the strange little village behind and rode on toward the mine. The sun had vanished behind the mountains by the time they reached the mouth of the canyon. The shadows that gathered inside it made it look like a black maw gaping in the rock wall. Bo heard some muttering behind him, and glanced around to see a worried frown on Hansen's face. The Swede's mouth was moving. Saying some more of those Lutheran prayers, Bo thought. Douglas looked a little uneasy, too.

But not Skinner, Jackman, Tragg, and Lancaster. They appeared eager to get where they were going. Jackman said, "I hope you got plenty of good whiskey in this place, Boss. After eatin' trail dust for a couple of days, I'm plumb thirsty."

"There's whiskey," Davidson said. An edge crept into his voice as he went on. "But I don't want you or anybody else getting sloppy drunk, Jackman. That makes a man careless. Just because those bandits haven't attacked the mine doesn't mean they never will."

"Sure, Boss, I understand," Jackman said. "Anyway, whiskey don't muddle me none."

"See that it doesn't," Davidson said.

Their eyes adjusted to the gloom inside the canyon. It ran fairly straight, and after a few minutes Bo spotted the yellow glow of lamplight up ahead. He was able to make out several buildings, and when he asked Davidson about them, the mine owner explained, "There's a bunkhouse for the workers, quarters for the foremen, a mess hall, and a cookshack. Plus storage sheds for the equipment, of course, and a barn for the mules we use to pull the ore wagons. There's another barn and a corral for our saddle horses. The shed where we store blasting powder is about two hundred yards farther up the canyon."

"That's a good idea, not keepin' that stuff too close," Scratch said. "I never have cared for anything that's liable to blow up."

"Well, you won't have to work with it," Davidson pointed out. "I have men who do that."

"How big is your crew?" Bo asked.

"I have between fifty and sixty men working here, plus a dozen more supervising the operation."

"You need that many foremen?"

"Mining can be pretty complex," Davidson said.

That didn't really answer the question, Bo thought, but he didn't press it. He had done some mining himself, and while it was grueling, back-breaking work most of the time, it wasn't really that complicated if you knew how to dig a tunnel and shore it up. That's what had been done here, he knew, because he could see the tunnel mouth in the canyon wall beyond the cluster of buildings.

Most of the buildings were made of adobe, but the biggest structure was of logs. Davidson nodded toward it and said, "That's the mine headquarters. My office is in there, as well as my living quarters. And there are extra rooms for you gentlemen as well, although I'm afraid you'll have to double up."

"I don't share a room with anybody," Skinner snapped.

"Reckon that's because nobody'd want to share one with you," Scratch drawled.

Skinner turned toward him angrily, but before things could turn into an argument, the door of the big log building banged open and a man hurried out onto the porch.

"Thank God you're back, Boss!" he exclaimed as the riders reined to halt. "We've got trouble!"

CHAPTER 7

The man was a tall, craggy-faced hombre in work clothes and lace-up boots. He had a revolver in a cross-draw military holster with a flap on it strapped to his belt on the left side. He went on. "Those blasted Mexes are causing problems again—"

"Hold on, Wallace," Davidson said sharply. "I just rode up after two days on the trail from El Paso. Can't you at least let me dismount and stretch my legs?"

The man called Wallace looked a little chastened, but still mostly angry and upset. "Sorry, Mr. Davidson," he said. "I just thought you'd want to know. I'm on my way into the mine now."

"I'll come with you and see what this is all about," Davidson said as he swung down from the saddle. "Is Alfred inside?"

"Sure. Where else would he be?"

Davidson ignored that question and turned to Bo, Scratch, and the other men. "You can put your horses in the corral," he said, pointing to the enclosure made of peeled pine poles. "There's water for them, and I'll have someone rub them down and put out some grain for them right away. You can go inside after that. My man Alfred will take care of you, see that you have something to eat and a place to sleep."

"Long as he don't try to give *us* a rubdown," Scratch said.

Davidson looked puzzled by that comment, but didn't hang around to question it. He started off toward the tunnel mouth instead, with Wallace striding along beside him and talking with a lot of animated gestures.

"I don't think Mr. Davidson understands your sense of humor," Bo said to Scratch as they led their horses toward the corral along with the others.

"Hell, sometimes *I* don't understand it, and it's my mouth the words are comin' out of. Say," Scratch went on, "did you ever see a Mexican village as plumb *quiet* as that one? There should've been kids and chickens runnin' around, and dogs a-yappin', and guitar music comin' from the cantina. Instead, the whole place was like a funeral."

"I noticed," Bo said. "I didn't like it very much either. Rubbed me the wrong way."

"You and me both, pard. Ain't the first thing about this job that's rubbed me the wrong way neither." Scratch cast a meaningful glance toward Jim Skinner. Bo just nodded in agreement.

When they reached the corral, Tragg opened the gate and the men turned their horses inside. The others all turned around to go back to the headquarters building, as Davidson had told them to do, but Bo and Scratch remained behind.

"You two fellows aren't coming?" Lancaster

asked from outside the corral fence as he paused to look back at Bo and Scratch.

"We're used to taking care of our own mounts," Bo said.

"That's right," Scratch added. "You never know when some other fella ain't gonna do it to suit you."

Lancaster shrugged and went on. Bo and Scratch led the dun and the bay through an open door into a flat-roofed adobe barn. The roof was made of thatch, and *vigas*—support beams made from logs—stuck out around the upper edges of the walls.

The barn was big, with about two dozen stalls in it, half of them occupied. Bo and Scratch led their mounts into a couple of the empty ones, unsaddled the horses, and began rubbing them down with handfuls of straw from the hard-packed dirt floor.

"Davidson's been working this mine for about six months," Bo said as he worked on the dun. "At least according to August Strittmayer. These buildings look older than that, though."

"Yeah, I'd say most of 'em have been here for at least a couple of years," Scratch agreed. "Davidson never said that he started the mine. Could be he bought it from somebody else."

"Yeah, I reckon." Bo saw a bucket in a corner of the stall, picked it up, and carried it outside to fill it in the corral's big water trough. He was going to take it inside so that the dun would have water in its stall.

As he was dipping the bucket in the trough, he noticed a man hurrying toward the corral. The fella was moving so fast he was almost running. He wore a straw sombrero, rope sandals, and the white shirt and trousers of a Mexican farmer. Somebody from the village who worked here at the mine, Bo supposed.

"Señor! Señor!" the man called as he came closer. "You do not have to care for your horses, Señor. I will do that. A thousand apologies for not getting here sooner!"

"That's all right, old-timer," Bo said as the man unlatched the gate and came inside the corral.

Enough red light left over from the sunset remained in the sky above the canyon so that Bo could make out the man's lined, leathery face and drooping white mustaches. He might not actually be much older than Bo and Scratch, but calling him an old-timer just seemed to fit. Repeating the explanation he had given Lancaster, Bo went on. "My partner and I are used to taking care of our own mounts."

"You will not tell Señor Davidson that you were forced to do so?" the man asked, worry evident both on his face and in his voice.

Maybe more than worry, Bo thought.

The old Mexican almost seemed *afraid*.

"Nobody forced us to do anything," Bo told the old man. "And anyway, what we do isn't really any of Señor Davidson's business."

The old-timer frowned, causing even more wrinkles to form in his forehead. "You do not work for the señor, like the other men?"

"Maybe. Maybe not. We haven't decided yet."

"But . . . but he brought all of you here to . . . to kill the men who try to take his gold, did he not?"

"Yes, he wants us to help protect his ore shipments from the bandits who have been holding them up."

"Sí," the old man said. "Bandits."

Something about his tone of voice made Bo's frown deepen. "What are you trying to say?" he asked.

Suddenly the old man looked even more nervous. "Nothing, Señor, nothing at all. I must tend to the horses."

With that, he grabbed the water bucket out of Bo's hand and scurried off into the barn, passing Scratch as the silver-haired Texan came outside.

"Where's that little varmint hurryin' off to?"

"Davidson sent him to take care of the horses," Bo said. "He was worried because you and I were already tending to our mounts. Didn't want us telling Davidson that we had to do it ourselves."

"We didn't have to," Scratch pointed out. "It was our own choice."

"Yes, but that old-timer didn't know that when he came up."

As they left the corral and started walking toward the headquarters building, Scratch said, "You make it sound like the little ol' fella was scared."

"I think he was."

"But scared o' what?"

"That's a mighty good question," Bo said.

They went up the steps to the porch and on inside the building. A stocky young man in a brown suit but with no tie appeared to be waiting for them in a small front room dominated by a pair of desks and some cabinets. With a smile on his round face, he said, "Mr. Creel? Mr. Morton?"

"That's us, sonny," Scratch confirmed. "He's Bo, I'm Scratch. Who're you?"

"My name is Alfred, sir. I'm Mr. Davidson's

bookkeeper and major domo, I suppose you'd say. The other men are in the dining room if you'd care to join them." Alfred held out a hand to usher them through a doorway into another room.

This chamber was considerably larger, with a long, brilliantly polished hardwood dining table in its center. A fireplace sat on one wall with a massive stone mantel above it. Mounted on that same wall were numerous wild-animal heads, including antelope, bighorn sheep, bear, and even a jaguar, the beast the Mexicans called *El Jaguar*, with its mouth open and fangs bared in a fierce snarl.

"Looks like Mr. Davidson is quite a hunter," Bo commented as he looked at the mounted heads.

"Yes, sir," Alfred agreed. "He's an excellent shot, and very daring. That jaguar would have been on him in another couple of bounds when he pulled the trigger on his rifle and killed it."

Bo wasn't sure whether a man endangering his own life like that just for a trophy was daring or foolhardy. He leaned toward foolhardy.

The other men had gathered around a sideboard on the wall opposite the fireplace. They held drinks in their hands, poured from a bottle that sat open on the sideboard. Hansen picked the bottle up by the neck and held it out toward Bo and Scratch, raising his bushy blond eyebrows in a questioning look.

Scratch glanced over at Bo and licked his lips. "Go ahead," Bo told his trail partner. "You don't have to ask my permission to take a drink."

Scratch sauntered over to Hansen and said, "Don't mind if I do." He got an empty glass from the sideboard, and Hansen spilled amber liquid into it from the bottle. Scratch took a sip and let out an appreciative "Ahhh."

Bo turned to Alfred, who had followed them into the dining room. "What sort of trouble is going on inside the mine?" he asked the young man.

"I wouldn't know, Mr. Creel," Alfred replied with a shake of his head. "I don't have anything to do with the actual mining operation other than keeping track of the books for Mr. Davidson. I also prepare meals for him and the supervisors . . . and now, I suppose, for you gentlemen as well."

Before Bo could say anything else, he heard a shot. From the deep, echoing sound of the report, it came from inside the tunnel. As it faded, it bounced back from the walls of the canyon as well.

There was only the one shot, but that was enough to send Bo striding quickly out of the dining room, followed close behind by Scratch. The rest of the men trailed along, too, with the exception of Skinner, Bo saw as he glanced at him. The skull-faced killer remained at the sideboard, casually pouring himself another drink. Unless somebody paid him to care or his own life was threatened, he clearly didn't give a damn what was going on.

By the time Bo, Scratch, and the others reached the porch, Davidson had emerged from the tunnel mouth, accompanied by Wallace, and was coming back toward the mine headquarters. He didn't seem upset.

"What was that shot?" Bo asked as Davidson and Wallace came up to the steps.

"Just now, you mean?" Davidson shrugged. "I

saw a little rattlesnake and got rid of it. Can't have them crawling in where they're not wanted."

"No, I suppose not. What about that other trouble you went to check on?"

"I'm not sure that's any of your business, Bo, since I'm hiring you to help guard the ore shipments, not to run my mine for me."

"Scratch and I haven't said for sure that we're going to work for you," Bo pointed out.

"I hope you will. I saw how well the two of you handled yourselves when those bandits jumped us last night." Davidson shrugged. "And I can understand your concern. But it's nothing for you to worry about. Just a dispute between a worker and one of my foremen. It's been resolved, and it won't happen again."

"Well, I reckon that's good to know. You were on your way back out of the tunnel when you spotted that snake?"

"That's right."

Bo wasn't sure he believed that. He couldn't help but wonder if Davidson had settled the dispute between miner and foreman with a bullet. He didn't want to think that. He had liked Davidson or he never would have agreed to come down here in the first place. And he had no proof that Davidson wasn't exactly the amiable sort he appeared to be, at least most of the time.

Bo believed in giving a man the benefit of the doubt. He would continue to do so—at least for now.

He would have felt better about things, though, if he had actually seen that rattlesnake himself.

The last of the light was fading from the sky. As

Davidson ascended the steps, followed by Wallace, he called, "Alfred, I hope you've prepared a suitable supper. After a couple of days on the trail, I'm hungry as a bear!"

"Of course, sir," the young man replied. "The meal will be ready shortly."

"And have Rosalinda serve."

"Yes, sir."

As Alfred spoke, Bo saw a troubled frown pass over the young man's face. The expression was there and gone so fast that if he hadn't happened to be looking directly at Alfred he wouldn't have seen it.

Something about Davidson's mention of a woman called Rosalinda bothered Alfred. Bo wondered who she was and why Alfred had reacted that way.

Like everything else, though, Bo figured that if he were patient, sooner or later he would have answers to all his questions.

CHAPTER 8

Rosalinda turned out to be a young woman; little more than a girl, in fact. She carried in a platter piled high with thick slices of roast beef, and set it on the table after the men had taken chairs around it.

From the way the gazes of several of the men followed her lithe form in her long skirt and low-cut blouse, they thought she looked as appetizing as the food. Her skin was a rich honey brown, and the long, thick hair that fell around her bare shoulders was as black as a raven's wing. She kept her eyes downcast as she backed away from the table.

"Thank you, Rosalinda," Davidson said. "That looks very good."

"*Sí, señor,*" she murmured. "I will bring the rest of the food."

She retreated to the kitchen and came back with bowls of beans, potatoes, chili peppers, and tiny onions, as well as plates piled high with tortillas. Davidson made an expansive gesture and said, "Dig in, gentlemen."

Rosalinda moved past him, and in what seemed a

natural extension of his gesture, Davidson's hand reached out and rested for a moment on the curve of her hip.

"We'll want coffee and brandy, too," he told her. *"Sí, señor."*

Davidson chuckled, squeezed her hip, and gave it a pat. It was a very possessive move, and Bo was willing to bet that none of the men around the table had missed it. Having Rosalinda serve the meal and then treating her that way served a dual purpose.

It showed her off to the men—and at the same time let them know in no uncertain terms that Davidson regarded her as his own personal property.

That rubbed Bo the wrong way, and he knew from the flicker of anger in Scratch's eyes that his partner felt the same way. That was no way to treat a lady, and to the Texans' way of thinking, all women were ladies unless and until they proved otherwise.

Several of the mine foremen had come to the headquarters building for supper, joining Davidson and the men he had brought from El Paso around the table. Wallace was among them, and at Davidson's urging he gave a brief accounting of the mine's production over the past week or so.

"You know we had quite a bit of ore on hand when you left here, Boss," Wallace said. "It's just grown since then. We really need to get it across the border."

Davidson nodded. "That's my thinking exactly. First thing in the morning, have it loaded on the wagons." He looked around the table at the newly hired guards. "Gentlemen, I hate to put you to work so soon after you got here, but I need to move that gold."

"You want us to turn right around and head back to El Paso with it?" Skinner asked.

"Is that a problem, Mr. Skinner?" Davidson asked.

Skinner shook his head. "Nope. Not as far as I'm concerned. You're payin' top wages, so you call the tune. Are you comin' with us?"

"No, I'll be staying here."

"Then I reckon you need to put somebody in charge for the trip back up there." Skinner bared his teeth in an ugly grin as he looked around the table. "I'll tell you right now, I ain't too good at takin' orders."

The implication was clear to all of them. Skinner preferred giving orders to taking them. He wanted Davidson to put him in charge of the guards who would accompany the ore shipment to El Paso.

Davidson looked around the table as well. "Do any of you men object to Mr. Skinner being in charge?"

Scratch opened his mouth to say something, but Bo caught his eye and gave a tiny shake of his head. Scratch frowned, but he didn't voice any complaints.

Neither did any of the other men. Jackman and Tragg both muttered, "Nope," and shook their heads. Hansen shrugged his broad shoulders. Lancaster said, "That's fine by me," and Douglas jerked his head in a curt nod of agreement with the Englishman. That left Bo and Scratch.

"No objections from us," Bo said, speaking for both of them.

"You've definitely decided to take me up on my offer of employment?" Davidson asked.

"We have," Bo declared. "And we appreciate you being patient while we made up our minds."

Davidson smiled. "Good men are worth waiting for. I believe that with the eight of you looking out for my gold, I can finally stop worrying about getting it to El Paso safely."

"I'll drink to that," Jackman said, reaching for his whiskey.

"That'll be the last drink tonight," Davidson said. "Since you'll be riding again first thing in the morning, none of you need hangovers."

"What about the señoritas?" Tragg asked. "We ain't had a chance to visit the cantina in that village, and you said they had some pretty gals there."

"Got at least one pretty one here," Skinner murmured as his deep-set eyes glanced toward the kitchen where Rosalinda had gone.

Bo saw Davidson's mouth tighten. "I'm sorry, that'll have to wait until you get back from this trip. But I'll see to it that there's a . . . bonus . . . waiting for each of you when you return." The mine owner forced a smile onto his face. "I believe you'll find that it's worth the wait."

That decision didn't set well with some of the men, but there wasn't anything they could do about it other than grumble, and none of them wanted to get on Davidson's bad side by doing too much of that. The meal continued, and after a few minutes Skinner said, "Figure we'll split up into four bunches of two men each tomorrow and fan out around the ore wagons. Lancaster, you're with me."

"All right," Lancaster said.

"Douglas and me will ride together," Hansen said.

The kid nodded his agreement. That left Jackman and Tragg, and Bo and Scratch, as the other two pairs. Everyone seemed satisfied with the arrangement. Skinner decided that he and Lancaster would ride about half a mile to the west of the wagons, with Jackman and Tragg in a similar position to the east. The other two pairs of riders would bring up the rear, several hundred yards apart from each other.

Davidson said, "The bandits have always laid an ambush for the wagons when they struck before. I think that arrangement should work fine to counter any frontal attack."

"Unless they decide to hit from some other direction since they know you've got extra guards now," Bo pointed out.

"We can't be sure they're aware of that," Davidson said. "The bunch that attacked us last night might not be the same ones who have held up the ore wagons in the past. There could be more than one gang of *bandidos* in these parts."

"Maybe," Bo said with a shrug.

"Anyway, no matter what direction the bandits attack from, with you men spread out around the wagons, there'll be reinforcements galloping in to attack them from the rear or the flanks."

"And you've got genuine fighting men protecting the wagons this time," Lancaster pointed out. "You strike me as a former military man, Mr. Davidson. Were you in the Army?"

"I was," Davidson replied with a smile. "I was a captain, in command of a company of infantry from Ohio during the War of Rebellion."

"You mean the War of Northern Aggression?" Scratch drawled.

"The Civil War's been over for nigh on to fifteen years," Bo said. "Let's not fight it all over again."

Davidson laughed. "Not at all. We're all allies now, Bo. And I'm glad of it." He turned back to Lancaster. "You served in Her Majesty's Army?"

Lancaster nodded and said, "I was a lancer in India."

Hansen spoke up. "I was in an infantry unit from Minnesota." Jackman and Tragg chimed in as well, saying that they had belonged to a company of irregulars in Missouri.

Guerrillas, that was what they meant, Bo thought. He wondered if they had ridden with Quantrill or Bloody Bill Anderson or some other guerrilla leader who was just an outlaw by another name.

Davidson turned to Skinner as the reminiscing continued. "What about you, Mr. Skinner?"

"I don't see any sense in war," the gunman snapped. "When I kill a man, it's for cold, hard cash, not some idea that don't mean a damn thing."

Davidson looked annoyed by Skinner's comment, but he turned to Bo and Scratch and asked, "What about you two? I assume that since you're Texans, you fought for the Confederacy?"

Bo shook his head. "We steered clear of the ruckus as much as we could."

"Reckon we got our bellyful of fightin' wars when Texas busted loose from Mexico and Santy Anny," Scratch added.

In truth, they had aided the Southern cause on a couple of occasions in the far western theater of war, helping out an old friend of theirs who was a member of the Confederate intelligence service. But being Texans, they had always considered themselves Westerners more than Southerners and had never actually donned the gray.

The subject shifted back to preparations for the trip to El Paso the next morning. Each pair of men would carry their own supplies, and they wouldn't rendezvous with the others, except in case of a bandit attack, until the wagons reached the border. They would make the return trip together, though. The *bandidos* wouldn't have any reason to jump empty wagons.

With everything settled, Davidson lifted his glass to finish off his whiskey. "To success, gentlemen," he said. "The more gold we get through to El Paso, the richer we'll all be."

"I'll drink to bein' rich," Jackman said.

"You're the only one that'll be rich," Skinner told Davidson. "Hired guns never stay in one place long enough—or live long enough—for that to happen to them."

"Stick with me, Mr. Skinner, and you might be surprised," Davidson said. "There's untold wealth in Cutthroat Canyon."

After supper, the men turned in, most of them eager to get some sleep since they had to be riding again early the next morning. Skinner was adamant about not sharing a room with anyone, so Alfred gave him one of the extra rooms to himself and set up a cot in a storage room for Lancaster, who volunteered for the less luxurious accommodations.

"Even so, it's much better than our quarters were in Peshawar, you know," the Englishman said.

Davidson stayed in the dining room to talk to Alfred after the others had left. Bo motioned Scratch to go on and lingered in the hallway, just out of sight, where he could hear what they were saying. He didn't like sneaking around and eavesdropping on folks, but he had a hunch that he needed to find out as much as he could about what was going on around here.

"Send Rosalinda to my room as soon as she's through cleaning up in here," Davidson ordered, his tone brisk.

"Yes, sir," Alfred said. Bo thought he didn't sound particularly happy about it either, but Davidson didn't seem to notice.

"The men will need a good breakfast in the morning," Davidson went on, "since they'll be riding all day. You'll see to that, and preparing supplies for them to take with them?"

"Of course, sir."

"And let Gomez know that we'll need girls here for them when they get back four nights from now."

"Yes, sir. Any, ah, particular preferences that you know of?"

Davidson chuckled. "No, I haven't really explored that with the new men yet. I'm sure they'll be satisfied with whatever Gomez can provide. If any of them want anything . . . special . . . we can deal with that later."

"Yes, sir."

Davidson yawned and said, "Good night, Alfred."

"Good night, sir."

Bo heard Davidson's footsteps retreating and Alfred moving around the room. Dishes clinked against each other a moment later. Bo ventured a glance around the corner, and saw that Rosalinda had reappeared from the kitchen and was cleaning off the table. Alfred helped her, and as he did so, he said in a quiet voice, "Señor Davidson wants you to come to his room when you're through here, Rosalinda."

A scared look appeared on her face as she shook her head. "Alfred, no. Not again, *por favor.*"

"I'm afraid you have no choice," he told her, then added in a mutter that Bo barely heard, "Neither of us do."

For a second, Rosalinda looked like she was going to argue, but then she lowered her eyes to the floor again and nodded. "*Sí,* Alfred. I will do as I am told."

Bo waited where he was, just out of sight of those in the dining room, until Rosalinda was gone and Alfred was moving around the room blowing out the lamps. Then he stepped around the corner and cleared his throat.

Alfred jumped a little in surprise as he turned around. "Oh, Mr. Creel," he said. "I didn't know you were still up. Can I do something for you, sir?"

Bo had a good idea why Alfred had reacted so guiltily. He had heard the young man muttering under his breath again as he moved around the room, and Bo suspected that whatever Alfred had been saying, it wasn't too complimentary to Porter Davidson.

"No, I don't need anything, son," Bo said. "What do you need?"

Alfred frowned in confusion. "I . . . I don't understand, sir."

"Are you happy here, doing the things you have to do?"

Alfred straightened his back. "I'm sure I don't know what you mean, sir. My job is quite satisfactory."

"All right. If you say so."

Bo wasn't convinced by the young man's answer, but he could tell from the stiff look on Alfred's face that he wasn't going to get anything else. Alfred wouldn't betray his boss. That sort of loyalty was usually an admirable quality.

Bo wasn't so sure that was the case here.

But he let it go and said, "Good night, Alfred. See you in the morning."

"Good night, Mr. Creel."

Bo went to the room that had been assigned to him and Scratch, and found the silver-haired Texan smoking a quirly and peering out the window at the night.

"Where have you been?" Scratch asked without turning around.

"Oh, skulking around the dining room, eavesdropping on Davidson and Alfred."

Scratch chuckled. "I knew you had some kind of burr under your saddle. Things ain't right around here, and if I can tell that, you sure as hell can."

"No, they're not," Bo agreed. "Davidson told Alfred to send that Rosalinda girl to his room after she got finished cleaning up after supper. Alfred didn't like it either."

"He's sweet on the gal his own self," Scratch said.

"That's what it looks like to me. He won't stand up to Davidson about it, though."

Scratch shrugged. "Davidson's his boss. Just like

he's *our* boss now." He finally turned away from the window. "You know it don't bother me none to let you do the thinkin' for us, Bo, but I ain't sure I want to work for that hombre after all. I'm startin' to think it's *him* the Mexes are so scared of, not any *bandidos.*"

"The same thought occurred to me," Bo agreed with a nod. "But I'd like to find out exactly what's going on around here, and I figure the best way to do that is if we're working for Davidson."

"We got to turn around and go right back to El Paso," Scratch pointed out.

"Yes, but we'll be coming back here, and after that, I expect it'll be a while before another ore shipment is ready. That will give us some time to poke around."

"Where we maybe ain't wanted, eh?" Scratch asked with a grin.

"If we never stuck our noses in where they're not wanted, we'd never find out anything interesting, now would we?"

Scratch chuckled. "Reckon not." He grew more serious. "Davidson ought to be ashamed of himself, messin' around with a gal as young as Rosalinda. Ol' Alfred's a lot closer to her age, and seems like a nice young fella to boot. Maybe before we leave Cutthroat Canyon for good, we can do somethin' about that."

"Yeah," Bo agreed dryly. "Just a couple of frontier Cupids, that's us."

"Speak for yourself, old-timer. I ain't ready to start wearin' no diaper again, and I sure as shootin' don't carry no bow and arrow! Say," Scratch went on, "you reckon ol' Cupid's really a Comanch?"

Bo didn't have any idea how to answer that question, so he just went to bed instead.

CHAPTER 9

The men were up before dawn the next morning, getting ready to ride. As Bo led his saddled dun out of the barn into the corral, he saw three wagons lined up in front of the headquarters building, each with a six-mule team hitched to it. Men in sombreros and sandals and rough peasant garb were carrying crates out of the big log building and placing them in the wagons.

There must be a strong room somewhere inside there that he hadn't seen yet, Bo thought, where Davidson stored the ore under lock and key until he could ship it out.

Leaving the horses in the corral, Bo and Scratch went to the headquarters building for breakfast. Alfred had outdone himself with piles of bacon and sausage, towering stacks of flapjacks, mounds of scrambled and fried eggs, thick juicy steaks, plates full of biscuits and bowls full of gravy, pitchers of molasses for the flapjacks, jugs of buttermilk, and several pots of strong black coffee.

Skinner, Jackman, and Tragg were already at the

table, eating enthusiastically. Jackman and Tragg gave friendly nods to Bo and Scratch as the Texans entered the dining room. Skinner didn't glance up or acknowledge their presence. Bo and Scratch sat down, poured cups of coffee, and started filling their plates.

"Ain't seen that Rosalinda gal around this mornin'," Tragg said.

"I reckon Mr. Davidson plumb wore her out last night, more than likely," Jackman added with a grin.

Alfred was coming in the door from the kitchen as Jackman made his crude comment. He had another pot of coffee in his hand, and for a second Bo thought he was going to haul off and smash the pot down on Jackman's head. Alfred controlled his emotions with a visible effort and placed the coffeepot on the table.

"Good morning, gentlemen," he said to Bo and Scratch. "You slept well, I trust?"

"Just fine," Scratch replied. "Where's the boss man this mornin'?"

Alfred shook his head. "I haven't seen Mr. Davidson yet. I assume that he's still asleep. Mr. Wallace is supervising the loading of the ore onto the wagons. He'll be driving the lead wagon as well."

"Wallace knows where to take the ore when we get to El Paso?" Bo asked.

"Yes, sir. He's Mr. Davidson's second in command and is familiar with all phases of the operation."

Douglas, Hansen, and Lancaster came in from saddling their horses and joined the others at the table. The kid was taciturn as usual, but Hansen and

Lancaster were talkative. Soon, conversation and laughter filled the dining room as the men bantered back and forth.

Wallace came in while they were still eating, and reported that the wagons were loaded and ready to roll. Skinner nodded, drained the last of his coffee, and scraped his chair back as he stood up.

"Davidson tell you that I'm in charge?" he asked Wallace in a challenging tone of voice.

Wallace's rugged jaw tightened. "He said that you were in charge of the guard detail. I'm still responsible for those wagons and that ore, though."

"Just don't go givin' me orders," Skinner warned. "I don't take kindly to it."

The two men glared at each other for a second; then Wallace shrugged and turned away. "Just let us know when you're ready to ride," he said over his shoulder as he started out.

"I'm ready now," Skinner snapped. He made a curt gesture at the other men. "Let's go."

Hansen still had food on his plate, and looked like he might complain about being forced to leave it, but he thought better of it and stood up along with the others. He picked up the couple of flapjacks he had left, though, rolled them into a cylinder, and shoved the whole thing into his mouth. He was chewing emphatically as they left the building.

There were two men on each wagon, armed with both rifles and shotguns. In addition, four heavily armed outriders would accompany the wagons, one at each point of the compass. Those defenders would be enough to discourage small groups of would-be thieves. And if a larger bunch tried to grab the gold, the men Davidson had hired in El Paso would rush in to put a stop to the robbery.

Bo and Scratch went to the corral with the other men and led their horses out. Alfred emerged from the house with four sets of fully loaded saddlebags. He handed out the supplies and then stepped back.

"Good luck, gentlemen," he said. "If all goes as planned, you'll be back here on the evening of the fourth day from now. I'll see you then."

"So long, Alfred," Scratch said as the men swung up into their saddles.

"Good-bye, Mr. Morton."

Bo lifted a hand in farewell as he heeled the dun into motion. Wallace, on the driver's seat of the lead wagon, gripped the reins tightly, and had already started slapping them against the backs of the mule team. He yelled at the balky critters, and the mules finally leaned forward in their harness. The wagon lurched ahead. The other teams followed.

Skinner, Lancaster, Jackman, and Tragg headed up the canyon ahead of the wagons. There was no point in spreading out until they were all out of the valley. The bandits weren't going to try anything this close to the mine. Bo, Scratch, Hansen, and Douglas followed the wagons, keeping their mounts at an easy walk to allow the vehicles to pull ahead.

"You want the right side or the left?" Hansen asked as they rode.

"It doesn't matter to us," Bo said. "Scratch and I are to the left now, so I guess we can stay that way."

Hansen nodded. "That's as good a way to choose as any." As they cleared the canyon mouth and started out into the valley, he went on. "Do you think the bandits will hit us this trip?"

"There's no way of knowing," Bo said. "I won't be surprised either way."

As the wagons followed the road that cut through the fields, Bo saw several men working with hoes or following teams of oxen pulling plows. At least the valley didn't appear as eerily deserted today as it had the day before.

Bo saw the furtive glances that the workers cast toward the wagons and the riders, too. And as they neared the village, he looked up at the bell tower in the church and spotted movement there.

"Fella in the tower," he said quietly to Scratch.

"I see him," the silver-haired Texan replied. "Hombre could cover a mighty big field of fire from up there. You reckon he works for Davidson?"

"I can't think of any other good reason for him to be up there, can you?"

Hansen asked, "What are you gents talking about?"

Bo decided to risk telling the big Swede what he and Scratch had noticed. "There's a rifleman in the bell tower of that church. That reflection we spotted from up there yesterday evening came from a rifle barrel, not the bell."

"He's probably just a lookout," Douglas suggested. "A man could see a long way from up there. He'd probably see that gang of bandits if they rode into the valley."

That was a long speech for the close-mouthed, cold-eyed youngster. What he said made sense, too—and yet Bo sensed that wasn't the full explanation for the presence of the rifleman in the tower.

"A fella with good eyes and a high-powered rifle, like, say, a Sharps Big Fifty, could hit just about anybody in this valley," Scratch mused, his thoughts obviously paralleling Bo's. "A few years ago down in the Texas Panhandle, a fella name of Billy Dixon shot an Injun's horse out from under him at a range of damn near a mile with a Sharps."

"And a pair of field glasses would let a man see everything that was going on around here," Bo added. "Sort of like the eyes of God looking down from Heaven."

"With a rifle instead of a lightnin' bolt."

Hansen laughed. "You fellas are loco. You're making it sound like Davidson rules this valley through fear. He gets along with these Mexes. He even buys fruits and vegetables and other supplies from them, he said."

"That's what he claims," Bo said.

"Well, I tend to take the word of the man who's paying my wages, at least until I've got proof that he's not tellin' me the truth."

Bo nodded. "That's reasonable. And maybe the fella in the bell tower really is just a lookout, like Douglas suggested. But I can't help being curious."

"Curiosity's sometimes a dangerous thing," Hansen said. "That's why I tend to keep any doubts I have to myself."

Scratch looked over at Douglas. "What do you think, kid?"

"I think I'm here to do a job," Douglas said. "That's all I care about."

Bo shrugged. "Fair enough. Let's let it go at that."

Douglas and Hansen could cause trouble, though,

if they went to Davidson when they got back to
Cutthroat Canyon and told the mine owner what Bo
and Scratch had said. Bo didn't think they would—
men who hired out their guns tended to mind their
own business—but it was a possibility.

He and Scratch would deal with that when and if
it happened. In the meantime, the reaction of the
two men had told Bo that he and Scratch couldn't
count on any help from them if it turned out that
Davidson really was running things around here by
fear and intimidation.

If that time came, Bo and Scratch would have a
decision of their own to make.

A few people were moving around in the village,
but they all retreated indoors when they saw the
wagons and the riders coming. Hansen seemed to
notice that. When Bo looked over at the man, he
saw a puzzled frown creasing Hansen's forehead.
Hansen thumbed his hat back and tilted his head so
that he could look up at the bell tower as they passed
the church. Bo could almost see the wheels turning
in the big Swede's brain as Hansen thought about
what Bo had said and what he had seen with his
own eyes.

They left the village behind, and a short time
later they reached the pass leading out of the valley.
By mid-morning, they were through the foothills
and out on the flats, heading north toward El Paso.
From their trip down here, Bo and Scratch knew
that for the most part the terrain was open, with only
a slight roll to it, not really good country for an
ambush.

But there were ridges and knolls here and there

that could conceal *bandidos,* not to mention arroyos of the sort that the bandits had used to sneak up on the camp two nights earlier. Appearances were deceptive. There were a lot more places to hide along their route than it looked like at first glance.

"Reckon we'd better split up," Hansen said. "The rest of the fellas are out of sight already."

That was true. Skinner and Lancaster had vanished to the northwest, while Jackman and Tragg headed northeast. They would parallel the course of the wagons, staying far enough away so that maybe bandits wouldn't notice them.

Bo and Scratch reined their horses to the left. Hansen and Douglas went right. They wouldn't separate as much as the others had and would stay within sight of each other, several hundred yards apart.

"I got to thinkin'," Scratch said after he and Bo had been riding by themselves for a few minutes. "It seems to me almost like Davidson's tryin' to tempt those *bandidos* into comin' after the gold again."

"Like maybe *he's* setting a trap for *them,* and wants us to wipe them out?" Bo suggested.

"Yeah. Exactly like that."

Bo nodded slowly. "Could be. After the things we've seen, I wouldn't put it past him."

Scratch rasped a thumbnail along his jawline, a habit he shared with Bo when either of them was deep in thought. "That young fella Davidson killed a couple of nights ago . . . he didn't look like much of a bandit to me. He wasn't much more'n a kid."

"You could say the same thing about Douglas," Bo pointed out, "and I wouldn't want to tangle with him."

"Reckon that's true enough. And the hombre *did*

try to ventilate me and was about to take a knife to Davidson. I ain't sayin' he was some sort of babe in the woods. But he didn't strike me as a hardened desperado either."

"No, not at all," Bo agreed. "I wish we could have asked him some questions."

"Well, Davidson saw to it that we couldn't."

"Yeah," Bo said. "He sure did."

That was something to ponder, too. Bo could tell from the palaver that Scratch's thinking was running along the same lines as his. Both of them had a pretty good idea what was really going on in Cutthroat Canyon and the adjacent valley. They just didn't have any proof of it.

It was another long, hot day in the saddle, the third such in a row for the Texans, but at least it passed peacefully, with no sign of trouble. As night fell, they made a cold camp and ate a supper of biscuits and jerky washed down with water from their canteens.

Scratch peered wistfully into the distance at the glow of the fire where the men with the wagons had made camp and said, "Those fellas got hot coffee tonight."

"You can have some coffee when we get to El Paso," Bo said.

"With maybe a little dollop of brandy in it?"

Bo chuckled. "I don't see why not."

Scratch sighed as he leaned back against the rock behind where he was sitting and tipped the brim of his Stetson down over his eyes. "I'll just think about that for a while."

"You do that," Bo told him.

The night passed as quietly as the day had, and everybody was on the move again at first light the next morning. Bo slipped a pair of field glasses from his saddlebags and used them to check on the wagons. Everything appeared to be fine as the vehicles rolled along northward. In late morning, they came to a range of small hills and mesas.

"If them bandits plan on hittin' the wagons between here and El Paso, this'd be about the best place," Scratch said.

Bo nodded. "I was just thinking the same—"

As if they had been waiting for that cue, somewhere up ahead guns began to roar.

CHAPTER 10

Bo and Scratch didn't hesitate. They heeled their horses into a run and headed for the wagons. Off to the right, Hansen and the kid did the same thing.

It was hard to hear anything over the thundering hoofbeats of the dun and the bay, but in that first moment Bo had heard rifles cracking, pistols popping, and shotguns booming. The wagons must have rolled into a full-scale ambush.

A moment later, they came in sight of the vehicles, which had halted a couple of hundred yards from a shallow mesa. Puffs of gun smoke came from the top of that mesa, telling Bo that some of the bandits had waited up there for the ore wagons to come along. Then they had opened fire, killing the lead mules in each team to stop the wagons. Bo could see that the animals were down in their traces.

The gunfire from the mesa had also driven the men on the stalled wagons to take cover. They had scrambled off the seats and were crouched behind the wagons as they returned the fire. The outriders had galloped in and taken cover behind the wagons, too, because to stay out in the open would have made them easy targets.

As if that weren't bad enough, bandits on horseback had entered the fray as well, circling the wagons like Comanches and taking potshots at the defenders. Their horses' hooves kicked up enough dust that it was difficult to see exactly what was going on.

Bo spotted riders converging on the mesa, though, and recognized them as Skinner, Lancaster, Jackman, and Tragg. He pointed them out to Scratch and shouted, "They're going after the bandits on the mesa! We'll take the ones on horseback!"

Scratch jerked his head in a nod, and hauled his Winchester from its sheath strapped to the bay's saddle.

Bo did likewise with his rifle. The dun was used to being in the middle of violent fracases. Gunfire and the smell of powder smoke didn't bother him. Bo guided the horse with his knees as he worked the Winchester's lever and jacked a round into the firing chamber. He lifted the rifle to his shoulder.

The back of a running horse was no place for accuracy. As Bo and Scratch opened fire on the bandits circling the wagons, they didn't try to place their shots. They just sprayed lead toward the *bandidos* as fast as they could. Some of the slugs were bound to find a target, or at least come close enough to spook the men attacking the wagons.

That was what happened. One of the bandits threw his arms in the air as his sombrero flew from his head. He pitched from the saddle, landed hard, bounced once, and then lay still.

His fall didn't go unnoticed. Several of the bandits

wheeled their mounts to confront this new threat. Smoke geysered from the muzzles of their pistols.

However, Bo, Scratch, Hansen, and Douglas were still out of effective handgun range. The bullets smacked into the ground and kicked up dust well ahead of their horses. The guards kept up a steady fire as they surged closer, and another bandit was hit, doubling over as a slug bored into his belly and then sliding out of his saddle to sprawl on the ground.

The bandits' nerve broke then. They whirled their horses and ran, pounding away toward the mesa where their compadres had lain in ambush. They didn't try to climb one of the paths up the rugged butte, though. Instead, they circled it and tore off into the hills as fast as their horses would carry them.

As Bo and Scratch slowed to a halt next to the wagons, Bo heard a fusillade of shots from the top of the mesa. Skinner and the others had made it up there and were battling against the rest of the gang.

"Reckon we ought to go give 'em a hand?" Scratch asked.

"Let's see how bad folks are hurt here first," Bo said.

He saw Wallace leaning against the lead wagon. Bright red blood had splashed out on the man's shirt. As Bo dismounted, Wallace sagged, and would have fallen if the man who'd been riding shotgun with him hadn't caught him.

"How bad is it, Wallace?" Bo asked.

Davidson's *segundo* shook his head. "Bullet just ripped across my side," he said between tightly clenched teeth. "Hurts like hell, but it probably looks worse than it really is."

"How about the rest of you boys?" Scratch called. "Anybody hurt bad?"

"Don't worry about us," Wallace snapped. "Get up on that mesa and help Skinner wipe out those damned bandits."

"I don't reckon that'll be necessary," Bo said with a nod toward the mesa. "Shooting's stopped."

So it had. Silence reigned atop the mesa now. They couldn't be sure what that meant, but in all likelihood Skinner, Lancaster, Jackman, and Tragg had been victorious. If the bandits had won the fight, they would be shooting at the wagons again by now.

Sure enough, while Bo was patching up the deep bullet graze in Wallace's side, Scratch said, "Here they come." Bo glanced up to see Skinner and the others riding slowly down the trail that led from the top of the mesa. When they reached the bottom, they came toward the wagons, and their deliberate pace and lack of urgency told Bo that there probably wasn't anybody left alive up there.

His mouth tightened at the thought. He didn't feel sorry for the bandits; it had been their own decision to ambush the wagons and try to steal the gold.

But he didn't like the idea of the slaughter that had probably taken place up there either.

"Get 'em all?" Wallace called to Skinner as the riders came up to the wagons.

"Yeah," Skinner replied.

"They're all dead?"

"That's right."

"Good," Wallace said vehemently. "The dirty bastards had it coming."

Again, Bo couldn't argue with that sentiment. As

men who had all too often lived by the gun, he and Scratch knew that someday they were likely to die by it, too. Still, the hatred that Wallace displayed, coupled with Skinner's cold-blooded callousness, bothered him.

"All right," he said as he finished tying the bandage around Wallace's midsection, "who else is hurt?"

A couple of the other men had minor wounds. Bo tended to them while Scratch rode out to check on the two bandits who had been shot off their horses during the fight. One or both of them might still be alive.

Bo could tell from the look on Scratch's face as he rode back to the wagons, though, that that wasn't the case. As Scratch came up and reined in, he shook his head.

"Nope, they're done for," he reported. "The first fella was drilled plumb through the head and must've died right away. The other hombre was gut-shot. Took him longer to die, the poor varmint."

"Don't waste your sympathy on them, Morton," Wallace said. "They're just bandits."

"Yeah," Scratch said. "I reckon that's right."

Bo could tell that something was bothering Scratch, though, and as soon as he got the chance, he pulled his trail partner aside and asked him what it was.

Scratch glanced at the other men and kept his voice pitched low enough so that his answer wouldn't be overheard. "They was even younger than that fella the other night, Bo," he said. "I don't figure either one of 'em was even twenty years old."

Bo frowned. "You're saying it was a bunch of kids who attacked these wagons?"

"I don't know about the rest, but those two sure were."

Bo looked toward the top of the mesa. "Now I'm mighty curious about the bandits Skinner and the others killed up there."

"Yeah, so am I. Reckon we ought to ask him about them?"

"I think maybe we should," Bo said.

They walked over to the other guards, who were getting ready to ride again while some of Wallace's men unhooked the dead mules from their harness. Having only four mules pulling each wagon would slow down the pace, but there was nothing anyone could do about that.

"We've got a question for you, Skinner," Bo said.

Skinner gave them a cold look. "I don't answer to you two, Creel."

"Scratch and I still want to know if you got a good look at those bandits up on the mesa?"

"Go to hell," Skinner snapped as he turned away.

Scratch started to step forward, his face taut with anger. Bo put a hand on his arm to stop him from confronting Skinner. They didn't want this to turn into a gunfight.

Lancaster spoke up, answering the question that Skinner had refused to. "We checked the bodies to make sure they were all dead," he said. "They were. We didn't have to finish off any of them."

"How old were they?" Bo asked.

"Why . . . I don't really know," Lancaster said with a puzzled frown. "I don't know about you, old boy, but I don't really make a habit of stopping to inquire a man's age when he's shooting at me."

"Nobody would expect you to." Bo jerked a thumb toward the pair of bandits who'd been shot off their horses. "But those two were just kids, and we were wondering if that was true of the ones who were up on the mesa."

Lancaster shrugged. "I'm afraid I didn't pay that much attention. You'd have to go take a look for yourself, if you're that interested."

"Maybe we'll just do that," Scratch said.

Skinner turned toward them again. "You do and I'll tell Davidson that you were neglectin' your job 'cause you were worried about some damn greasers. What do you think he'll do then?"

"It won't take long to check it out," Bo said. "How did you manage to wipe all of them out so fast anyway?"

Jackman grinned and provided the answer to that question. "There's a trail up the back side of that mesa. They should've put a guard on it, the damn fools. We made it up there and were practically on top of 'em before they knew what was goin' on. And there were only three of 'em. It wasn't much of a fight."

Skinner turned to Wallace. "You got those damn dead mules unhitched? We need to get movin' again. This is already gonna slow us down."

"We're ready to roll," Wallace replied stiffly. He was pale from losing so much blood, but didn't seem to be on the verge of passing out.

"All right, then." Skinner swung up into his saddle and motioned for the other men to do likewise. "Let's get this gold to El Paso."

Bo and Scratch mounted up as well, but instead

of falling in behind the wagons, they started riding slowly toward the mesa.

Skinner saw that and called after them, "Damn it, stop wastin' your time! Do what you're supposed to, or you can forget about workin' for Davidson! I'll tell him it's either you two or me!"

"Do what you have to do, Skinner," Bo said over his shoulder.

"And so will we," Scratch added.

They heeled their horses into a trot and left the cursing Skinner behind. They reached the main trail and started up. By the time they made it to the top of the mesa, the wagons were lumbering past.

"You think they'll get jumped again before they get to El Paso?" Scratch asked.

Bo shook his head. "I don't know. It's doubtful. The bandits who got away know now that the wagons are well guarded. Anyway, we'll catch up in a little while. I don't care whether Skinner wants us along or not. We'll finish the trip."

Scratch nodded. "That's what I was thinkin'. I don't like to break my word . . . even if the fella I gave it to turns out to be a low-down skunk."

It took them only a moment to find the bodies sprawled behind some rocks at the edge of the mesa. The men wore rough clothes more suited for farming than for robbing gold wagons. Two had fallen on their sides when Skinner and the others cut them down. The third man lay on his back, staring sightlessly at the deep blue, cloudless sky.

"Son of a bitch," Scratch breathed. "That hombre can't be more'n sixteen years old."

"Lancaster must've known that, too," Bo said.

"He just didn't want to admit that they'd slaughtered a bunch of kids."

"Kids who were doin' their best to kill the fellas on those wagons," Scratch reminded him as Bo dismounted. "That bullet crease in Wallace's side is proof of that."

Bo shrugged as he handed the dun's reins to Scratch. "Yeah, there's no denying that. A bullet can kill you just as dead no matter how old the finger is that pulls the trigger."

He used a foot to roll the other two bodies onto their backs as well. Not surprisingly, those two bandits were very young, too, not out of their teens.

"Varmints hadn't even been shavin' long," Scratch commented, the grim tightness of his voice revealing that what he and Bo had discovered bothered him, too, despite the circumstances.

Bo nodded and hunkered on his heels next to the bloody corpses. Each of them had numerous gunshot wounds. Skinner and the others had riddled them mercilessly with lead.

The sudden scrape of boot leather on the rocks behind them made Bo start to straighten up. His hand started toward his holstered Colt.

"Don't move, damn you!" a shrill voice cried. "I'll kill you! I'll kill you both!"

CHAPTER 11

Bo finished straightening up, but kept his hand well away from his gun. On the bay, Scratch kept his hands half lifted as he used his knees to make the horse turn toward the newcomer. Both Texans had heard the fear and panic in the voice, and knew that someone so spooked might be quick to pull the trigger.

Not only that, they had recognized the tone as female. Sure enough, they saw as they swung around, it was a young woman who stood there pointing a revolver at them. The gun barrel wavered back and forth as her hand trembled. Whether that was from her fear or the weight of the weapon or a combination of both, Bo didn't know and didn't care. He just didn't want to get shot.

"Hold on, Señorita," he said, keeping his voice calm and steady. "My partner and I don't mean you any harm."

"Liar!" she cried. "Filthy liar! I saw you shooting at my friends."

"You mean you're part of this bunch of bandits?" Scratch asked.

That probably wasn't the best way to phrase the question, Bo thought as the young woman jerked the barrel of the gun toward Scratch. But that pulled the gun away from him, and since it looked like she was about to shoot Scratch, Bo lunged forward, diving at her.

She let out an alarmed yell, yanked the gun back toward Bo, and jerked the trigger. She shot high, though, as most amateurs did when they hurried, and Bo had already left his feet. The blast slammed against his ears, but the bullet whistled harmlessly over his head. He wrapped his arms around the young woman's hips as he crashed into her and bore her over backward.

She cried out again, this time in pain, as she hit the rocky ground with Bo on top of her. He grabbed her wrist and twisted it enough to make her drop the gun without actually injuring her. By that time, Scratch was off his horse, and leaned down to snatch the weapon from the ground so that the young woman couldn't get her hands on it again.

Well aware that he was lying on top of a gal young enough to be his granddaughter, Bo pushed himself to his hands and knees and stood up quickly. He stepped back, picked up his hat, which had come off when he tackled her, and said, "I'm sorry I had to do that, Señorita. Couldn't let you shoot my pard here, though, or me for that matter."

The young woman rolled onto her side, put her hands over her face, and began to sob. The grief-stricken spasms wracked her body. Bo and Scratch looked at each other, and Scratch shrugged as if to say that this was Bo's problem.

"You're the one who's such a hand with the ladies," Bo said.

"Yeah, but my saddle's older'n this one," Scratch pointed out. "Gals don't respond to my charms until they got a mite more seasonin'."

"Well, you can help me help her up anyway."

They reached down and each of them took hold of an arm. "Come on, Señorita," Bo urged as she began to struggle against them. "We just want to talk to you. Let's go somewhere away from here to do it."

They lifted her to her feet despite her struggles and led her away from the bodies. She stumbled, and would have fallen if Bo and Scratch had not had hold of her. When they were well away from the dead men, Bo stopped and said, "Why don't you start by telling us your name?"

"Wh-why do you care?" she asked through her sniffles. "You have to know my name before you rape me and kill me?"

"Doggone it!" Scratch exclaimed, clearly shocked. "Why would we want to do a terrible thing like that?"

"You work for *him.* That is what his men do. They rape the women and kill everyone who opposes them, men, women, and children alike." Growing steadier on her feet, she gave a defiant toss of her head and went on. "I may be a woman, but I can fight like a man! So you'll be better off if you just go ahead and kill me!"

"Nobody's going to hurt you," Bo said. The young woman's words made him feel hollow inside, because they confirmed all his suspicions that had been growing stronger the past couple of days. Porter Davidson wasn't the man he had appeared to be at first. He was a lot worse.

"You were shooting at my friends," she said again. She wiped her eyes with the back of a hand. "For all I know, it was your bullets that killed some of them."

Bo couldn't argue with that. What she said was true. He told her, "You're right. But we didn't know what the situation was. And your amigos were shooting at us, too."

"Have you been to San Ramon?"

"Where?" Scratch asked.

Bo guessed, "You mean the village in the valley outside Cutthroat Canyon?"

"*Sí*. The village is called San Ramon."

"We've been there," Bo said.

"Then how could you *not* know the sort of man Señor Davidson is? Did you not see how the people of San Ramon cower in fear of their lives?"

"We saw," Bo said, his voice grim. "And we figured something was wrong. We just hadn't had a chance yet to talk to anybody and find out exactly what's going on around here."

She gave him a contemptuous look. "And what difference would it have made if you had known? Would you not have continued to take Davidson's money to terrorize my people?"

"We damn sure—I mean, we darn sure wouldn't," Scratch said. "Fact of the matter is, ma'am, we already figured somethin' was wrong around here, and we were plannin' to get to the bottom of it when we got back from El Paso."

The young woman looked back and forth between them. Bo could see in her eyes that a part of her wanted to believe them, but she was too afraid, too embittered, to embrace that hope. She couldn't bring herself to trust them.

He reached down to his hip and palmed out his Colt. The young woman flinched when she saw what he was doing, but her look of fear changed to one of confusion when he flipped the gun around and extended it to her, butt first.

"I don't think you're going to believe us until you see for yourself that we're telling the truth," Bo declared. "Take the gun. Do what you want with it. Nobody's going to stop you."

Scratch saw what Bo was doing. He had tucked the young woman's gun behind his belt, but he pulled his Remingtons, turned them around, and offered them to the young woman as well. "We're almighty sorry, Señorita. If we hurt any of your pards, it truly was because we didn't know for sure what's been goin' on around here. But I reckon we know now, and we want you to trust us when we tell you we aim to put a stop to it."

"That is," Bo added, "if you're telling us the truth about Davidson."

Anger flared in the young woman's dark eyes. She snatched the Colt away from him and lifted it with both hands, earing back the hammer as she did so. Bo just looked at her unflinchingly as she pointed the revolver at him.

She didn't pull the trigger. After a moment, she lowered the gun and let down the hammer again. "How did you know I would not kill you?" she asked.

Bo shrugged. "I figured you could tell we mean you no harm. And that we didn't know for sure Davidson was as bad as you've painted him."

"If we'd known," Scratch said, "you can bet a hat we never would've signed on to work for him."

"So why don't you fill us in?" Bo suggested as he took his Colt out of her limp hands. "You can start by telling us your name."

She swallowed hard. "It is Teresa . . . Teresa Volquez."

"All right, Señorita Volquez. It is Señorita, isn't it?" Teresa nodded. *"Sí."*

"Why don't you go on back down off this mesa with my partner, Señorita, and then we'll talk in a little while. First . . . I reckon we've got some burying to take care of."

Bo thought that Teresa Volquez might take off if they left her alone, but if she did it would have to be on foot. The men who had fled had taken all the horses with them. Instead, Teresa found a tiny bit of shade at the base of the mesa, and sat down to wait while Bo and Scratch dug graves and then brought the bodies down on the dun and the bay. They also used the horses to fetch the two corpses that lay out in the open near where the wagons had been stopped earlier.

Digging graves in the stony ground was difficult, and the Texans weren't as young as they used to be. Both men were drenched with sweat by the time they were finished with the grim chore. The graves weren't quite as deep as Bo would have liked either, but there were plenty of rocks along the base of the mesa that could be piled up to make cairns over the holes in the ground.

"I reckon we've given up any thought of catchin' up to the wagons," Scratch said as they worked on those cairns.

"Yes, considering what the girl's already told us, I think that's true," Bo said. "I've heard enough to know that I don't want to work for Davidson anymore."

"What *are* we gonna do?"

"Find out just how bad things really are in that valley. Then we'll decide."

"From the sound of it, those folks could use some help."

"Yeah," Bo said. "I was thinking the same thing."

Teresa joined them beside the graves, making the sign of the cross and muttering prayers for the souls of the young men who had been killed there today. Then she and Bo and Scratch walked back over into the shade, and Bo said, "Start from the beginning and tell us everything you know about Davidson."

"You mean when he came to San Ramon and murdered Don Alviso, who owned the mine in Cañon del Despiadado? Or when he forced the men of the village to abandon their crops and work in the mine instead? Or perhaps when he took the young women and forced *them* to . . . to degrade themselves with his men? These are the things you want to know about Señor Davidson?"

Scratch said, "Looks like we were wrong about the fella, Bo."

Bo nodded. "Yes, I'm afraid you're right. Señorita

Volquez, is there a rifleman in the bell tower of the church in San Ramon?"

"*Sí*. He keeps watch over the valley, and anyone who tries to escape, or to fight back against any of Davidson's men, the man in the tower can kill them with one shot." Her voice caught a little. "I . . . I have seen it happen."

Scratch shook his head. "That dirty son of a gun."

"What about the holdups?" Bo asked. "Were you and your friends just after the gold?"

"We thought that if we made it impossible for Davidson to ship his gold to El Paso, he might abandon the mine and leave us alone." Teresa gave a harsh, bitter laugh. "We should have known better. He just brought in even more hired killers." She looked pointedly at the Texans.

"We were told that his gold shipments were being robbed by bandits," Bo said. "You've got to admit, that's the sort of thing that can happen down here."

"Of course," Teresa said with a shrug. "But in this case, we were simply striking back at him the only way we could think of."

"Were all of you from San Ramon?"

"*Sí*. There were a dozen of us who managed to slip out, one at a time. Now . . ." She struggled to get the words out. "Now there are only a handful left alive."

Scratch asked, "What did you do with the gold you took before?"

"It's hidden in the mountains. We thought that . . . perhaps if we had enough . . . we could go to El Paso and hire some gunmen of our own." Teresa grimaced. "A foolish hope, I know. Anyone we could have found would have come down here and simply stolen the gold from us, or gone to work for Davidson instead. We cannot hope to stop him now."

"Now, don't go getting ahead of yourself," Bo said. "How come you were riding with the men who escaped from the village?"

She tossed her head again, making her long, midnight-black hair swirl around her shoulders. She was dressed like a man, in whipcord trousers and a faded shirt, with a flat-crowned hat that hung behind her back by its chinstrap and a gunbelt around her waist. There was no mistaking her femininity, though.

"You think a woman cannot fight?" she asked, her dark eyes blazing.

"I've lived long enough to learn a few things," Bo said with a smile, "including that most women can do anything they set their minds to. I was just curious how it came about."

"I knew when Davidson took my sister Rosalinda to his house, I had to do something. If I had waited in the village, he would have just taken me and forced me into slavery sooner or later. The only way I could help Rosalinda was to escape and fight back against that evil man." She hesitated. "You have been to the mine. Did you . . . did you see a girl called Rosalinda?"

Bo and Scratch exchanged a glance, and then Bo nodded. "We did. She works in the headquarters building as a servant. In fact, she served us our supper last night."

"How did she look? Is she all right?"

"Seemed to be," Bo said. "She looked like she hadn't been mistreated."

That wasn't strictly true, but Teresa didn't have to know the extent of the servitude her sister was being forced to endure. Not yet anyway.

"Ah, thanks to the Blessed Virgin! Perhaps I can save her yet!" Teresa's face fell. "But how?" she went on miserably. "My few remaining friends have fled, and I do not know if they still have the heart for fighting. What can I do, alone against Davidson and all his gunmen?"

"That's just it, Señorita," Scratch told her as a grin spread across his rugged face. He glanced at Bo, who nodded without hesitation. "You ain't alone anymore."

CHAPTER 12

They couldn't leave Teresa out there alone and on foot in the middle of nowhere, so she climbed up onto the back of the dun with Bo and wrapped her arms around him as they started riding northward again.

Feeling her plump breasts pressed against his back like that was a mite awkward, but he put his mind on other things, such as indulging his curiosity about something else.

"How did you manage to live through the fight on that mesa?" he asked her, turning his head a little.

"There was a crevice in the rocks, near the edge of the mesa. My friend José made me slide down in it before he and the others ambushed the wagons. He told me . . . he told me not to come out until he came for me."

Bo wondered if maybe this hombre José had been more than just a friend to Teresa. As fiery and defiant as she was, he figured that she must've had strong feelings for José in order to go along with hiding instead of taking part in the battle.

Her voice was still choked with emotion as she

went on. "I could see some of what was going on from there. I saw the wagons stop, saw the fighting around them. Then I heard the horses coming up the trail and started to climb out, but I slipped and slid back down. When the shooting started on top of the mesa, I knew there was nothing I could do except wait and pray that José and the others would be all right. Then the shooting stopped and the horses went back down, and I knew . . . I knew that nothing would ever be all right again."

"How come you jumped us?" Scratch asked.

"By the time I heard your horses, I realized that I had nothing left to live for. I was determined to die fighting, striking whatever blow I could against Davidson's men. So I climbed out of the crevice and came up behind you."

Bo said, "I'm mighty glad you didn't just start shooting without saying anything first. That gave us a chance to explain to you how things are with us."

"I still do not know whether to believe you completely," Teresa said. "I do not know if I can trust you. Perhaps you are taking me to El Paso to turn me over to the rest of Davidson's men."

"Not hardly," Scratch protested. "Once you've known us a while longer, you'll see that we ain't like that."

"You expect me to believe that you are honorable men? You sold your guns to Davidson. You must have done such things in the past, too."

"We're no angels," Bo said. "Wouldn't claim to be. We've lived rough lives and done some things we probably shouldn't have. We've even had the law after us a few times."

"But we ain't complete skunks," Scratch said. "There are lines we don't plan on crossin' . . . like helpin' Davidson mistreat any more folks."

"In fact," Bo added, "we sort of plan on stopping him from doing it."

Teresa rode in silence for a few moments, then finally said, "I believe you are telling the truth . . . but you are only two men. What can you do?"

"Well, I've been studying on that," Bo said. "Seems to me like what we've got to do is find Skinner and Wallace and the others and try to mend our fences with them."

He felt Teresa stiffen against his back. "Madre de Dios!" she exclaimed. "Then you *have* been lying to me!"

"Not at all," Bo insisted. "You're right when you say two men can't do much against Davidson and the rest of his bunch . . . if we go against them out in the open. But if we're working against them from inside . . ."

Scratch nodded. "I see what you're sayin'. We can do more good if Davidson thinks we're still workin' for him. That's a mite sneaky, Bo." He chuckled. "I like it."

"But you would be putting yourself in great danger if you did that," Teresa said. "If Davidson found out that you were working against him, he would have you killed immediately. That is, if he did not decide to have you tortured to death to serve as an example to his other men of what will happen if they turn against him."

"Don't worry about us," Bo told her. "We've been

in a few tight spots before. We don't plan on letting Davidson know what's going on."

"Leastways, not until we're durned good and ready," Scratch added.

Evening had fallen by the time they reached Juarez. Bo reined in and asked Teresa, "Do you know anybody here in town where you can stay for a while?"

She shook her head. "I have been here before, but only twice. Nearly all my life has been spent in San Ramon. I know no one in Juarez."

Scratch had brought the bay to a halt beside Bo's dun. He rubbed his jaw in thought, the fingertips rasping over a couple of days' worth of silvery beard stubble. "We need a place to stash the señorita, don't we?"

"That's what I was thinking," Bo said.

"How about Luz's?"

Bo frowned. "You reckon the place is still there?"

"It was the last I heard." Scratch chuckled. "I would've gotten around to checkin' to make certain, happen we hadn't gotten mixed up with Davidson instead."

"Yeah, I'm sure you would have," Bo agreed dryly. "All right. I reckon it's as good a place as any, and better than most." He turned his head to speak to Teresa. "My apologies in advance, Señorita. You're about to see some things that aren't entirely proper."

"You forget what I and the others of San Ramon have lived through in the past six months, Señor Creel. I assure you, there is nothing more improper than what that monster Davidson has done to my people."

"You're probably right about that." Bo hitched the dun into motion again.

They rode through the streets of Juarez until they reached a good-sized adobe house with a red tile roof and a small courtyard behind a wrought-iron gate. Bo and Scratch brought their horses to a halt beside the gate, and Bo reached out to tug on a rope that rang a bell inside the house. A moment later a massive broad-shouldered man appeared at the gate, carrying a lantern.

"Howdy, Pepe," Scratch said. "Still at your post, I see."

"Señor Scratch!" the man greeted him with a big grin. "And Señor Bo. It is good to see you again. Too many years have passed since you have honored us with a visit."

"And yet you remember us," Bo said, smiling.

"*Caramba!* How could I forget, after all the . . . excitement . . . last time?"

"Now, that ruckus wasn't our fault," Scratch insisted. "We weren't lookin' for trouble when we came here that night. It just sorta followed us."

Pepe nodded. "*Sí,* it often does, I hear." He leaned to the side to look past Bo at Teresa Volquez. "What do you have there, Señor Bo? A present for Luz?"

"Not really. More like a guest."

That brought a frown to Pepe's round face. "This is not a hotel, Señor Bo."

"I know. But if we can talk to Luz, I think she'll be willing to help us out."

Pepe's huge shoulders rose and fell in a shrug. "After the last time, she told me not to let the two of you in again. But then, just a few months ago, she was saying something about missing you, so I think it will be all right."

Scratch chuckled. "Luz always was a mite sweet on me."

"I would advise you not to let her hear you say that, Señor Scratch," Pepe said as he took a large key from his pocket and unlocked the gate. He swung it back to let them ride inside the courtyard.

Bo glanced at the long shed on one side of the compound and saw that only a few horses waited there. "Not very busy tonight," he commented.

"It is early yet," Pepe said with another shrug. "Many men are still drinking or gambling. Their thoughts will not turn to women until later in the evening."

Bo and Scratch swung down from their saddles. Bo turned to help Teresa dismount, but she slid off the back of the dun and landed lightly on her feet beside him before he could do anything.

In a low voice, she asked, "Is this a . . . house of ill repute?"

"You could say that," Bo admitted, feeling a little embarrassed.

"Some folks feel that way," Scratch added. "Me, I think its repute is just fine."

Bo took Teresa's arm. "Come on. We'll introduce you to the lady who runs the place."

She tried to pull away. "I will not be turned into a *puta*! If I wanted to do that, I could have stayed in San Ramon and let that bastard Gomez take me to the house he runs for Davidson's men."

"It's not like that at all," Bo insisted. "Like I told

Pepe, if Luz is agreeable, you'll stay here as a guest, as a favor to us, not as one of her girls."

Teresa sniffed. "That is the only way I will stay." She rested her hand on the butt of her gun, which Scratch had returned to her before they started to El Paso. "I mean that, Señor Creel."

"I know you do. Believe me, I know you do."

Bo steered her along a flagstone walk bordered with flower beds. Pepe led the way, and Scratch brought up the rear.

They went through a heavy, ornately carved wooden door and into a hallway lighted by candles in brass wall sconces that gleamed in the warm light. The corridor opened out into a large parlor with Navajo rugs on the floor and massive furniture. Brightly colored tapestries hung on the walls. Curtains made of loosely woven strings of beads hung over several arched doorways.

On one of the divans, two young women half sat, half reclined. They wore silk wrappers that clung to their bodies and left little to the imagination. One was dark, mostly Indian; the other fair-skinned, with long, thick hair the color of honey.

Both of them smiled at Bo and Scratch, then looked surprised and puzzled as they caught sight of Teresa. She was attractive and sensuous enough to fit right in at a place like this, but the mannish clothing she wore, along with the gunbelt, made it clear she was no soiled dove.

"This is Magdalena and Helen," Pepe said as he nodded toward the two young women on the divan. "They were not with us the last time you were here."

"Ladies," Scratch said with a smile as he tugged

politely on the brim of his cream-colored Stetson. "It's a pleasure to meet you."

"I will get Luz," Pepe said. He went over to a door and knocked on it. A voice came from the other side of the door, and Pepe said, "Visitors out here you should greet, Luz."

She jerked the door open and stepped out, wearing a scowl on her face. Several inches shorter than Pepe but almost as broad, Luz Flores looked mighty formidable—formidable enough that Pepe moved back a step and appeared slightly nervous.

"What is this?" Luz demanded. "I was working on the books, and you know I don't like to be interrupted—"

She stopped short as she caught sight of Bo and Scratch. A beaming smile flashed onto her face and she seemed like she was about to say something, but then she stopped herself and forced a scowl.

"You two loco gringos!" she said, practically spitting out the words. "I thought I told Pepe never to let you in here again."

"We forced him to bring us to you, Luz," Bo said, not wanting to get Pepe in any more trouble than was necessary. "So don't hold it against him."

Luz snorted. "Nobody could force that big bull to do something he didn't want to do. Why are you here?" She frowned at Teresa. "Who is this? You hope to appease my anger over what happened last time you were here by bringing me a new girl?"

Bo saw fury flash in Teresa's eyes. Before she could say anything, he replied quickly, "No, we're here because we need your help. This is Señorita Teresa Volquez, from the village of San Ramon."

Luz nodded, clearly interested even though she didn't want to admit it. "I have heard of this place. It is down in the foothills at the edge of the mountains."

"That's right," Bo said. "Near a place called Cañon del Despiadado."

"Cutthroat Canyon. I have heard of it as well. Why is she dressed like a man and toting iron, as you gringos would put it?"

"Because there's been trouble down there, a lot of trouble. Señorita Volquez has been trying to put a stop to it. Scratch and I are going to help her, but we need a place for her to stay for a while. A safe place. We thought of you."

"Actually, I'm the one who suggested it," Scratch added with a grin. "I've never forgot the other times I was here, Luz. Nor that time when you and I—"

She stopped him with a slashing motion of her hand. "Enough! Why would I wish to do the two of you any sort of favor? You come in here, you shoot up my place, you upset my girls—"

"That shooting wasn't our fault," Bo said. "We didn't know those fellas who had a grudge against us had followed us here. Anyway, everybody in Juarez knows that such things aren't allowed in Luz's place. They were to blame for the ruckus, not us."

Again, Luz looked doubtful. "I have a feeling you make that claim quite often, Señor Bo."

Teresa said, "If she doesn't want to help us, let's go. I don't want to stay here anyway."

"You think we are not good enough for your presence?" Luz demanded. Now her dark eyes were the ones glittering with anger.

"That ain't what she said—" Scratch began.

"Listen," Bo said, "we'll tell you all about it as soon as we know that Señorita Volquez is safe. There are some men in El Paso who might try to kill her if they knew the whole story."

"Then why don't you tell it to us, Creel?" a hard voice said from behind them. "And don't reach for those guns, because we got you covered, damn it!"

CHAPTER 13

Neither Bo nor Scratch said anything for a moment. Then, Scratch drawled, "I don't know about you, but I'm gettin' sort of tired of folks sneakin' up behind and pointin' guns at us."

"Yeah," Bo said. "It gets old in a hurry."

Both of them had recognized Jackman's voice. Turning slowly and keeping their hands in plain sight, they saw the hired gun standing just behind one of the beaded curtains. The barrel of his revolver stuck out between two strands of beads. Tragg was with him—no surprise there—standing just behind and to one side of Jackman. He had his gun drawn as well.

Bo put a smile on his face. He figured that the two men had overheard too much to be fooled now, but he gave it a try anyway. "Good to see you boys," he said. "I was hoping we'd catch up to you in El Paso, but I didn't figure it would be in Juarez."

With a clicking and clattering of beads, Jackman pushed into the room. Tragg followed right behind him.

"You can forget about those buffalo chips you're

tryin' to sell us," Jackman snapped. "We heard what you said. That gal was in with the bandits, and you've gone over to her side now. I didn't expect a double cross like that from somebody who looks as much like a preacher as you do." He sneered. "Why'd you decide to betray Davidson, Creel? Because of the girl . . . or the gold?"

"I don't consider it a double cross when Davidson didn't tell us the truth to start with," Bo said. "If you want to hear about it, we can tell you what's really going on down there."

"Sure, that's what I said before. You go ahead and tell us."

The sneer on Jackman's face made it clear, though, that it wouldn't really matter what Bo said.

"Davidson killed the legal owner of that mine, a Mexican named Don Hernando Alviso," Bo explained. Teresa had told them the man's full name during the ride to El Paso. "He's been murdering anybody who stands up to him and ruling the others through fear. I'm pretty sure he murdered one of the miners who got in an argument with a foreman the day we reached Cutthroat Canyon. We all heard the shot."

"He said he killed a rattlesnake," Tragg said.

Teresa couldn't hold her emotions in. "A lie!" she burst out. "We heard about what happened. One of the men Davidson forces to work in the mine asked for compassion for an old man who had collapsed and could no longer work. The foreman kicked the old man, and the one who had begged for mercy lost his temper and struck the foreman. Some of the guards grabbed him and held him until Davidson got there and . . . and shot him in the head."

"We weren't there to see it happen," Jackman said. "All we got is the word of some greaser slut. I'll trust the word of the man who puts money in my pocket."

"Damn right," Tragg added.

The tension in the room had grown thicker, but since Tragg and Jackman were the only ones with guns in their hands, they still had control of the situation—for the moment. Jackman gestured with his iron and said, "Go on, Creel. We're still listenin'."

"Davidson's posted a sharpshooter in the bell tower of the church in San Ramon," Bo said. "The fella has a high-powered rifle and a pair of field glasses. He guards the passes in and out of the valley and acts as another of Davidson's enforcers if any of the people there get out of line."

"Man's got a right to protect his property and the folks who work for him," Tragg said.

"Ain't you been listenin'?" Scratch said. "Davidson's *forcin'* those folks to work for him. And it's not just the men who dig the gold out of that mine neither. He's got himself his own private whorehouse, too, and the gals from the village have to work in it."

Jackman said, "I wouldn't act so high-and-mighty if I was you, Morton. You're standin' in the middle of a whorehouse your own self, right now, and from the sound of the conversation that was goin' on when we came up the hall, you're pretty friendly with that fat madam, too."

Luz said, "If I had known what *cabrones* you are,

I would have had Pepe throw you out on your ears
as soon as you got here!"

"Shut up, *mamacita,*" Jackman snapped. "You
were quick enough to take our money, and glad to
get it."

One of Luz's pudgy hands came up and delved
into the deep valley between her huge breasts, which
hung halfway out of her low-cut blouse. When she
brought her hand out, she flicked her wrist and sent
coins spinning through the air at Jackman and Tragg.
"There!" she screamed. "Take your filthy *dinero*
back!"

The coins pelting them made the two men grimace and step back. Tragg yelled, "Shit!" and
brought his free hand up to his left eye, which had
been hit by one of the coins. With his other hand he
swung his gun toward Luz. "You bitch! I'll—"

What he was going to do remained unknown, because in moving as they had, Jackman and Tragg
had brought themselves within reach of Magdalena
and Helen, the two whores sitting on the divan. Both
women lunged to their feet at the same time, and
the lamplight flickered on cold steel as they each
plunged a knife into Tragg's back. Tragg howled in
pain and stumbled forward. The gun in his hand
roared as his finger involuntarily jerked the trigger,
sending a bullet into the floor.

At the same time, Bo and Scratch slapped leather.
Even though Jackman's gun was already in his
hand, he got only one shot off before Bo's Colt and
Scratch's twin Remingtons blasted. The explosions
came so close together, they sounded like one shot
and were deafening in the relatively close quarters.

Jackman was thrown backward by the impact of all three slugs smashing into his body. He hit the divan where Magdalena and Helen had been sitting and flipped over the back of it to thud to the floor. Bo took a couple of swift steps that brought him around the piece of furniture so that he could cover Jackman.

That caution wasn't necessary. Jackman had dropped his gun, and his shirt was already soaked by the blood that welled from the wounds in his ruined chest. Eyes wide, he turned his head and stared at Bo in shock for a second before his features went slack in death. The stench of voiding bowels mixed with the acrid reek of burned powder.

"Damn it!" Luz screeched at Bo and Scratch. "It always winds up smelling like shit and gunpowder in here when you two show up!"

"We're mighty sorry about that," Bo told her. He glanced at Scratch. "What about Tragg?"

The gunman had fallen on his face so that the handles of both knives protruded from his back as crimson stains bloomed around them. Keeping Tragg covered with both Remingtons, Scratch hooked a boot toe under his shoulder and rolled him onto his side, then let him flop on his face again.

"Dead," Scratch announced. He looked at Magdalena and Helen. "Where'd you gals come up with them pigstickers anyway?"

The two women smiled, and Helen said, "It's probably better that you don't know, Mr. Morton. Trade secrets and all that."

Scratch grunted. "Sure. I reckon you're right."

Magdalena said, "We would not have killed that

man if he had not threatened Luz. We could not let him shoot her."

Bo finished thumbing fresh shells into his Colt and snapped the cylinder closed. "That's all right, ladies. I reckon we would've had to kill 'em both sooner or later anyway."

"Yeah," Scratch agreed. "They weren't gonna turn on Davidson. They would've sold us out to him if they got a chance."

Luz had calmed down a little. She said to Pepe, "Haul this *carne muerta* out of here." She turned to the other hallways leading off this central room and spoke to the frightened women who peered through the beaded curtains. "Go back to your customers. The trouble is over."

"If they got any customers left," Scratch said to Bo from the corner of his mouth. "When them shots went off, I'll bet most of the hombres in here crawled out the nearest window and lit out for the tall and uncut."

"More than likely," Bo replied with a nod.

Pepe dragged the bodies of Jackman and Tragg out of the room, leaving smears of blood on the floor. Bo and Scratch didn't know how Luz's bodyguard would dispose of the corpses, and neither of them particularly wanted to know.

Luz motioned to the Texans. "Come into my office." With a nod toward Teresa, she added, "Bring the girl with you."

Teresa didn't look shocked by the violence she had just witnessed. She had probably seen enough during the past six months of Davidson's reign of terror in the valley to be hardened to most such displays, although she had been shaken by the deaths of José and the other men on the mesa earlier that day. She went with Bo and Scratch into Luz's office without objection.

The madam sat down behind a desk on which a ledger book lay open. There was only one other chair in the room, and she said to Teresa, "Have a seat, Señorita."

Teresa did so, but rather gingerly, and that brought a laugh from Luz. "Do not worry, little one," she said. "Nothing improper has ever taken place in that chair. Although one cannot say that about very many places in this house." She turned her attention to Bo and Scratch. "You want to leave this one here with me, you said?"

"That's right," Bo said. "As long as you understand that you can't, uh, try to put her to work."

"Food and a place to sleep cost money . . ."

"We'll pay for her keep," Scratch said.

Luz laughed. "I would never force a girl to work for me. I am not like this man Davidson you spoke of. He sounds like a vile creature."

"He is," Teresa said. "That is why we must defeat him."

"What are you going to do?"

"Davidson thinks that we're working for him," Bo explained. "Scratch and I figured to join up again with the other men who came here with those wagons of ore and head back to the valley to see what we can do from inside Davidson's camp."

"Wagons of ore?" Luz said with growing interest. "You must tell me about this. Start from the beginning."

Bo did so, going back to the night they had met
Porter Davidson in August Strittmayer's Birdcage
Saloon and then saved his life during the ruckus
with Little Ed Churchill and the rancher's men.

Scratch put in, "I reckon if we'd known then what
we know now, we might've let Little Ed ventilate
the son of a bitch."

"It's too late for that," Bo said. He resumed the
tale, sketching in what they had discovered in Cutthroat Canyon and the adjacent valley, as well as the
events of the trip to El Paso with the gold wagons
and the attempted holdup that afternoon that had
backfired on Teresa and her companions.

"Poor little one," Luz murmured as she looked at
the young woman. "You are all alone now. Your
amigos are either dead or have abandoned the fight."

"She's not alone," Bo said. "We're on her side
now . . . and I hope you are, too."

Luz shrugged. "I have no stake in what goes on
down in that valley. I am a businesswoman, as you
well know, Señor Bo."

"Don Alviso had no family," Teresa said. "The
mine rightfully belongs to the people of San Ramon
now. If you help us, a share of it could be yours."

"You have no power to make such an arrangement," Luz said with a shake of her head. "This man
Davidson still holds the mine, and until it is otherwise . . ." She shrugged again. "Anyway, I deal in
what is, not what might be. Cash, in other words."

Bo said, "All we want is a safe place to leave
Señorita Volquez. Scratch and I can come up with
enough money to pay you for that."

"And for cleaning the blood off my parlor floor? And for getting the stink out of the air?"

"Name your price," Bo said.

"Five hundred dollars."

Scratch let out a low whistle. "That's a heap of *dinero*."

"We don't have anywhere near that much," Bo said. "Might be able to get it, though."

"You have until tomorrow," Luz declared. "For tonight, I will keep the girl here and personally guarantee her safety. This much I will do out of the goodness of my heart, but no more."

Bo thought calling it the goodness of Luz's heart was stretching it a mite, but he didn't say that. He just nodded and said, "We'll see you tomorrow then. Right now, there's one other thing you can do for us that won't cost you anything."

"What is that?"

"I'd like to talk to the girls who were with Jackman and Tragg."

"The two men you killed?" Luz thought it over and nodded. "I think I can do that. Wait here."

While the madam was gone, Teresa turned in the chair to look at Bo and Scratch. "Why are you doing this for me?" she asked. "You never even knew I existed until earlier today."

"I reckon we knew Davidson wasn't telling us the truth, though, even if we didn't have the proof yet," Bo said.

"And we don't take kindly to bein' lied to," Scratch added. "We don't cotton to hombres who try to take advantage of other folks neither . . . and I'd say Davidson qualifies, in spades!"

"I guess you could say that we're just natural-born meddlers," Bo went on.

Teresa looked at them for a long moment, then said softly, "At first I did not want to believe you. But now I see that you are telling the truth. You want to help because it is the right thing to do. You are like the knights in the old stories."

"Oh, Lord, don't go callin' us knights," Scratch protested. "If we were, our armor'd be so tarnished by now . . . Shoot, we just can't go too long without gettin' in some sort of scrap. We'd get bored otherwise."

"Say what you will," Teresa said. "Now I know the truth."

Luz came back to the office a moment later with two of the young women who worked for her, one Mexican, one Chinese. The Chinese girl didn't seem to speak any English or Spanish, so Bo hoped that the other whore could tell them what they needed to know.

"Did you have a drink or anything with those two hombres before you took them back to your rooms?" he asked her.

She nodded. "*Sí.* They passed a bottle of tequila back and forth and drank half of it."

"Did they say anything about the men they came with to El Paso? Were they supposed to meet the others anywhere in particular?"

The girl frowned in thought as she tried to recall. "I am not sure," she said slowly. "They talked and laughed a lot, but I did not pay too much attention." She shrugged, making her breasts move under the silk wrapper she wore. "Men prattle all the time. Most of it means nothing."

"Try to remember," Luz urged. "I may have money riding on this."

"I think they said something about a place called . . . Encinal's. That was it."

Bo and Scratch looked at each other. The name meant something to them.

"Encinal's is a café across the river in El Paso," Bo said. "Davidson's men must be planning to get together there in the morning before they start back to the mine."

"Makes sense," Scratch said. "They got to El Paso all right, Wallace and the other fellas with the wagons delivered the ore wherever it was supposed to go, and the rest of the bunch split up to have themselves a good time tonight. That's got to be the way it is."

"So we can catch up to them at Encinal's first thing in the morning, I reckon."

"And my money?" Luz asked.

"That gives us tonight to lay our hands on it."

"You are sure you would not want to lay something else?"

"Some other time," Scratch said. "I don't reckon we can afford it tonight."

CHAPTER 14

Coming up with the five hundred dollars to pay Luz for looking after Teresa was surprisingly easy. Bo had figured that an all-night poker game and a lot of luck would be required, but all it took was a visit to the Birdcage.

August Strittmayer greeted them heartily when he spotted them coming across the saloon's big main room toward him. "Herr Creel! Herr Morton! I did not expect to see you two fellows again so soon. Didn't you leave town with Herr Davidson just a few days ago?"

"We did," Bo agreed. "We're back. You haven't happened to see Jim Skinner in here tonight, have you?"

Strittmayer made a face, as if a bad taste had suddenly come into his mouth. "That one! I don't want him in here. He's nothing but trouble. I heard a while back that he was in El Paso, but I have not seen him."

"You know a big Swede named Hansen?" Scratch asked. "Or a Britisher called Lancaster?"

"Nein," Strittmayer replied with a shake of his head.

"A baby-faced kid with killer's eyes?" Bo asked. "He goes by Douglas, but I don't know if that's his first name or his last."

"Now, him I have heard of, but he has not been in here." A frown creased Strittmayer's broad face. "You are looking for these men because there is trouble between you and them? The bullet holes in my walls are just now patched!"

Bo chuckled. "Don't worry, August. We won't be starting any trouble. We've got some business to discuss with those hombres, that's all."

"I would not do business with Jim Skinner. That man is no good."

Scratch said, "You won't get any argument from us on that score."

Bo looked around the room at the gambling tables. "Have you got a high-stakes game going on tonight, August? Scratch and I need to come up with some money as quickly as we can."

"How much do you need?" the German asked.

"Five hundred bucks," Scratch said.

Strittmayer inclined his head toward the door that led to his office. "Come with me. I will let you have the cash."

Bo and Scratch glanced at each other. "We couldn't take your money like that, August," Bo said.

"Then consider it a loan. I will even charge you interest, *ja*?"

"Why would you want to help us out that way?" Scratch asked. "It ain't like we're old pards or anything."

"Of course we are friends," Strittmayer insisted. "Little Ed Churchill came in here and caused trouble every time he visited El Paso from his ranch. His men were just as bad. Now he is no longer a problem."

"So what you're talking about is blood money," Bo said flatly.

"Nein, nein. You were friends as well with Three-Toed Johnny. That is the main reason I wish to help you. And I know your reputation. The law may consider you scoundrels, but if you say you will pay back the money, I know it is true."

"Unless we go off and get ourselves killed first," Scratch muttered.

"That is a gamble I am willing to take. Come with me to my office. I give you the money."

"You don't even want to know what it's for?" Bo asked.

"Does it matter?"

"Well . . . I reckon not."

Bo would have told Strittmayer about Teresa if he'd needed to, but it was better this way, he thought as he and Scratch followed the German into his office. The fewer people who knew where Teresa was—the fewer people who even were aware of her existence—the safer it would be for her.

Strittmayer opened a bulky safe in his office, using his body to shield the combination from view as he spun the dial. He might feel indebted to Bo and Scratch, but that gratitude only went so far, especially balanced against his natural caution. He took a wad of cash from the safe and counted out five hundred dollars onto the desk. Then, after a second's hesitation, he added another hundred to it.

"In case you need some for anything else," he said.

"We could use some more supplies, I reckon," Bo said as he picked up the money, folded it, and stuck it in a pocket inside his black frock coat. "We're much obliged to you, August."

Strittmayer waved a hand. "*De nada,* as our friends across the border say. What else can I do for you?"

"We ain't had any supper yet," Scratch said.

"That can be remedied. Come with me. I take you to the best German restaurant in El Paso!"

"I only know of one German restaurant in El Paso," Bo said.

Strittmayer grinned and slapped them both on the back. "That is why it is the best!"

Figuring that Davidson's men would want to get an early start, Bo and Scratch were at Encinal's Café before dawn the next morning. Strittmayer had let them borrow a spare room at the Birdcage, and they had slept soundly, full of beer and bratwurst and potatoes. Both of the Texans were still a little sluggish from all the food, in fact.

Bo recognized some of the horses tied at the hitch rack in front of Encinal's as they walked up, and so did Scratch. Skinner and the others were here. Scratch said, "I'll go back to the livery stable and get our horses, too."

Bo nodded. "All right. I'll go inside and talk to them."

"Don't you reckon it'd be better if you waited until I got back, so we can brace 'em together?"

"I don't think anybody's going to slap leather in the middle of breakfast."

"You better be right about that," Scratch cautioned. "If you ain't, you're liable to get some hot lead with your coffee."

He headed for the livery stable where they had left the dun and the bay, while Bo stepped up onto the boardwalk in front of the café.

As soon as Bo went inside, he spotted Lancaster, Hansen, and Douglas at one of the tables. Skinner was alone at another table, brooding over a cup of coffee as he sat with his back to the wall so that an enemy couldn't come up behind him. Encinal's was a fairly popular eatery, and despite the early hour, several other customers sat at the tables with their blue-checked tablecloths, as well as at the counter, behind which the menu was chalked on a board.

Lancaster and Hansen were talking, but they fell silent when they noticed Bo coming toward them. Skinner glanced up with a dark scowl from the adjacent table and demanded, "What the hell are you doin' here, Creel? You don't work for Davidson anymore."

"Everybody's got to be somewhere," Bo said, "and I reckon it's a free country. Anyway, it's up to Davidson whether or not I'm still working for him, not you."

Skinner's lips curled in a snarl. "You run out on us! You rode up onto that mesa because you were more worried about a bunch of damn greaser *bandidos* than you were about doin' your job!"

The gunman's loud, angry voice drew some looks of displeasure from the other customers, about half of whom were Mexican. Bo pulled back a chair and sat down without asking, across the table from Skinner.

"I'll admit, I don't much cotton to killing kids," Bo said, "but those hombres who ambushed the wagons called the tune. They had to dance to it. And as for running out on the rest of you, that never happened. We were behind you all the way to El Paso. We just hung back far enough so that you wouldn't spot us."

From the other table, Lancaster asked, "Why would you do that, old boy?"

Bo smiled at him. "If you couldn't see us, then we figured those bandits couldn't either, if they doubled back and tried to hit the wagons again. If we'd heard any shooting, though, you would have seen us in a hurry."

It was a plausible lie, and one that none of the others could disprove. Bo and Scratch had worked it out the night before.

Douglas said, "I thought I heard a shot back there behind us a little while after we passed that mesa. You know anything about that?"

That would have been the shot that Teresa took at him as he tackled her, Bo thought. He nodded and said, "Yeah, I fired it. Wanted to scare off the damn buzzards. They were already starting to work on those corpses when Scratch and I rode up."

"Let me guess," Skinner said with a sneer from the other table. "You and Morton buried all those poor dead Mexicans."

"We thought about it." Bo shrugged. "But in the end, we decided it was too hot and too much work."

"So the *zopilotes* got 'em anyway."

Bo didn't say anything to that. Let Skinner think whatever he wanted. At least, it seemed like the gunman accepted the story about Bo shooting at some buzzards to scare them off.

"So you followed us to El Paso after all," Hansen said.

"That's right. I figure we were doing our job, too. Hell, the gold got here all right, didn't it?" Bo looked around the café. "Are you supposed to meet Wallace and the others here, too?"

"No, we'll rendezvous with them at the wagon yard," Lancaster said. He frowned in thought. "How did you know that you could find *us* here, Creel?"

"We didn't." Bo grinned. "That was pure dumb luck. Scratch and I like to eat here when we're in El Paso. We figured we'd have some breakfast and then scout around for you fellas. It just happened to work out the other way around."

"Where is Morton anyway?" Skinner asked.

"When we saw your horses tied up outside, he went back up the street to fetch our mounts." That answer was true, although it didn't tell the whole story. "We might as well all head back to the valley together."

"I still don't think Davidson's gonna want you workin' for him," Skinner said.

"Then he can tell us that himself."

Skinner glared across the table for a second longer, then shrugged. "Suit yourself," he said in a surly voice. "If it was me, though, I'd skin your hides."

"Good thing it's not you who's in charge then."

Skinner bristled a little at that, but didn't make an issue of it. He picked up his coffee cup and pointedly carried it to a table that was even farther away, where he sat down and proceeded to ignore the others.

Bo ordered breakfast for himself and Scratch from a busy, white-aproned waiter who finally made it over to the table. While he was waiting for the food, he asked the others, "Where are Jackman and Tragg? Were they supposed to meet you here, too?"

Lancaster frowned again. "We haven't seen them. I'm worried that they're lying somewhere in squalid surroundings, having drunk and debauched themselves into oblivion."

"I reckon there are plenty of places in El Paso and Juarez where they could've done just that," Bo agreed. "What if they don't show up by the time you're ready to leave?"

Lancaster shrugged. "I suppose we'll go without them. They knew what the plan was. It's their responsibility to be back in time. Perhaps they can catch up to us later if they wish to."

Scratch came into the café a minute later, and looked around until he spotted Bo and the others. He nodded to the men at the other table and said, "Howdy, boys. I reckon Bo's already told you about how we followed y'all on into town."

"I did," Bo said. "We've been welcomed back into the fold."

Skinner's contemptuous grunt testified as to how he felt about that.

Their food arrived as Scratch sat down at the table

with Bo. They dug in, even though the enormous
meal they'd had with Strittmayer the night before
hadn't left them with much of an appetite even now.
But they had a lot of long, hard hours on the trail in
front of them, and likely their meals until they got
back to the mine would be on the sparse side. Bo and
Scratch had done enough cowboying to learn that it
was smart to eat and sleep whenever you had the
chance, because it might be a while before those opportunities came around again.

The six men left Encinal's together, mounted up,
and rode through the streets of El Paso toward the
wagon yard where the rest of Davidson's men would
be waiting. As they did, Bo wondered whether any
of the men could be swayed over to the other side
if they knew the truth about what Davidson was
doing to the people of the valley. Skinner was out of
the question, of course; he didn't care about anything except the money Davidson had promised to
pay him.

Hansen and Lancaster, on the other hand, might
be uneasy enough to switch sides. Bo didn't really
think so, because men who hired out their guns
weren't usually troubled overmuch by their con-
sciences, no matter what the circumstances. It was
a hard, dangerous life that soon wore calluses on the
souls of most men who took it up. But it was possible he might get through to them, Bo supposed.

With the kid, who could tell? Douglas was an
enigma, hiding behind that cold, hard face.

Wallace had bought some more mules to replace
the ones killed by the bandits, Bo saw as he and
the others rode up to the wagon yard. The teams

were already hitched to the wagons, which weren't completely empty. Some supplies had been loaded into them.

"Didn't expect to see you again," Wallace said to Bo and Scratch. "I thought you'd decided not to work for the boss after all and lit a shuck."

"Nope," Scratch said. "We were still keepin' an eye on you boys, like guardian angels."

Wallace grunted. "Scruffiest old angels I ever saw." He looked at Skinner. "Where the hell are Jackman and Tragg?"

Skinner shrugged. "Haven't seen 'em."

"We can't sit around here all day waiting for them. We need to get back to the mine as soon as we can. I thought I'd made that clear to all of you."

"There you go again, soundin' like you think you're the boss," Skinner said, his voice dangerously soft.

Wallace's face darkened with anger, but all he said, "We'll have to leave without them if they don't show up in the next couple of minutes."

"Fine by me either way."

"For all we know," Lancaster said, "they got themselves in some sort of drunken brawl and may be in jail . . . or dead."

Wallace jerked his head in a nod and said, "Let's get started then." He climbed onto the driver's seat of the lead wagon and unwound the reins from the brake lever. The other drivers did likewise. The outriders swung up into their saddles.

The sun was just peeking over the eastern horizon when the wagons rolled across the bridge over the Rio Grande, headed back to Cutthroat Canyon.

CHAPTER 15

The trip south through Mexico was uneventful. They saw no sign of the men who had been with Teresa at the mesa, those who had survived the battle and fled. Skinner and the others were surprised that Jackman and Tragg hadn't followed them from El Paso and caught up to them, but they didn't seem worried about it. According to Wallace, Davidson had advanced them some money against their wages, but not much.

"If they want to give up the job, it's their loss," Wallace commented with a shrug of his shoulders as the group camped the first night on the trail. "After killing as many of those bandits as we did yesterday, I'm not sure the rest of them will ever give us any more trouble."

That appeared to be the case. Bo figured that Teresa's remaining compadres might summon up the gumption to resume the fight against Davidson sooner or later, but for now they were demoralized, their spirits broken.

While Davidson's group was camped, Bo tried to

sound out Lancaster, Hansen, and Douglas about how far they would go for Davidson, all in the guise of idle conversation, but he didn't get very far, especially with the taciturn youngster. None of them gave any indication that they would be willing to turn on their employer as long as he continued paying them.

The lightly loaded wagons moved faster than they had when they were full of the heavy gold ore. Because of that, an hour or more of daylight remained on the second day when they rolled into the valley. Bo and Scratch glanced at the church's bell tower, then at each other. They knew one of Davidson's marksmen was up there, watching the wagons and the accompanying riders through field glasses.

If the day ever came when the people of the valley rose in open revolt against Davidson, somebody would have to do something about the hombre in the tower. Otherwise, he could sit up there with his Sharps and pick off the Mexicans as long as he had ammunition.

It might not come to that, however. Bo hoped that it wouldn't, because then it would amount to war, and innocent folks always got hurt in a war. It was the nature of the beast, as the old saying went.

The villagers stayed out of sight as the wagons rolled through. By the time they reached the mouth of the steep-sided canyon, shadows were starting to gather despite the fact that the sun was still up.

And even though the air was still hot, Bo felt a chill go through him as he and Scratch rode into the canyon with the others.

Davidson was waiting for them when they got to

the mine. He strode forward wearing an expression that was relieved and anxious at the same time.

"I'm glad to see that you're back," he said as Wallace and the other drivers hauled on the reins and brought the teams to a halt. "You got the ore through all right?"

Wallace wrapped the reins around the brake lever. "We did," he said. "Turned it over to the express agent for shipment on the train coming through that very evening."

Davidson heaved a sigh and nodded. "Excellent work. Any trouble?" He glanced around at the riders. "Wait a minute. Jackman and Tragg aren't with you. Were you attacked? Were they killed?"

Wallace put a hand on the driver's seat and climbed down to the ground, moving a little gingerly because of the wound he had suffered.

"Yes to your first question, no to the second," he told Davidson. "Those bandits jumped us again on the second day out. They had an ambush prepared for the wagons. But your plan worked, Boss. Skinner and the others came charging in and took them by surprise. We killed five of the bastards, and the others gave up and ran off."

Davidson pounded his right fist into his left palm and said, "By God, I'm glad to hear that! Was anyone hurt?"

"I got a bullet crease in my side, and a couple of the other fellas picked up a nick or two. But the only ones hurt bad were those five *bandidos* who wound up dead."

"Then where are Jackman and Tragg?" Davidson asked with a puzzled frown.

"They went off to carouse somewhere in El Paso or Juarez, and they never came back."

Davidson's frown deepened. "They just quit?"

"Don't know," Wallace replied with a shrug. "Like I said, we never saw them again after we split up in El Paso. You didn't tell us to stay together while we were there."

A look of displeasure flashed across Davidson's face. "Maybe I should have," he snapped, "if you're not capable of keeping up with the men who work for me."

From the back of his horse, Skinner drawled, "I reckon we need to have a talk about that, Boss. These two"—and he made a lazy motion with his left hand toward Bo and Scratch—"ran out on us."

Davidson turned toward the skull-faced gunman. "I don't understand. Creel and Morton are here. How could they have run out?"

Bo said, "Skinner's talking about the fact that Scratch and I stopped at the scene of that ambush long enough to check the bodies of the bandits who were killed. Then we followed the wagons on to El Paso, staying far enough back so that we wouldn't be spotted if the bandits who lived through the fight tried to attack again."

"That's your story anyway," Skinner said. "You don't have a lick of proof for it."

"And you don't have any proof that I'm not telling the truth," Bo pointed out. To Davidson, he went on. "We found the other fellas once we got to El Paso, and we rode back down here with them. Now, to me, it seems like Scratch and I did our jobs. We helped fight off those *bandidos,* and the ore made it to El Paso. What more could anybody want?"

"Why did you go to the time and trouble of checking on those bandits?" Davidson wanted to know. "You weren't going to help any of them that were just wounded, were you?" His voice hardened. "Those men are my enemies."

"They weren't men," Scratch said. "More like boys."

"What the hell does that matter? They take up arms against me, they deserve whatever happens to them."

Skinner leaned over in the saddle and spat. "Damn right."

Davidson made an obvious effort to control his irritation with Bo and Scratch. "Look, I'm paying you good wages to defend my interests from anyone who threatens them. If that doesn't sit well with you, you're free to ride away any time you want."

Scratch said, "Fact of the matter is, we haven't collected any wages yet. Some of the other fellas asked for advances, but Bo and me didn't."

"Are you saying you want to draw your time?"

"That's not what we're saying at all," Bo said. "Look, this is getting blown up into something bigger than it is. Yeah, it bothered us a little that those dead bandits were as young as they were, and to tell you the truth, we thought about staying there long enough to bury them. But we didn't. We went on to El Paso, keeping an eye on the wagons along the way just like we were supposed to. Skinner and the others might not have seen us, but that doesn't mean we weren't there. And nobody said anything about quitting." Bo shook his head. "If those youngsters didn't want to get shot, they shouldn't have tried to steal that gold. Simple as that, and nobody's arguing it."

Davidson thought over what Bo had just said, then turned to look at Skinner. "How about it?"

"I still wouldn't trust 'em if I was you, Boss," the gunman said with a shake of his head.

Douglas spoke up unexpectedly. "I would."

Davidson looked at him. "You would?"

The kid nodded. "Sure. The only real trouble we had, they were right there fighting beside us. They may be a mite older, but they've still got the bark on. That's the sort of man I want backing any play I make."

"Thanks, kid," Scratch said.

Davidson turned to Lancaster and Hansen. "What about you two?"

Hansen shrugged. "I got no trouble with Creel and Morton."

"They seem like splendid chaps to me," Lancaster added.

Davidson nodded and said, "All right then. It's settled. I know you don't like them, Skinner, but just steer clear of them while you're here at the mine. The money I'm paying, you can stand to put up with them during the trips to and from El Paso."

"Whatever you say," Skinner responded, but the scowl on his face made it clear that he didn't like Davidson's decision.

"In the meantime," Davidson went on to Bo and Scratch, "what I said before still goes. You two, or any of the rest of the men, for that matter, can draw the wages you've got coming to you and ride away any time you like, with no hard feelings on either side. I don't want anybody working for me who doesn't want to be here."

Bo thought about the men from the village being herded at gunpoint into the mine to chip gold ore from the hard rocks, and the women who had to labor in Davidson's brothel. Lying obviously came easy to Davidson. Or maybe he truly believed that the villagers just . . . didn't count. Maybe to him, they were just animals he could use any way he saw fit in order to make himself richer.

Bo didn't allow any of what he was thinking or feeling to show on his face, and Scratch kept his features just as expressionless. With a nod, Bo said, "I'm glad we cleared the air. I reckon there won't be any more problems."

"No, no problems at all." Davidson laughed. "Except figuring out how to spend all the money that all of us are going to make before this is over."

Dusk had settled over the canyon by the time Bo and Scratch finished tending to their horses. The dun and the bay had been hard used the past week, and they needed a nice long rest. Once again, the Texans took care of rubbing down, graining, and watering their mounts while the old Mexican hostler looked on nervously and tended to the other horses. The old-timer knew by now that they wouldn't complain to Davidson about having to care for their own animals, that in fact they preferred it that way.

When they went into the headquarters building, they found Alfred waiting for them. "The other gentlemen are having drinks," he said. "Would you care to join them?"

"We're a mite tired," Bo said. "You reckon we could get something to eat up in our room?"

"Of course. I'll bring a tray up in just a few minutes. Will beef and beans and tortillas be all right?"

Scratch grinned. "Sonny, you're talkin' our lingo."

They went up to their room, took off their hats and jackets, but left their gunbelts on. Keeping his voice low, Bo said, "I believe that fella Alfred is sweet on Teresa's sister Rosalinda."

"Yeah, I noticed that the other night, too," Scratch said with a nod. "You reckon we can turn that to our advantage somehow?"

"I don't know. Alfred seems pretty loyal to Davidson, but maybe he doesn't know all the things that have been going on around here. Maybe he just knows that he doesn't like Davidson taking advantage of Rosalinda like that. We'll have a talk with him and see if we can figure out how much to tell him."

"I'll follow your lead," Scratch said. "You handle the thinkin' part better than I do." He chuckled. "That leaves the fightin' and the lovin' parts to me, and I like them more anyway."

When a soft knock sounded on the door a few minutes later, though, it wasn't Alfred who stood outside in the hallway with a tray containing several platters of food. It was Rosalinda.

"I have brought your supper, Señores," she said.

Bo had answered the knock on the door. He stepped back and ushered her into the room. "Just put the tray over there on the table," he told her, then glanced at Scratch and cocked an eyebrow. The

silver-haired Texan nodded. After all the miles—
and all the years—they had ridden the trails together, often they didn't even need to speak to know
what each other was thinking.

Rosalinda set the tray on the table and turned to
go, but Bo eased the door closed and said, "We'd
like to talk to you for a minute, Señorita."

"I must get back downstairs," she said, nervous-
ness flaring up in her eyes. "Señor Davidson will
expect me to serve dinner, and then—"

She stopped short, clearly uncomfortable and un-
willing to say anything else about what Davidson
would be expecting from her this evening. Probably
the same thing he expected from her every evening,
Bo thought grimly.

"This won't take long," he told her.

"If you want a woman, there is a place you can
go. One of the buildings is set aside for that, and
there are women of the village there who . . . who
serve the needs of Señor Davidson's men . . ."

Bo shook his head and said, "You're getting this
all wrong, Rosalinda. We know what's been going on
here in the valley, and we'd like to put a stop to it."

She seemed confused as she looked back and
forth between Bo and Scratch. "I do not understand," she said. "You work for Señor Davidson,
and yet you say that you want to make him stop
what he is doing?"

"That's right. We know about all of it . . . the rifleman in the bell tower at the church, the women who
are forced to prostitute themselves, the men of the
village who have to slave in the mine for him."

"And we don't like it one little bit," Scratch added.

"But how do you know these things?" Rosalinda asked. "Has he admitted them to you?"

"He didn't have to," Bo said. "We saw some of the signs ourselves, and then . . . we talked to your sister."

Her dark eyes widened in shock. "My . . . my sister?"

Bo nodded. "Teresa. She was with the bandits who ambushed the wagons and tried to steal the gold on its way to El Paso."

Rosalinda's face paled. "She . . . she was hurt? I heard there was shooting—"

"She's fine," Bo assured her. "We took her to El Paso with us and left her in a safe place. She'll be all right there until we've had a chance to put things right here in the valley."

Suddenly, Rosalinda's strained composure seemed to crumple. Tears welled from her eyes and coursed down her smooth cheeks. She threw herself at Bo, wrapped her arms around his neck, and buried her face against his chest as she continued to sob.

Scratch looked on with a slight frown. "You know," he mused, "it'd be all right one of these times if the pretty gal wanted to hug *me* in gratitude, too."

CHAPTER 16

Bo stood there for a minute, awkwardly patting Rosalinda on the back as her tears continued to dampen the front of his shirt and vest. Finally, he put his hands on her shoulders and gently but firmly moved her back a step so that she wasn't hugging him anymore.

"Tell me about it," she begged. "Tell me about Teresa. For all I knew, she was dead."

"She's very much alive," Bo said. "And she's worried about you, too. She knows that Davidson is forcing you to work here."

"She is with the men who escaped from the valley? The ones Señor Davidson calls bandits, even though they fight only for our freedom?"

Bo nodded. "That's right." His voice and expression were solemn as he went on. "And I'm afraid I've got some bad news there. Several of those young men were killed when they ambushed the wagons and tried to steal the ore. Only a few were left alive, and they were running away the last time we saw them."

Rosalinda's face fell. "They have given up the fight? This cannot be."

Scratch said, "They know now that Davidson's brought in some real fightin' men and not just a bunch of run-o'-the-mill hardcases. They probably feel like they can't stand up to him no more."

"But they must!" Rosalinda cried. "Someone has to fight! Otherwise, he will continue making slaves of us, working us to death, killing the ones who defy him, until either all the gold is gone . . . or all the people of the valley are."

She was probably right about that, Bo thought. He said, "Somebody *is* going to fight . . . Scratch and me, and when the time is right, anybody we can get to stand with us."

Rosalinda clutched his shirt sleeve. "You would do that?" she asked. "You would lead us in battle against Señor Davidson and his killers?"

"If it comes to that, yes. We'd like to try to find some way to deal with him without getting a lot of innocent people hurt or killed, though."

Gravely, Rosalinda shook her head. "You cannot. The only way a man like that gives up his power is when he is dead. You will have to kill Señor Davidson in order to defeat him, and you cannot kill him without others sacrificing their lives."

"Maybe not, but we intend to try."

A look of wariness suddenly came over her face. She tensed like an animal realizing that it was about to step into a trap. "How can I believe you?" she asked. "You work for Señor Davidson."

"Not anymore, although he still thinks we do."

"We've done quit," Scratch said with a grin. "He just don't know it yet."

"If you'll help us, you can see for yourself that we intend to help your people," Bo told her.

"What can I do? I have no power. I . . . I cannot even save myself."

"Do you ever talk to any of the others who are forced to work for Davidson?"

"Sometimes," she said hesitantly. "Most of the time I stay here, so that I can serve him . . . however he wishes." She took a deep breath. "But once a week or so, he allows me to go see my mother and father in the village. They are old, too old to work in the mine or . . . or in the house of the women."

"He lets you go there alone?"

She shook her head. "No. Someone always goes with me. Alfred sometimes, or one of the other men."

"Alfred is very fond of you," Bo said.

Rosalinda nodded. "I know. And I am fond of him as well. But there is nothing we can do about it."

"Would he help us if you asked him to?"

"You mean would he betray Señor Davidson?" Rosalinda frowned as she thought. Finally, she went on. "I . . . I do not know. He has worked for Señor Davidson for several years, since well before they came to San Ramon."

"Does he know everything that's been goin' on?" Scratch asked. "Seems to me like it wouldn't set well with a decent young fella like that, the way Davidson treats folks around here."

"He does not like it. I know this from the look on his face when one of the men is punished, or when a new woman is brought from the village and taken sobbing into the house. But you have seen Alfred. He . . . he is not like the other men who work for Señor Davidson. He is kind, when he can be." Her eyes dropped to the Colt holstered on Bo's hip. "And he is not the sort of man who uses a gun or his fists."

"Not a hardcase like us, in other words," Scratch said.

"I mean no offense—"

"None taken, Señorita," Bo told her. "You're only speaking the truth. We don't want him to pick up a gun and start shooting, although it might come to that sooner or later. Like you said, it's mighty hard to get rid of a tyrant without at least a little bloodshed along the way."

"You speak to a Mexican, Señor Creel," Rosalinda said. "We know all about tyrants and bloodshed."

Scratch said, "Yeah, I recollect a fella name of Santy Anny—"

"What we want from Alfred is information about things that Davidson may be planning," Bo said. "Also, he could tell us exactly how many men Davidson has working for him—the foremen, I mean, not the men from the village who are being forced to work in the mine—as well as things like where the extra guns and ammunition are kept."

"But if you ask him these things," Rosalinda said with a frown, "he will know that you plotting against Señor Davidson. Alfred is very smart."

"That's why I reckon it would be better if *you* were to ask him instead of one of us."

Her eyes widened again, this time in understanding. "You want me to spy for you!"

"For your people actually. And when you see your parents the next time, tell them that things are going to change around here. Tell them to spread the word, but to be careful about it. They should speak only to people they're sure they can trust. But when the time comes to fight, if it does, they'll know they're not alone. They'll know they've got a chance if they all stand together."

Rosalinda thought it over for a moment and then nodded. "I can do these things. If nothing else, it will give the people hope. And that is something they have not had for a very long time." She gave a little gasp. "I must get back downstairs. Alfred will wonder what is taking me so long."

"All right." Bo smiled at her. "Keep your courage up. Your sister has plenty of it, that's for sure."

"Teresa was always bold . . . too bold for her own good sometimes." Rosalinda stepped forward and gave Bo an impulsive hug. "Thank you for helping her, and for what you intend to do for my people."

Scratch cleared his throat.

Despite the depth of emotion that gripped her, Rosalinda managed to laugh softly. "And thank you as well, Señor Morton," she said as she turned to him and hugged him, too.

Scratch grinned. "Now that's more like it."

The next few days passed peacefully—at least for the men who were in power in the valley. Bo and Scratch didn't figure things were all that peaceful for the men being forced to swing pick and shovel in the mine tunnel for fourteen to sixteen hours at a stretch, or for the women who had to endure the bestial grunting of Davidson's men when they were taken against their will.

For now, though, the Texans had to bide their time. Several times during that interval, Rosalinda found opportunities to speak to one or both of them privately and pass along what she had found out from Alfred.

Davidson had no plans that Alfred knew of except to continue working the mine, sending the gold ore to El Paso, and then shipping it out from there by train. There were fourteen supervisors or foremen at the moment, plus the six hired guns, giving Davidson a total of twenty men to do his bidding. Of course, that number included Bo and Scratch, but even without them, Davidson's forces were large enough to control the people of the valley, who had always been peaceful farmers, not gunhands or fighters of any type.

It didn't help matters that Davidson and his men had confiscated all the weapons in the valley when they took over. That hadn't amounted to much—a few old single-shot rifles, some rusty pistols, knives and machetes more suited for work than fighting—but losing them had meant that the people had nothing with which to fight back except their bare hands. It was no wonder that Davidson had been able to seize power and hang on to it with relative ease. The bandits going after his gold shipments had really been his only problem.

As for the extra guns and ammunition belonging to Davidson's men, those were stored in the bunkhouse used by the supervisors. If the people of the valley were ever going to be able to fight back, it would sure help if they could get their hands on those weapons, Bo thought after Rosalinda told him and Scratch about the guns.

There was one more somewhat puzzling item that Rosalinda reported. Those two long crates that Davidson had brought back from El Paso on the pack mules were still unopened in the supply shed. Davidson had said that they contained mining equipment, but if so, it wasn't being put to use.

Not only that, but he had instructed his men to leave the crates alone. The Englishman, Lancaster, was the only one who was allowed to touch them.

That convinced Bo that whatever was in the crates, it wasn't intended for mining. He decided to try to find out more.

For that reason, when he saw Lancaster, Hansen, and Douglas playing cards one evening, he said, "Poker's better with four than three. Mind if I join you?"

"Not at all, old boy," Lancaster said as he waved a hand at the empty chair. "By all means."

Bo sat down, played a couple of hands and lost both, and joined in the casual conversation going around the table. Eventually, he said to Lancaster, "You mentioned you were in the British Army, didn't you?"

"That's right. Posted in India. I left the service a few years ago and decided to see some of the world." Lancaster laughed. "I landed here in your American West. Not all that different in many respects from India and Pakistan and Afghanistan. You have your red Indians and desperadoes instead of the Sikhs and the sort of hill bandits we dealt with over there. But I must say, I feel almost as much at home here as I did in the Khyber."

"What did you do in the army?" Bo asked as he studied his cards, keeping his tone one of idle curiosity.

"I was a machine-gunner. The Gardner gun, you know. A refinement of your country's Gatling gun."

Bo shook his head. "Don't think I've heard of it."

"It has two barrels that fire in an alternating pattern, rather than the six revolving barrels of a Gatling gun, but the feed system is superior, in my opinion, and allows for just as great a rate of fire, if not better. In tests, I've personally seen the Gardner fire up to ten thousand rounds in a little more than twenty minutes."

Hansen let out an impressed whistle. "That's a lot of lead to sling in that amount of time."

A superior smile curved Lancaster's lips. "There's a reason the sun never sets on the British Empire, my friend. In addition to our indomitable spirit, we usually have the greater firepower in any battle as well."

"I'd like to see one of those Gardner guns in action sometime," Bo said.

Still smiling, Lancaster said, "Perhaps you shall have that chance someday."

Bo knew for sure then what he had suspected before. Mining equipment, hell! Those crates contained a disassembled Gardner gun. Davidson had bought himself a machine gun—and a man to use it.

That was an even bigger potential threat than the marksman in the bell tower. Even if the villagers managed somehow to arm themselves and tried to throw off Davidson's brutal hold over them, that machine gun could mow them down in droves. It would have to be knocked out early if an uprising were to have any chance of success.

Otherwise, it would just be a bloody massacre.

Later, Bo told Scratch what he had found out. "Damn," Scratch said. "I've seen them Gatling guns at work, and so have you, Bo. If that Gardner gun of Lancaster's spits out even more rounds than a Gatling, these poor folks won't stand a chance against it."

"That's why *we* can't take a chance on letting Lancaster put it to work. If trouble comes, I'm going to knock out the machine gun first. You'll go after that hombre in the bell tower."

Scratch nodded in understanding. "That'll go a long way toward evenin' out the odds. When do we make our move?"

"I don't know yet," Bo said with a shake of his head. "But soon, I hope, so the folks here don't have to put up with being enslaved for any longer than necessary."

He figured there still had to be some among the villagers who would be willing to fight. Those were the men he needed to talk to, and he decided that he would ask Rosalinda to try to get word to them through her parents. Somehow, Bo and Scratch needed to get together with the villagers they could count on and start discussing some plans.

That was as far as he had gotten in his thinking by the next night, when a sudden rattle of gunfire from somewhere in the canyon made Davidson and his men boil out of the headquarters building to see what was going on. Bo and Scratch had no choice but to go with them, since they were still pretending to be loyal to Davidson.

The shooting continued as Davidson looked up the canyon and exclaimed, "It's coming from the shed where the blasting powder is stored."

Several of the men took an involuntary step back. One spark, or a stray bullet, could set off a keg of that blasting powder, and that would cause all the other kegs to blow up, too. An explosion like that would blast out a big crater in the ground and a hole in the canyon wall that the shed backed up to.

Davidson saw the men's hesitation and snapped, "Damn it, don't just stand there. Go find out what's happening."

"I don't much cotton to bein' around blastin' powder," Hansen muttered.

"If you want to keep your job, you'd better get moving." Davidson's flint-hard tone didn't leave any room for argument.

Luckily, the shooting eased off as the six hired gunmen approached the powder shed. Guards were normally posted at the shed, so Skinner called, "Hey, up there! What the hell's the shootin' all about?"

"We caught somebody sneakin' around," one of the guards replied. The two men came closer, prodding a stumbling figure ahead of them at gunpoint.

The second man gave the captive a hard shove. The prisoner tripped and fell, sprawling on the rocky ground. "Look what we grabbed," the guard said, gloating.

The moon had risen, and enough of its silvery glow penetrated the canyon for Bo, Scratch, and the others to be able to see the captive's face as she lifted her head and glared up at them. Bo and Scratch tensed in surprise and alarm.

The person the guards had caught sneaking around the powder shed was none other than Teresa Volquez.

CHAPTER 17

Teresa was dressed in range clothes, as usual, and had a gunbelt strapped around her waist. The holster was empty at the moment.

"Damn little minx was gonna blow up the powder shed," the first guard said. "She had matches and some fuse on her when we got hold of her."

"We saw her before she could get the fuse going," the second man added. "She ducked behind some rocks and started shooting at us. I was able to trade shots with her while Matthews slipped around and got behind her."

"She put up a hell of a fight when I jumped her," the first guard said, resuming the story with a note of pride in his voice. "I thought for a second I was gonna have to wallop her with my gun just to get her to settle down."

Bo and Scratch stood there listening, waiting to see what was going to happen. If Teresa called out to them to help her, that would give away their connection with her and all hell would break loose. Bo was sure that Jim Skinner would use that as an excuse to try to kill both him and Scratch.

Teresa must have been smart enough to realize that, because she didn't say anything. She just glared darkly at her captors, and her gaze held just as much venom when she directed it toward Bo and Scratch as it did when she looked at the other men.

"Who the hell is she?" Skinner demanded.

"I dunno. Some greaser bitch, that's all I can tell you. But she's gonna be sorry she tried to blow up the boss's blasting powder. You can be sure of that."

"Davidson's gonna want to see her," Skinner said. "A couple of you fellas get her on her feet. But hang on to her. We don't want her gettin' away."

Before any of the other men could move, Bo and Scratch stepped forward, each of them reaching down to grasp one of Teresa's arms. They lifted her to her feet, being none too gentle about it.

"All right, Señorita," Bo told her. "You're going to see the boss man. Do you *habla inglés*?"

"I speak your gringo tongue." Teresa practically spat the words. "And if you do not let me go, you will be sorry!"

A harsh laugh came from Skinner. "I reckon you're confused. We're the ones who've got you, not the other way around." He jerked his head toward the mine. "Bring her along."

Teresa struggled in the grip of the two Texans, but they didn't ease their holds on her. This had to look real, for all their sakes. Bo and Scratch represented her only chance of getting out of this, and she had to know that.

Bo wondered what in blazes she was doing here,

and why she had tried to blow up the powder shed. Actually, the answer to that second question was pretty obvious. She had been trying to hurt Davidson and his mining operation any way she could. Setting off a big explosion would have shaken things up in Cutthroat Canyon in more ways than one.

Davidson would have been able to recover from the damage as soon as he had more powder freighted in from El Paso, but he couldn't shake off the blow to his power and prestige quite so easily. It would have made him appear at least a little vulnerable—and vulnerability was one thing no tyrant could afford.

As they drew closer to the headquarters building, Davidson stepped forward with a lantern that someone had brought out to him. He lifted it so that its yellow glow fell over the men and their prisoner, and as he realized that the captive was a woman, he exclaimed, "What the hell!"

"We caught her tryin' to blow up the powder shed, Boss," one of the guards said. "When we spooked her, she started shootin' at us."

"Good job, good job," Davidson commended them. He strode up to Teresa and held the lantern so that it was close to her face. She glared at him defiantly. He studied her angry features for a moment and then demanded, "Who are you?"

Teresa spat in his face.

Bo couldn't have done anything to stop her, but he wished she hadn't done that. Davidson's free hand flashed up and cracked across her cheek in a hard slap that rocked her head to the side. She might have been knocked off her feet if the Texans hadn't been holding her arms.

Bo heard a low growl coming from deep in Scratch's throat. He looked over at his old friend and narrowed his eyes. That was all the warning he could risk, but it was enough. Scratch didn't let go of Teresa and go after Davidson, as Bo had worried for a second that he might.

Davidson wiped the spittle off his cheek and then grinned. "You've got spirit, Señorita, I'll give you that," he said. "And more courage than most of your countrymen." He frowned suddenly as he looked more closely at her. "There's something familiar about you. Have we met?"

Bo knew that Davidson was recognizing the family resemblance between Teresa and Rosalinda. He wasn't sure if it would do any harm for Davidson to know that the young women were sisters, but it might complicate matters more.

Teresa didn't answer the question. She just stared at Davidson in stony silence. After a moment, Davidson chuckled. "You're a stubborn one, aren't you?"

"Give her to us, Boss," one of the guards suggested. "We'll work that stubbornness out of her."

Bo knew what Teresa would be in for if Davidson turned her over to his men. They were experienced in mining operations, but more than that, they were all brutal, hard-nosed bastards who kept the workers from the village beaten down and broken in spirit. They would subject Teresa to even greater degradation than the women who worked in the brothel. In all likelihood, they would rape her repeatedly, perhaps even to the point of death.

"Sorry," Davidson responded curtly. "You can't have her." Bo didn't have a chance to be relieved by the decision, though, because Davidson continued. "At least not yet. I'm going to take care of this one myself." He jerked his free hand toward the corral. "Take her over there and tie her wrists to the top rail."

Scratch couldn't restrain himself. "Boss, I ain't so sure—"

"Do what I said, Morton," Davidson snapped. "It's time you see—it's time *everyone* around here sees—that I won't be trifled with." He put his hand on Scratch's shoulder and gave him a shove. "Do it."

Bo and Scratch started toward the corral with Teresa. Bo bent his head toward her and said in a low voice, "When you get a chance, run into the barn and find a horse. You'll have to ride bareback. Scratch and I will cover your escape."

"Davidson will kill you," Teresa whispered.

"We'll take our chances. We can't stand by and let him go ahead with whatever he's got planned for you."

Bo thought he knew what Davidson's intentions were. That hunch was confirmed when Davidson turned and called, "Alfred!"

The young man had followed the others out of the headquarters building. "Yes, sir?" he asked nervously.

"Go inside and get my whip."

"Sir . . ."

"Do what I told you, Alfred." Davidson turned to Lancaster and handed him the lantern. "Hold this. Raise it good and high so I can see what I'm doing."

Bo glanced around, and saw troubled frowns on the faces of Lancaster and Hansen. They didn't like where this was headed. But Lancaster shrugged and took the lantern. "You're the boss, as you Americans say," he told Davidson.

"And don't you forget it," Davidson said.

Bo and Scratch had reached the corral fence. A coiled lariat hung on one of the posts. Bo took it down and used his barlow knife to cut a couple of short lengths from it. He muttered to Teresa, "We'll tie your wrists so that you can slip right out of the bonds."

"No!" she breathed. "Let him do his worst. I can stand it."

"Maybe you can, Señorita," Scratch said, "but I don't reckon we can."

They had steered Teresa toward the big gate, and in fact it was to the gate that they loosely tied her wrists after lifting her arms over her head. When Bo lowered his hand, he brushed it against the latch, seemingly accidentally, and knocked it open.

"Rip her shirt off," Davidson called.

Bo and Scratch looked back at him. Alfred had brought him a long bullwhip, and with a flick of his wrist Davidson sent the length of it snaking out. Another flick made it coil at his feet and resemble a serpent even more.

Hansen spoke up. "This don't sit all that well with me, Boss—"

"Shut up," Skinner broke in. "Whatever Mr. Davidson's got in mind, I want to watch it."

"It'll be entertaining, I can promise you that," Davidson said with an ugly grin. At this moment, with the lantern light washing over his face and the whip in his hand, he looked like Satan himself, Bo thought, nothing at all like the affable businessman he had seemed to be back in El Paso. With that evil smile of anticipation, Davidson went on. "I'm going to flay the skin right off her naked back. Then the rest of you can have her . . . if you still want her."

He turned toward the corral, moving his wrist so that the whip hissed and writhed. His smile disappeared and his face darkened with rage as he said, "You still haven't torn her shirt off? Strip her, damn you, and do it now!"

"When I shove the gate open," Bo told Teresa, "pull your hands loose and get in the barn as fast as you can."

"Señor Creel, I am sorry—"

"No time for that now," Bo said. He gave the gate a hard push. "Go!"

As the gate swung open, the Texans whirled toward Davidson and the other men. Bo didn't know who would be faster in a showdown, although he suspected that Skinner could shade both him and Scratch. But in this case, they took the others by surprise, so Bo's Colt and Scratch's twin Remingtons were out and leveled before anybody else had a chance to slap leather.

"Nobody move," Bo snapped. "We'll kill the first man who reaches for a gun."

He heard the swift footsteps behind him and knew that Teresa had pulled loose and was running into the barn.

Davidson stared at the Texans in surprise for a second before fury took over. "Kill them!" he screamed as he lashed the whip at his feet. "Shoot them both and stop the girl!"

"Better think about it," Bo advised. "Scratch will kill the first man who tries it. *I'll* kill *you*, Davidson."

The mine owner threw the whip down and pointed a trembling finger at the Texans. "I'll have both your hides for this!" he cried. "You . . . you . . ." He was so angry he couldn't talk. He just started sputtering instead.

A man like that gets a little money and power and thinks he owns everything and everybody. Davidson himself had said those exact words about Little Ed Churchill back in the Birdcage, on the violent night that had started all this, Bo recalled. And now Davidson was a living example of that sentiment. He was so furious at the very idea anyone would challenge his orders that he was shaking with rage.

Bo heard hoofbeats, and knew that Teresa had managed to get on a horse, open the rear door of the barn, and ride out that way. If she could reach the mouth of the canyon, she could get into the valley and slip away under cover of darkness.

"Five hundred dollars to any man who kills Creel and Morton!" Davidson said. "No, a thousand!"

"Each?" Skinner drawled.

"No . . . but I'll throw in another thousand for any man who kills them and brings back that girl!"

Bo kept a close eye on Skinner. The skull-faced gunman was supremely confident in his gun-handling skill, Bo knew. Skinner was probably figuring the odds on getting lead into both of them before they could get lead into him.

"Do it!" screamed Davidson.

Skinner finally shook his head. "Man can't out-draw a gun that's already drawn, not even me."

"Five thousand!"

"Now you're startin' to tempt me . . ."

"By God, I'll take it!" Hansen said. He lunged to the side, clawing at the gun on his hip as he did so.

Bo wished the big Swede hadn't done it. Hansen wasn't a bad sort for a hired gun.

But he wasn't nearly fast enough either. His revolver had just started to clear leather when the Remington in Scratch's left hand roared.

As the .44 round punched into Hansen's beefy torso, Lancaster slung the lantern toward Bo and Scratch. Bo fired at Davidson, as he had promised, but the bullet struck the lantern in midair and shattered it. Flaming kerosene sprayed through the air, lighting up the scene in a hellish glare. Bo ducked away from it, and as he did he saw that Davidson had thrown himself to the ground. Davidson rolled over and came up with the whip in his hand again. Its weighted tip leaped out toward Bo.

The whip struck Bo's hand and bit deep like the snake it resembled. The pain as a gash opened up in the back of his hand made Bo drop the Colt. Smoke and flame continued to erupt from the muzzles of Scratch's Remingtons as he called to Bo, "Head for the barn! I'll cover you!"

If they could reach their horses, they stood a chance of getting out of this ruckus. A slim chance, to be sure, but better than nothing. Lancaster and Douglas had their guns out by now and were blazing away, firing through the flames that still rose from the spilled kerosene. Bo felt the wind-rip of a slug past his ear as he darted toward the barn.

Then Scratch grunted in pain and went to one

knee, and Bo knew he couldn't run out on his trail partner. Not after more than forty years of friendship and riding together. He wheeled around and saw that Scratch had dropped his left-hand gun. That hand was now pressed to Scratch's side, with crimson streams welling between the fingers.

Bo dived for the fallen Remington and scooped it up with his left hand. He knelt beside Scratch and felt the gun buck against his palm as he triggered it.

"Looks like this is the end of the trail, old-timer," Bo said over the roar of guns.

"Yeah," Scratch said. "Wish we could've helped those folks—"

That was when a giant fist slammed against the side of Bo's head, knocking him backward. He didn't know it when he hit the sandy ground in front of the open corral gate. Black oblivion had already claimed him.

CHAPTER 18

Bo would have bet that he'd never wake up again. But after an unknowable time, the darkness that surrounded him slowly began to fade. Like a long night giving way to dawn, awareness seeped back into his brain.

Consciousness brought with it thundering pain, and that dull, aching throb was welcome because it meant that he was still alive, Bo realized. If he'd been dead, he wouldn't feel anything.

The pain in his head wasn't the only one. Agony gripped his arms and shoulders, too, and every time he took a breath, what felt like sharp knives jabbed him somewhere inside. Gradually, he figured out that his arms were fastened somehow above his head, and he was hanging from them with all his weight being borne by his wrists.

The darkness continued to fade, and as it did so, a blindingly powerful light replaced it. Bo squeezed his eyelids shut as hard as he could, but the light grew more and more intense despite his efforts. It increased the pain in his head as well, until finally it was so bad he couldn't help but gasp.

"Bo! Bo! Thank God you're alive, old son!"

The voice was fuzzy and distorted, but Bo recognized it anyway. He ought to, after all these years. Even though it pained him considerably to do so, he forced his eyes open, wincing as the bright light struck them with even more force. He blinked rapidly as his vision tried to adjust.

After what seemed like an eternity of eye-searing brilliance, Bo was able to see well enough to tell that he was still in Cutthroat Canyon. Sharp, scraping pains in his back as his body shifted slightly told him that he was hanging against the canyon's rocky wall.

Even though the movement made the world spin crazily around him, he turned his head toward the sound of Scratch's voice as the silver-haired Texan said, "Are you all right, Bo?" A hollow laugh came from Scratch, followed by, "That's a hell of a dumb question, ain't it?"

Bo's sight was still blurry, but he could see well enough to make out his friend and partner. Scratch hung by his arms, too. His wrists were tied together with rope, and that rope was looped over a spike of some sort that had been hammered into the canyon wall. Scratch's bare feet dangled about ten inches off the ground.

Scratch wore only his trousers. He had been stripped to the waist, and mottled bruises from a terrible beating covered his torso. His face was a mass of bruises and dried blood. Blood that had flowed from a wound of some sort had caked into a dark brown patch on his left side.

Bo recalled that Scratch had been shot during the fight with Davidson's men in front of the corral. From the looks of the injury, the bullet had plowed a furrow in Scratch's side, not a serious wound other than the loss of blood.

"You . . . look like . . . hell," Bo managed to say.

"Reckon I could say the same thing about you." Scratch was more alert and had been conscious longer.

"I take it I'm . . . hung up like a side of beef, too."

"Yep. They whaled on us good and proper, then hung us up here to cook in the sun."

"Feels like . . . it's working." Heat gripped Bo like a giant, blazing hand. He didn't have the energy to talk much, but he managed to ask, "Teresa . . . ?"

"She got away," Scratch said, and relief flooded through Bo. "I heard 'em talkin' about it. Davidson sent Lancaster and Douglas to look for her, but I got my doubts about 'em bein' able to find her."

If Teresa had any sense, Bo thought, she would keep running until she had put this canyon and the evil it held far behind her.

But if she'd had any sense, he reminded himself, she wouldn't have come back here in the first place. She would have left it to him and Scratch to do something about Davidson. Now that possibility was gone. They couldn't work against the mine owner from within. They would be extremely lucky just to stay alive. Bo was surprised they weren't dead already.

He hung there silently in the heat for several minutes, as still as a lizard, gathering the feeble remnants of his strength. When he felt a little better he asked, "Was I wounded?"

"Yeah, a slug nicked you on the side of the head," Scratch replied. "Bled like a stuck pig, too. I thought you were a goner for sure. Reckon it just knocked you out, though. Another inch to the left and your brains would've been splattered all over that corral fence." He chuckled. "You ought to see yourself. You got so much dried blood on your face you look like somethin' out of a nightmare."

"You're not what I'd call pretty as a picture yourself." Bo turned his head again to look around. "Where are we?"

"Up the canyon from the mine, not far from the powder shed Teresa tried to blow up. Say, what do you think made that gal come back down here instead of stayin' at Luz's place like we told her to do?"

"Old as I am, I still haven't lived long enough yet to figure out how a woman thinks," Bo said. "My guess is that she got tired of waiting, or she just felt like it was her fight, too, and had to do something about it. Or maybe something happened at Luz's to upset her and make her leave. We'll have to find her and ask her about it . . . when we get loose from here."

"You sound pretty sure we ain't gonna just hang here until we die," Scratch commented.

"Damn right we aren't," Bo said. "We'll get out of this somehow."

But for the life of him, he sure couldn't see how.

* * *

That day was an eternity long, but thankfully, Davidson had miscalculated when he told his men where to hang Bo and Scratch on the canyon wall. By the afternoon, when the sun was at its hottest, the blazing orb had moved far enough west in the sky so that the canyon itself gave the Texans a little shade. Midday had been the worst, with the sun beating down fiercely from directly overhead.

The heat had been helpful in a way, though, because it had numbed some of their other aches and pains. Bo dozed off from time to time, even though he didn't want to and fought against it. In the back of his mind lurked the fear that if he went to sleep, he might not ever wake up again.

He couldn't tip his head back far enough to see his own wrists, but he had studied the way Scratch was tied and hung from the spike. For a while, Bo had thought that if they could somehow start their bodies swinging back and forth, they might work up enough momentum to slip the ropes off the spikes. That wasn't going to happen, though, because of the way the ropes were tied to the spikes themselves, not merely looped over them as Bo had thought at first.

The only way they would get down was if someone cut them down, and that seemed mighty unlikely to happen.

Bo's mouth felt like it was filled with cotton. In fact, it seemed like all the moisture in his body had been leeched out by the sun. His tongue swelled, filling his mouth until it threatened to choke him.

If they could make it until nightfall, he told himself, things would get better. The air cooled off considerably at night in these parts, and that would help soothe their blistered skin.

But another day like this would kill them. Bo had absolutely no doubt about that.

Sometime during the afternoon, curiosity prodded him to ask Scratch, "Do you know if you killed Hansen when you shot him?"

"Yeah, he crossed the divide," Scratch answered. "Damn shame, too. I sort of liked that big Scandahoovian. He wasn't such a bad hombre for a hired gun. Wish we hadn't wound up on opposite sides." With his arms tied above his head as they were, Scratch couldn't shrug, but the shrug was in his voice as he added, "Not much you can do about it when a fella starts shootin' at you, though. You got to shoot back. At least I do."

"Yeah," Bo agreed. "Me, too. But like you say, it's a shame. What about Skinner and Lancaster and Douglas?"

"They all came through the fight without gettin' ventilated. Skinner took particular delight in kickin' the hell outta both of us, after Davidson told his men to work us over before we was strung up here."

"Lancaster and Douglas get in on that?"

"Nope. It was the hombres who run the mine for Davidson, along with Skinner."

That made Bo feel a little better. The Englishman and the kid hadn't struck him as the sort who would take part in torturing a helpless enemy. They preferred to fight their battles straight up and out in the open.

"Remember we talked about Lancaster's Gardner gun?" Bo asked.

"Yeah. Just what Davidson needs," Scratch muttered. "A newfangled way to run roughshod over these poor folks."

"If we could get our hands on it . . ."

"Right after we get loose from here, you mean?"

"Yeah."

"You know what? If you keep studyin' on it, Bo, I really do believe you'll come up with a way to do it."

More time dragged by. Shadows covered the whole wall of the canyon now, although the air was still stiflingly hot. Bo's hands and arms were completely numb by now, which was a relief in a way because he could no longer feel it where the rope had chafed and bloodied his wrists. He dozed again, and when he jerked awake, he saw two people coming along the canyon floor toward him and Scratch.

Bo glanced over at his partner, saw that Scratch's head lolled forward loosely on his neck. For a terrible second, Bo thought that his old friend had died, but then he saw the faint movement of Scratch's chest that told him the silver-haired Texan still lived.

"Scratch," Bo croaked. "Scratch, wake up. Somebody's coming."

They were close enough now for Bo to make out who they were. Rosalinda came first. Trailing behind her was Alfred, who carried a bucket with a long-handled dipper in it. Bo's parched and blistered lips stretched in a half-smile, half-grimace as he saw that. A desperate yearning for water filled his entire being.

Scratch muttered something unintelligible and slowly lifted his head. "Wha . . . Is that . . . Teresa?"

"No," Bo told him. "It's Rosalinda. And Alfred."

"Thought maybe . . . Teresa had come back . . . to let us loose."

Rosalinda looked sorrowful and horror-stricken as she came to a stop in front of the prisoners and gazed up at them. Alfred kept his eyes averted, as if he was too ashamed of what was going on to look at them.

"Señor Creel . . . Señor Morton . . . I am so sorry," Rosalinda began.

"Not your fault . . . Señorita," Bo told her.

"But if you had not been trying to help me, and the people of the valley—"

"Shoot, don't . . . worry about it," Scratch broke in. "We just got . . . a natural dislike for . . . varmints like Davidson." He summoned up a grin. "No offense, Alfred."

The young man finally looked up with a tormented expression on his face. "For God's sake, don't apologize to me!" he cried. "It's the man I work for who's responsible for the terrible things that have happened to you! I swear, he wasn't always that way. The gold . . . it changed him somehow. He used to just speculate in mining claims, but then he heard about Don Alviso's mine somehow . . . We came down here to look it over, and when Mr. Davidson saw the quality of the ore . . . But even then, I never dreamed he would . . . would . . ."

"Murder Don Alviso and take over the mine for himself?" Bo asked.

A shudder ran through Alfred. "I tried to tell myself at first that it must have been an accident when the gun went off. I didn't think Mr. Davidson would do such a thing. But then I saw how he began to treat the people around here . . . the sort of men he brought in to run things for him . . . I hoped it wasn't as bad as it looked . . ."

"I'm sure you did, son," Scratch said. "And it ain't that I'm not sympathetic. But if that's water in that bucket, I'd be powerful obliged if I could have some."

"Oh, Lord, of course!" Alfred pulled the dipper full of water out of the bucket and raised it to Scratch's mouth. Even though it was awkward, Scratch gulped down as much as he could. Bo was next, and he didn't think anything had ever tasted sweeter than the water that spilled from the dipper into his mouth.

His body was so dry that it sucked up the moisture immediately, leaving him still thirsty. He figured he could drink for a week without quenching his thirst. But he knew if he guzzled down too much water, he was liable to get sick and throw it back up, and he didn't want that. So he settled for running his swollen tongue over his lips to get every last drop he might have spilled, and he then asked thickly, "What's Davidson going to do with us?"

"I . . . I don't really know," Alfred said. "He told me to bring you some water so that you wouldn't . . . wouldn't die too fast. Maybe he'll let you go later."

Scratch chuckled. "You know better than that, son. He's gonna leave us out here and let the sun bake us again tomorrow. We'll be dead 'fore the day's over."

Rosalinda put her hands over her face and sobbed. "Why did Teresa have to come back? Why?"

"You told Alfred about her?" Bo asked.

"*Sí.* I told him everything, all about how you said you were going to try to help me and my people. I did not think it mattered now if he knew the truth."

Scratch said, "I don't reckon it does. What do you say, Alfred? Now that you know what's goin' on, are you gonna keep helpin' that polecat?"

"There's nothing I can do," Alfred said, looking and sounding miserable as he did so.

"You could cut us loose," Bo suggested.

Alfred shook his head. "No, I can't. Mr. Davidson told that man Skinner to keep an eye on us while we brought the water to you. He told Skinner that if we did anything besides give you the water . . . if we tried to help you in any way . . . Skinner was to shoot me. And then Rosalinda would be sent to the brothel."

Bo turned his head enough to look back down the canyon toward the mine. His vision had gotten better since the sun hadn't been shining directly into his eyes for a while, and he could make out Jim Skinner's lean form as the gunman lounged on the porch of the headquarters building.

"He has a pair of field glasses," Alfred went on. "He's been watching us. I can feel his eyes following us, like . . . like . . ."

"A snake's?" Scratch suggested.

"Exactly." A shudder went through Alfred.

"How about Lancaster and Douglas?" Bo asked. "Maybe they could do something for us."

Alfred shook his head. "Mr. Davidson's already talked to them. He knows they're upset about what's happened. But he promised them a bonus if they go along with what he's doing to you, and they're going to take it."

"That ain't surprisin'," Scratch said. "Hombres like that, *dinero* means more to 'em than anything else."

Bo said, "It looks like there's nothing you can

do without risking your life, Alfred, and I reckon Rosalinda here is going to need you to look out for her. So that's what you need to do. Don't worry about Scratch and me."

"If there was any way I could help . . ."

"No, you run along," Scratch told him. "Might give us a little more of that water before you go, though."

"Of course." Alfred used the dipper to give each of them another drink. Then he and Rosalinda headed back down the canyon toward the mine, both of them glancing back from time to time.

"Reckon the boy's gonna do the right thing?" Scratch asked when the young people were gone.

"I don't know," Bo said. "I don't know what to hope for. Alfred's no fighter. If he tries to help us, he's liable to just get himself killed. Might be better in the long run for him and Rosalinda if he just turned his back on the whole thing."

"You don't believe that," Scratch said. "It'll eat away at him the rest of his life if he does."

Bo sighed. "Yeah. You're probably right about that."

They fell silent again. Exhaustion caught up to Bo a while after that, and he drifted off to sleep again, even though he didn't really want to.

When he awoke, darkness had descended once more over Cutthroat Canyon. With it had come a chill. During the heat of the day he had looked forward to cooling off, but now it quickly became a bone-numbing cold that settled into him. He shivered, and his teeth began to chatter. A clicking sound from beside him told him that Scratch was having the same reaction to the lower temperature.

That was when something hit him on the head. It felt like a pebble, and it was followed by several more tiny rocks that struck his head and shoulders as they fell, along with some dust and grit that drifted into Bo's eyes and made him blink. He heard a faint scraping sound above him.

He twisted his head as far as he could in an attempt to look up the canyon wall. Stars were visible against the ebony sky, but then some of them were blotted out by a moving patch of darkness.

"Scratch!" Bo whispered. "Scratch, wake up! Somebody's climbing down into the canyon!"

CHAPTER 19

Another shower of rocks pelted down around them. Scratch stirred and lifted his head, muttering, "Wha . . . what the hell?"

Bo watched as the shadowy form lowered itself toward them. The canyon walls were too sheer for anybody short of an ape to climb them, so whoever it was had to be using a rope to let themselves down.

Maybe it *was* an ape, Bo thought wildly as he saw how big the figure was. Feet pushed against the rock face, the shape swung out from it, and then dropped to the ground between them with surprising grace for someone so bulky.

"Señor Bo! Señor Scratch! *Caramba!* Tell me that you are alive, and we are not too late!"

"Pepe!" The whispered exclamation burst from Bo's cracked lips. "What in blazes are you doing here?"

Starlight penetrated the canyon and winked on the blade of the knife the massive bodyguard from Luz's place in El Paso pulled from behind his belt. He reached up with a long arm and started sawing through the rope that bound Bo's wrists to the spike in the canyon wall.

"Thanks be to El Señor Dios that you are still alive," Pepe said in a low, rumbling voice. "There will be time for explanations later, once you and Señor Scratch are safe."

Pepe put his left arm around Bo's waist and held him up easily as the rope parted. Gently, he lowered Bo to the ground and finished the job of freeing the Texan's wrists. Then, as Bo sat slumped at the base of the canyon wall, leaning against it, Pepe went to work freeing Scratch.

A million tiny knives stabbed into Bo's shoulders, arms, and hands as the blood began to flow freely again into the numbed extremities. In its own way, the pain of that was as bad as anything else Bo had experienced in the past twenty-four hours. He clenched his jaw to keep from groaning in agony, and rolled his shoulders in an attempt to speed up the process. He looked down at his hands and tried to clench and unclench the fingers, but the muscles refused to work just yet. Those hands might as well have belonged to someone else, for all the good Bo did in trying to control them.

Pepe lowered Scratch to the ground beside him. Scratch husked, "*Gracias, amigo.* If you weren't such an ugly ol' varmint, Pepe, I reckon I'd kiss you right about now."

"Save your kisses for Luz, Señor Scratch," Pepe advised. "I think she will appreciate them much more than me."

"Well, I'll settle for sayin' thanks then."

Bo said, "I never expected to see you here, Pepe."

"I will tell you about it later. Are there guards nearby?"

"There haven't been any guards out here all day. I reckon Davidson figured we were in such bad shape and in such a bad fix that he didn't need to post any."

"Then he will be very surprised in the morning when he finds that you are gone, eh?"

"Very," Bo said. For a second, he worried that Davidson might blame Rosalinda and Alfred for their escape, but then he recalled that Skinner had been watching those two as they came back to the mine headquarters late that afternoon. The gunman would know that the youngsters hadn't had anything to do with Bo and Scratch getting away.

Of course, they hadn't gotten away yet, Bo reminded himself. This canyon was a dead end, and he thought it was highly unlikely they could sneak out past the mine without being discovered.

Pepe hunkered in front of them and said, "How do you feel? Your arms are not as numb, yes?"

"That's right," Bo said. All those little knives hadn't gone away yet, but at least they weren't jabbing as deeply or as painfully as they had been a few minutes earlier.

Pepe reached over and grasped the rope he had used to let himself down into the canyon. "Can you climb?"

"I don't know about that," Bo replied. "I reckon it might be a little too much right now."

"That is what we thought. Let me help you stand. I will tie the rope around you, and Luz and Teresa can pull you up."

"Teresa is with you?"

"*Sí.* It was she who persuaded us that we should come down here from El Paso and try to help you drive that hombre Davidson out of the valley."

Bo didn't mention the fact that Teresa's "help" had come mighty close to costing him and Scratch their lives. All that could be hashed out later.

"I'm not sure a couple of women can lift me," he said as Pepe helped him to his feet and passed the rope under his arms, knotting it in front of his chest.

"Don't worry. Luz is as strong as an ox. And if you tell her I said so, I will deny it to my dying breath."

Bo managed to chuckle. "Don't worry. I won't say anything."

When the rope had been made fast around him, Pepe gave it a couple of tugs. Bo felt the slack go out of it. Pepe made a stirrup out of his hands, and Bo put a bare foot in it and stepped up. The rope held most of his weight as he began to walk up the canyon wall.

He was never quite sure where he found the strength to do that, but he managed to reach the top a few minutes later. Luz and Teresa were waiting for him, as Pepe had promised. They reached out to grasp his arms and pull him onto a ledge. Bo sprawled out on it, his chest heaving.

He stayed there catching his breath for only a couple of seconds, though, before he sat up and started fumbling with the knot that held the rope. Scratch was still down there.

His fingers still didn't want to work right. Teresa knelt in front of him and said, "Let me." She pulled at the knot and had it untied in moments. She dropped the rope back down over the rim.

The other end was tied around Luz's waist, Bo noticed. She wore trousers and a man's shirt, like Teresa. The top button was unbuttoned so that the upper halves of her big breasts spilled out of the shirt. Bo had a hard time imagining the madam on horseback, and wondered if that was how they had come down here into Mexico, or if they had brought a wagon.

While Bo sat there and rested, Teresa and Luz hauled Scratch up out of the canyon. Then they dropped the rope down to Pepe again, and the body-guard scrambled up it like the ape he had reminded Bo of earlier. As he coiled the rope after Luz untied it from around her waist, he said, "I am sorry we could not bring the horses up here. We will have to walk out."

"Don't worry about that," Scratch told him. "It'll feel mighty good to be on our feet again, I reckon, after danglin' like that all day."

Pepe helped them up, and when they proved to be unsteady, he got between them and looped an arm around each of them. Their progress was slow but steady as they followed Teresa off the ledge and onto a narrow, winding trail that twisted upward into the mountains. Luz brought up the rear, carrying a Winchester.

"When we get higher up, this trail will lead to an-other that goes down into the valley," Teresa ex-plained. "We left the horses there."

"What about Davidson's man in the bell tower?" Bo asked.

"He cannot see in the darkness. As long as we are

in hiding before daylight, we will be safe from his eyes . . . and his gun."

"We've never cottoned much to hidin' out," Scratch said. "I reckon under the circumstances, though, it ain't such a bad idea."

"You are in no shape to fight a battle right now," Teresa said. "You must rest and recover from what Davidson has done to you." Her voice caught a little as she went on, "I . . . I am sorry you had to endure such torture because of me."

"I reckon you had your reasons for doing what you did," Bo said. "And if you'd gotten away with blowing up that shed, it would have done considerable damage to Davidson's operation, at least for a while. We can talk about that later, once we get out of here."

"Yeah," Scratch said, "and we can start figurin' out how we can get our hands on some guns, too . . . because I aim to pay another visit to Cutthroat Canyon later on."

"Count on it," Bo said.

The trek out of the mountains took more than an hour and used up all the reserves of strength the Texans had left, and the rocky ground was terribly hard on their bare feet. By the time they reached the horses, Pepe was carrying them more than helping them walk. He lifted each of them onto the back of a horse. Teresa swung up behind Bo, while Pepe rode behind Scratch. Even at a slow walk, they had to hold the Texans on the mounts. Luz followed on a third horse, answering the question that had gone through Bo's mind earlier.

They took a roundabout route toward San Ramon. Having grown up in the valley, Teresa knew all the trails, both there and in the surrounding mountains and foothills. That was how she had been able to lead Luz and Pepe to the ledge above the canyon.

Eventually, Teresa whispered, "We must go the rest of the way on foot. Pepe will take the horses back into the hills and hide them."

Bo and Scratch had regained some of their strength during the ride. They were able to dismount with only a little help. Pepe took the reins of the other two horses and set off into the night while Teresa and Luz led the Texans through the cultivated fields toward the cluster of adobe huts.

When they reached the village, Teresa went to the door of one of the huts and called through it, "Evangelina!" Bo heard the sound of a bar being removed from its brackets on the other side of the door, which swung open a second later. No light came from inside the hut. All the lamps had been blown out.

A young woman in a long skirt and low-cut peasant blouse ushered them inside. When she had closed and barred the door behind them, she commanded in a low voice, "Light the lamp, Enrique."

A match rasped. Flame moved through the darkness, caught the wick in a crude oil lamp. A flickering glow welled up.

Bo saw that they were in a small, spartanly furnished room. A rough-hewn table, a couple of chairs, and a stone fireplace filled up most of the room. Thick curtains hung over the single window. Through an arched doorway, he saw another room with a rope bunk in it. A straw-filled mattress rested on the bunk.

"Welcome to my home, Señores," the woman said. "Teresa tells me that you are enemies of the man Davidson. This means you are my amigos."

Bo looked at her in the lamplight, and his jaw tightened. She was a little older than Teresa, but still young and beautiful. At least, she had been beautiful before someone had taken a knife to her and left an ugly red scar down each side of her face. From the looks of the scars, her cheeks had been sliced open down to the bone.

"Son of a—" Scratch exclaimed before stopping himself.

The woman called Evangelina smiled, but the pain in her eyes remained. "I know. No man can bear to look at me now save Enrique, and he is . . . well, not right in the head."

The white-whiskered old man who had lit the lamp grinned and chortled. "I still think you are pretty, Evangelina, even after the gringo cut you."

"Who did it?" Bo asked. "Davidson?"

Evangelina shook her head. "The one called Wallace. I thought at first he was nicer than the others who came to me in . . . the place where they took us. But then one night, he grew angry at me when he could not . . ." She shrugged. "He became angry and took out his knife and said that no man would ever want me again." She laughed, but the sound held no humor. "He was right about that. And in a way it was a blessing. Señor Davidson told Gomez, the *cabron* who runs the house, to send me away."

"Wallace will pay for that," Bo said.

"Bet a hat on it," Scratch added.

Evangelina said, "You must sit down and rest. I have food and wine. Not much, but whatever I have I am willing to share."

Bo sank gratefully into one of the chairs at the table. Scratch took the other. Bo said, "You know you're taking a big chance by helping us, don't you, Señorita?"

Evangelina shook her head. "I don't care. All that matters to me is striking back against the men who have invaded our home and ruined our lives. From what Teresa tells me, you two are the best chance of doing that."

She brought them cups of wine, and tortillas and beans. There was a gourd full of clean water from the stream, and Bo and Scratch passed it back and forth, drinking deeply. After being empty for so long, Bo's stomach threatened to rebel at first, but then it settled down and the food began to make him feel better.

When they had finished eating, Teresa said, "We should clean those wounds."

"I can do that," Evangelina offered. "I had plenty of experience with my own."

"Got any tequila or pulqué or mescal?" Scratch asked.

"Fetch the tequila, Enrique," Evangelina said. "You are right, Señor Morton. It will help to cleanse the wounds."

"Well, yeah, that, too," Scratch said with a smile.

Bo grimaced and his breath hissed between his teeth as Evangelina used a tequila-soaked rag to wash the blood away from the gash the bullet had left on his head. She did the same with the deep graze on Scratch's side. Then she heated water in a pot over a small fire in the fireplace and pressed hot, damp compresses to the bruises and scrapes on their torsos. They soaked their bruised, lacerated feet in pans of hot water as well.

A great weariness stole over Bo as this was going on. He knew he wasn't going to be able to stay awake much longer, so he told Teresa, "Somebody better stand guard all the time. Davidson's liable to send some men to search the village tomorrow when he finds out we're gone. Wake us before dawn and Scratch and I will slip out of here so they won't find us. We don't want to bring any trouble down on your friend's head."

"Let us worry about that," Teresa said.

Bo would have argued, but he was too blasted tired to do so. He dozed off, not knowing where or when he would wake up, but too far gone to do anything about it.

CHAPTER 20

Cool darkness surrounded him when awareness came back to him again. At least, he hadn't died in his sleep and gone to hell, Bo thought. It would be a lot hotter and brighter if he had.

He opened his eyes. He was lying on something soft, and when he shifted a little, it rustled underneath him. A straw-filled mattress like the one he had seen in Evangelina's bedroom, he decided. But he wasn't on that bunk. Some sort of roof was fairly close overhead, so that he couldn't stand up without banging his head on the planks. He could see that much because faint light filtered down to wherever he was through cracks between the boards.

A soft snore made him turn his head. Scratch was sleeping on another mattress beside him. Under the mattresses was a hard-packed dirt floor, and the walls of the chamber were made of stone. They were in some sort of underground room, Bo realized, a hidey-hole underneath one of the huts in the village, probably Evangelina's. And it was day now, because the light coming through the cracks was sunlight, not the flickering glow of the oil lamp.

Bo heard the mutter of voices overhead, and opened his mouth to call out to whoever was up there and let them know he was awake. He stopped without saying anything, though. Instead, he pushed himself up on an elbow, reached over, and clamped a hand over Scratch's mouth.

The silver-haired Texan jerked away and started to bolt upright, but Bo's other hand on his shoulder held him down. When he saw awareness come into Scratch's eyes, he took his hands away and held a finger to his lips in a signal for silence.

Someone had wrapped bandages around Scratch's midsection where the bullet had grazed him. Bo put a hand to his head and felt a bandage there as well. He sat up—there was room in the hiding place for that—and Scratch did likewise. Both men listened intently, trying to make out what was being said above them.

The voices suddenly grew louder as boots thumped on the boards. "If you see any sign of those two, you'd damn well better let us know, or you'll be sorry," a man said in harsh tones.

"Don't worry, Señor, we will come to the mine immediately and tell you."

That was Evangelina. Her words were meek and submissive, and she didn't sound at all like the fiery, defiant young woman she had been the night before.

Bo had figured out that it was the next morning now, and Davidson's men had come to the village to search for him and Scratch, just as he thought they would. The search had reached Evangelina's hut.

It hadn't taken long, though, for the men to see that no one was there except the scarred young woman and the somewhat addlepated old man. Footsteps clomped out. Bo and Scratch breathed a little easier then, but they didn't relax until part of the floor above them rose, forming a trapdoor. More light flooded into the hidden chamber, making both men narrow their eyes against its brightness.

Evangelina leaned over the opening, blocking some of the light. "You can come out now," she told them. "Davidson's men are gone."

Bo and Scratch stood up, hoisted themselves onto the edge of the opening in the floor, and climbed out. They saw that they were inside Evangelina's bedroom. A woven rug had covered one side of the trapdoor, the other side of which was flush with a wall. Unless someone knew the opening was there, they wouldn't spot it without a thorough search. Obviously, Davidson's men hadn't been that diligent.

Enrique stood to one side, grinning as usual. He wore a serape today, and one hand came out from underneath the coarsely woven cloak holding an ancient cap-and-ball pistol. "I don't need to shoot anyone, Evangelina?" he asked.

"No, no shooting," she told him as she gently took the heavy revolver out of his gnarled hand. She looked at Bo and Scratch and added, "If they had found the trapdoor, Enrique was going to kill them. The shots would have brought the rest of Davidson's men, but at least you would have had their guns to make a fight of it."

"I'm glad it didn't come to that," Bo said. "I

thought Davidson confiscated all the guns in the valley, though."

Evangelina shrugged. "His men missed a few that our people were able to hide, like this one. But we have only a handful, and a limited amount of ammunition. Not enough to stand up to Davidson and his men." She made a face. "Not enough *cojones* either, when it comes to that."

"Where are Teresa and Luz?"

"They went into the hills before dawn to hide with Pepe during the day," Evangelina explained. "They will be back tonight. In the meantime, Teresa told me to keep you safe and let you rest. Would you like something to eat?"

Bo realized that he was famished. He said, "Yes, ma'am, we surely would."

"Yeah, my backbone's ticklin' my belly button," Scratch added. That struck Enrique as funny and sent him off into spasms of laughter.

Evangelina heated a pot of stew filled with savory wild onions and chunks of goat meat. Bo and Scratch wolfed down bowls of the stuff, and cleaned up the last drops with pieces of tortilla. Evangelina had coffee as well, and as Bo was sipping the thick, strong brew, he thought that the woman was probably emptying her larder for them. People in villages such as this one never had much, and the people of San Ramon probably had less than most because of Davidson's harsh treatment of them. With many of the men off in the canyon slaving in the mine, their farms had gone neglected.

As soon as they could, he and Scratch would

have to leave here. They didn't want to be a burden to the very people they were trying to help.

So far, that hadn't worked out very well, he mused. They hadn't accomplished a damned thing except to kill three of Davidson's hired guns. And as dangerous as Jackman, Tragg, and Hansen had been, there were hundreds more men like them scattered throughout the West. Davidson could replace them without much trouble. Skinner, as well as Lancaster and his blasted Gardner gun, represented much bigger threats.

"I have to go work in the fields," Evangelina told them when they had finished eating. "It will be better if you get back in the hidden space under my bedroom." She smiled. "Cooler there during the heat of the day, too."

"Sounds good to us," Bo said. "How did you happen to have a hiding place like that anyway?"

"A number of houses in the village have them, but Davidson and his men do not know that. We used them to store food, goat milk, things like that."

Bo nodded. Such cool places weren't unusual in hotter climates. Folks had to do what they could to make food last longer, because it tended to spoil quickly because of the heat.

They climbed back into the underground room, taking a gourd of water and some tortillas with them, and Evangelina lowered the trapdoor into place. She left Enrique's old hogleg with them.

"I think you could probably make better use of it than him, if the need arose," she said. "He will come with me to the fields, so no one should disturb you."

Once she was gone and the Texans were alone,

Scratch suggested, "One of us ought to stay awake, I reckon, just in case anybody comes snoopin' around."

"Good idea," Bo agreed. "You can sleep first, if you want to."

"No, I'm wide awake. And you're the one who got shot in the head. You probably need more rest."

"You lost more blood," Bo pointed out.

"I ain't so sure about that. Head wounds bleed like the devil."

That was true. Bo shrugged and rolled onto his side. He was asleep within minutes.

They spent the day like that, alternating dozing and staying awake. No one disturbed them until Evangelina and Enrique returned as the light coming through the cracks in the floor began to fade, signifying that another day was over. When the trapdoor rose, Enrique looked in at them with his toothless grin and motioned for them to come out.

The curtains had been drawn over all the windows. Evangelina looked tired from her day's labors as Bo and Scratch joined her in the hut's main room. She told them to sit down at the table, but Bo said, "We've been taking it easy all day, Señorita. Why don't you sit down and let us see what we can rustle up for supper."

"I'm a pretty fair hand at cookin', if I do say so myself," Scratch put in.

Evangelina smiled. "That would be nice, for a change. Very well, Señores."

Bo realized that when she smiled, the scars on her cheeks weren't as noticeable. Or maybe he was just getting used to them.

Either way, he hoped that before he and Scratch

left this valley, Evangelina and everyone else who lived here would have reason to smile again, because they had been freed from Porter Davidson's tyrannical hold on them.

An hour after dark, a soft tapping on the door announced the arrival of Teresa, Luz, and Pepe. Evangelina blew out the lamp and then let them in. Once they were inside, Enrique relit the lamp, as he had the night before.

"You look better," Teresa said with a smile as she looked at Bo and Scratch. Bo wore one of Enrique's old shirts. It was too small, but better than nothing. Scratch had a serape draped over his shoulders. Both Texans had rags wrapped around their feet. Walking barefoot out of the mountains the night before had left their feet bruised, scratched, and swollen.

"I reckon we've still got a ways to go before we're up to snuff again," Bo said with a smile. "But we've got some of our strength back already."

"Did Davidson's men come to the village looking for you?"

"They did," Bo confirmed, "but thanks to Señorita Evangelina here, they didn't find us."

Luz said, "What are we going to do now? How long can you keep hiding like that? For that matter, how long must the three of us hide in the hills like animals?"

"It was your choice to come down here," Bo pointed out. "And speaking of that, what in blazes made you do such a thing?"

Luz shrugged, making her breasts move under

her shirt. "This little one"—and she gestured toward Teresa—"spoke of how much gold there was for the taking in that mine. I asked myself, why shouldn't some of it belong to me?"

"And I go where Luz goes," Pepe added.

"Anyway, I knew Teresa would not stay in El Paso," Luz went on. "I could tell by looking at her how restless she was as soon as the two of you left. If we had not come with her, she would have run away from my house, stolen a horse, and ridden back here by herself."

Teresa got a defiant look on her face as she said, "This is my home. These are my people. Should I turn my back on them while others fight the battles I should be helping to fight?"

"We did ask you to stay put," Bo said.

"I sort of figured you wouldn't, though," Scratch added.

Teresa tossed her head. "I am here now and ready to wage war against Davidson. Just because I failed the first time does not mean that I will again."

Bo frowned and tugged at his earlobe. "And how are you going to go about waging that war, Señorita? You don't have an army."

"I have the people of San Ramon. Some of them will fight. I swear it."

"That's all well and good, but an army has to have weapons."

Evangelina said, "As I told you, we have a few guns that we were able to hide."

Bo shook his head. "That won't help you against Davidson and his men. There are too many of them, and they are too well armed."

Teresa blew out her breath in exasperation. "Then what do you suggest that we do, Señor Creel? Sit back and wait until Davidson is finished brutalizing us and killing us?"

"Not at all," Bo said. "I was thinking that it would go a long way toward evening the odds if we could get our hands on a certain item that's stored in a couple of crates in one of those sheds . . ."

CHAPTER 21

Scratch let out a low whistle and exclaimed, "That doggone machine gun!"

Bo nodded. "That's right."

"What is this . . . machine gun?" Luz asked. "I have never heard of such a thing."

"I'll bet you've heard of a Gatling gun," Bo said.

"*Sí.* I have heard men speak of a weapon by that name."

"Well, they call this a Gardner gun, and it spits out a bunch of bullets in a hurry, just like a Gatling. Lancaster used one when he was posted with the British Army in India. We brought it with us the first time we rode down from El Paso, even though I don't reckon any of us except Davidson and Lancaster knew it at the time."

"You reckon we could figure out how to use such a contraption?" Scratch asked.

Bo shrugged. "We've both used a Gatling gun before. If we had a little time to study on it, I think we could figure it out."

A look of anticipation came into Scratch's eyes.

"After the things we've seen down here, it'd feel mighty good to cut loose like that on Davidson and his bunch. I'd say they got it comin' to 'em."

Bo turned to Teresa. "Davidson said that a man could probably climb in and out of the canyon at its far end. Do you know if that's true?"

She nodded and said, "Yes. It would not be an easy climb, but it could be done. And we could always let men down with ropes, as we did with Pepe."

"The thing is," Scratch said, "Davidson's liable to have some guards posted along the canyon now, 'cause he knows we got out of there somehow. We can't just waltz in, grab them crates with the machine gun from the shed, and waltz back out again."

"No, we'll probably have to knock out the guards," Bo said. "It's going to take a considerable amount of stealth, and I don't think Scratch and I are up to it right now. We're going to have to rest and recover for a few days first. I hate to ask you folks here in the valley to put up with Davidson for any longer than you have to—"

"Better to wait until our chances of success improve," Evangelina said. "We have endured Davidson's cruelty for months now. A few more days will not make any difference."

"So you say," Luz muttered. "As for me, I can almost see that gold glittering in my hands."

"The gold would make a lot of difference for the people in this valley," Bo pointed out. "It could make life a lot better for them."

Luz shrugged. "I will not take all of it."

Bo was grateful for the help she and Pepe had given them—without it he and Scratch would be dead by now, more than likely—but he told himself it might be a good idea to keep an eye on her anyway.

For the next four days, the Texans stayed with Evangelina and Enrique, resting and regaining their strength. Their bullet wounds began to heal. Teresa, Luz, and Pepe slipped into the village every night and came to Evangelina's hut. Some of the other villagers knew that Bo and Scratch were there, but Bo warned Evangelina not to spread the word of their presence any more than she had to. While it was unlikely that anyone would sell them out to Davidson, it wasn't impossible for such a thing to happen.

Evangelina brought them clothes that fit better, although she couldn't get boots for them. They would have to wear rope sandals when they ventured out next. She found another gun for them, too, a rusty Colt that was newer than Enrique's old cap-and-ball pistol but hadn't been taken care of as well. The Colt had four rounds in the chamber; that was all the ammunition they had for it.

Davidson's men showed up again to search the village, showing that he hadn't forgotten about the Texans. But Bo and Scratch were hidden safely in the little chamber under the hut when the searchers came, and once again the men didn't spot the trapdoor.

Bo knew that they had been lucky so far not to be discovered. Eventually, Davidson might become frustrated enough to order his men to tear the village apart looking for them. They needed to make their move before that could happen.

Scratch was getting a mite restless, too. When the

silver-haired Texan suggested after four days that they pay another visit to Cutthroat Canyon, Bo nodded and said, "Yeah, I reckon it's about time."

That night when Teresa, Luz, and Pepe came to the hut, Bo told them, "We're going after that machine gun tonight."

"Are you well enough?" Teresa asked with a worried frown.

"We're feelin' right spry again," Scratch told with a grin.

"It has been less than a week since you were wounded—"

"We're in pretty good shape for a couple of old fellas," Bo said.

Scratch snorted. "Speak for yourself. I ain't all that old, ladies."

"I can vouch for that," Luz said, which made Scratch's grin grow even wider.

"We'll need some rope," Bo said, dragging the conversation back on track. "And a couple of knives would come in handy, too. If there are guards, we'll need to kill them as quietly as possible."

The matter-of-fact way in which he said it made Teresa and Evangelina glance at each other, Bo noted. They had their own grudges against Davidson and his men, to be sure, and he had no doubt that they would fight and kill their enemies if the need arose, but they were still young women who had lived most of their lives in a peaceful farming community. They weren't used to battle, bloodshed, and sudden death—and with any luck they never would be.

Teresa, Luz, and Pepe had each had a lariat on

their saddle when they rode down there from El Paso, so ropes wouldn't be a problem. They had pistols and rifles as well. Bo and Scratch each borrowed a pistol from them, tucking the guns inside their belts, so the Texans had two guns apiece now. Evangelina left the hut, and came back a short time later with a pair of knives. Bo and Scratch added them to their makeshift arsenal as well.

"Can I come with you?" Enrique asked with a hopeful expression on his whiskery old face.

"I don't know if that would be a good idea," Bo said. Seeing the disappointment that replaced the enthusiasm on Enrique's face, he added, "We need you to stay here and look after Evangelina. She'll need someone to help her if there's any trouble."

"Oh." Enrique nodded. "I can do that."

As they were getting ready to leave, Evangelina found a moment to speak to Bo privately, keeping her voice low so that they wouldn't be overheard. "Thank you for what you said to Enrique. He just wants to help."

"I know that," Bo told her with a smile. "And he's mighty devoted to you. Is he your grandfather?"

She shook her head. "We are not related. He lived with his daughter and her husband until a fever took them both a few years ago. Someone had to look after him, so I asked him to come live with me. He thinks of me as his granddaughter at times, but as you know, he is easily confused."

"Well, what I told him was the truth. Scratch and I will feel better about things with the old-timer here to help you if you need him."

Over the past few days, Evangelina had rounded

up serapes and sombreros for them, too, so when Bo and Scratch slipped out of the hut late that night, after the moon had gone down, they looked like villagers themselves. Teresa, Luz, and Pepe went with them, and once again a couple of them had to ride double after they reached the place where they had left the horses.

Teresa led the way into the mountains. With the moon gone, the stars provided the only light, but it was enough. Ever since she was a little girl, Teresa explained, she had roamed over the hills that bordered the valley, climbing from them into the mountains as well, so she knew every step of the trails.

"Reckon you must've been what we call a tomboy," Scratch commented. "You grew up ridin' horses and explorin', didn't you?"

"What of it?" Teresa said. "Woman's work never appealed to me."

"Why should it?" Luz asked. "Women work twice as hard as men and receive half the credit. I was married once. I know. That is why I decided to put my skills to better use."

"By prostituting yourself?" Teresa said. "Is that really better?"

"For me it was," Luz declared. "And now no man tells me what to do."

Bo didn't want them to get into an argument. He said, "We'd better be quiet. I doubt if Davidson has any guards posted outside the canyon except the rifleman in the bell tower, but we can't be sure of that."

They climbed through the hills, eventually dismounted, and began working their way on foot toward the canyon. Pepe had two of the coiled lariats draped over his shoulder.

At last they found themselves at the top of a steep, rugged slope. Teresa leaned close to Bo and Scratch and whispered, "This is the end of the canyon. If you climb down here, it is a little less than a mile to the mine."

"Toss one of the ropes down," Bo told Pepe. "We may not need it, but it'll be there if we do."

When Pepe had anchored one end of the rope around an upthrust finger of rock and thrown the other end into the canyon, Bo went on. "I'll go down first. When I get to the bottom, I'll give the rope a tug, and that's how you'll know to start down, Scratch."

"*Bueno*," Scratch said in agreement. He grasped the rope so he could feel the tug when Bo was finished with the descent.

Quickly, Bo went over the rest of the plan. "Scratch and I will dispose of any guards we encounter and get those crates from the storage shed. We'll bring them back here one by one, and then Pepe can toss down the other rope. We'll tie a rope around each end of a crate, and the three of you can haul them up. Everybody understand?"

The others nodded, and with a grim nod of his own, Bo swung over the edge of the canyon wall and began searching for handholds and footholds.

The darkness made the climb more difficult, since Bo had to feel his way down, but he was grateful for it anyway. In the thick shadows that cloaked the canyon, no one could see him, and he was careful not to dislodge any rocks that might clatter down and alert any guards that Davidson had posted up here at the canyon's end.

The descent covered fifty or sixty feet, he estimated, but it took him a full half hour to make it. Scratch and the others were probably getting a mite worried, he thought as his sandaled feet finally touched the ground. He tugged on the rope and got an answering tug from Scratch. Then he stepped back and slipped out the borrowed Colt, leaving the old cap-and-ball pistol tucked inside his belt. A gunshot would ruin everything, of course, because it would echo down the canyon and warn Davidson and his men that trouble was on their doorstep, but he would fire if he had to in order to save his life or Scratch's life.

Long minutes dragged by. Scratch was being careful and quiet about climbing down, too. At last, though, Bo heard the faint whisper of sandals on rock and then Scratch dropped down beside him.

"I ain't all that fond of heights, you know," Scratch breathed.

"Then it's a good thing it's so dark tonight. You couldn't see where you would have landed if you'd fallen."

Scratch grunted, and Bo knew his old friend was laughing. "Let's go," Scratch whispered.

They started down the canyon toward the mine, staying close to the wall and still taking it slow and easy. Bo sniffed the air with every few steps because he knew that most sentries couldn't resist the urge to roll themselves a smoke every now and then. As late as it was, weariness and boredom were even more likely to have set in by now, and a man might risk firing up a quirly.

He figured they had covered maybe a quarter of a mile when he scented the faint aroma of tobacco smoke. Reaching out unerringly in the darkness, he touched Scratch's shoulder. In the darkness, he could barely make out the nod Scratch gave him to signify that he had smelled the smoke, too.

They stood absolutely still for long moments, searching the shadows with their eyes and ears for the guard, or guards. Finally, Bo spotted the tiniest pinprick of orange light. The sentry was trying to hide his cigarette in his hand, but the coal on the end of it had winked out between his fingers for just an instant.

That was enough for the Texans. They began creeping toward the man with stealth worthy of an Apache or Comanche.

Their approach took several minutes, but at last they were close enough for Bo to hear the almost inaudible rustle of clothes as the guard shifted position just slightly. A second later, the man sighed tiredly, which helped Bo pin down his position even better. With the knife Evangelina had given him gripped tightly in his hand, Bo stepped forward and brought the blade up. He reached around the sentry with his other hand and clamped it over the man's mouth as he drove the knife into his back.

Bo felt the blade scrape on a rib and then slide on through. The way the guard spasmed as Bo jerked him backward told him that the knife had penetrated the man's heart. His death was almost soundless.

Almost, but not quite. A couple of yards away, a man said, "Hey, Rockwell, what—"

That was as much as he got out before Scratch struck. The Texans had dealt with this sort of danger many times in the past and operated with smooth efficiency. Scratch knew that it was his job to take care of a second guard, if there was one, so when the man spoke up, Scratch lunged forward and lashed out with the revolver he held. The gun butt crunched against the man's skull with devastating force. The guard went down without another sound, and a quick slash across the throat as Bo knelt beside him finished him off.

Bo didn't like this sort of killing, never had. But sometimes it was necessary, and he wasn't going to lose any sleep over ridding the world of a couple of varmints like these two. He had no doubt in his mind that they had helped brutalize the people of San Ramon, he thought as he and Scratch collected the six-guns and the Winchesters carried by the sentries.

They didn't let their guard down as they moved on toward the shed where the Gardner gun was stored. At least, that was where it had been a few days earlier, Bo reminded himself. They had no way of knowing whether or not it was still there. If it was, more sentries might be between them and it.

They didn't smell any more smoke or hear anything else, though. Davidson was being cautious because the Texans had disappeared from the canyon somehow, but he couldn't know where they were or even if they were still alive. The silence that lay over the canyon convinced Bo that the men he and Scratch had disposed of were the only ones who'd been standing guard.

The shed loomed ahead of them. Bo could make

it out in the shadows, a deeper patch of darkness than what surrounded it. It was an open structure, with two sides, a roof, and the canyon wall itself forming the back wall. While Scratch kept an eye open for trouble, Bo slipped into the shed and began searching for the crates containing the parts of the machine gun.

It took him only a few moments of feeling around inside the shed to reach the exact conclusion that he was hoping to avoid.

The Gardner gun was gone.

CHAPTER 22

With the bitter taste of defeat under his tongue, Bo backed out of the shed. He leaned close to Scratch's ear and breathed, "It's not here."

"Dadgum it! I was afraid of that. Davidson must've had Lancaster uncrate it and put it together."

Bo thought the same thing. He couldn't help but wonder what that meant. If Davidson was getting ready to use the machine gun for something, it couldn't be anything good.

"What do we do now?" Scratch asked.

"Let's take a look around," Bo whispered. "Maybe we can find the gun."

They couldn't risk poking around for too long, though. They had no way of knowing when the guards were supposed to change. If a new pair came to relieve the ones he and Scratch had killed, their presence in the canyon would be revealed. They needed to be out of Cutthroat Canyon before that happened.

They checked the other storage sheds, but the crates that had contained the Gardner gun were nowhere to be found. Trying to slip into the headquarters building was too much of a risk; they couldn't chance it. Both Texans knew they represented the last hope for the people of the valley to live normal lives again, free of Davidson's reign of terror.

Bo motioned toward the far end of the canyon, signaling that they were leaving. He and Scratch catfooted past the shed where the blasting powder was kept. It would have been nice to blow the shed to kingdom come, but Bo hadn't thought to bring matches or anything to make a fuse with him.

They slipped past the bodies of the guards they had killed, and reached the end of the canyon a short time later. The rope still dangled there. Pepe would be waiting up above for three tugs on the rope, which was the signal for him to throw down the other lariat.

Instead, Bo only pulled sharply on the rope twice, which meant that he and Scratch were coming back up.

This time, he was able to grasp the rope himself and walk up the canyon wall with the Winchester under his arm, rather than having the others lift him. Pepe was there when Bo reached the top, ready to reach out and grasp his arm to help him over the rimrock.

"What happened?" Teresa asked in a tense voice. "What about the gun?"

"Gone," Bo said. "Lancaster must've assembled it already. Chances are it's in the headquarters building, ready to be used whenever Davidson gives the word."

"Used for what?"

"Nothing good," Bo said, echoing his earlier thought.

Pepe helped Scratch scramble out of the canyon. "What now?" the silver-haired Texan asked. "We head back to San Ramon empty-handed except for the Colts and Winchesters we got off those varmints we killed?"

"I don't see that we have much choice in the matter," Bo said. "We're still outnumbered and outgunned. We'll have to figure out some other way to make the odds more even."

But as they started out of the hills, Bo had to admit, at least to himself, that he didn't see any way of doing that.

The look of disappointment on Evangelina's face when she heard that their mission had failed sent a pang of regret through Bo. Everyone in the village had suffered under the iron fist of Porter Davidson, of course, but the scars on her cheeks were a poignant reminder of just how much suffering the people had undergone.

"Don't worry," Bo told her. "We'll think of something else."

"What can we do?" Evangelina asked dejectedly. "We are only a handful against an army."

"I wouldn't go so far as to call Davidson and his men an army," Bo said.

"Anyway," Scratch said, "I recollect a time when a handful of men stood up to a whole army and did pretty well for themselves. Place called San Jacinto."

He added hastily, "No offense, you folks bein' Mexicans and all."

"You think we care about such things now?" Teresa demanded. "Evil is evil, whether it takes the form of General Santa Anna or that dog Davidson. He is as much a dictator as Santa Anna ever was."

"You're right about that," Bo said. He glanced at the window, where gray light was beginning to come in around the curtain. "It'll be dawn soon. Scratch and I will get back in our hiding place and try to figure out what to do next."

"You must have some breakfast first," Evangelina said. "Sit down, and I will prepare it."

Bo knew she couldn't keep feeding them for much longer. The few people in the village who knew of their presence were helping out, but these folks didn't have much to start with, and having to provide food for him and Scratch was putting a serious drain on their resources.

That was just one more reason, as if they needed it, to put a stop to what Davidson was doing down here.

After everyone had eaten a meager breakfast, Bo and Scratch lifted the trapdoor and climbed back down into the hidden chamber under Evangelina's bedroom, taking the liberated firearms with them. Once they were alone, with the door closed over them and narrow shafts of light poking down through the cracks, Scratch said, "You got any ideas, Bo? Because for the life of me, I can't think of a damn one."

"Not yet," Bo admitted. "If there was some way we could draw Davidson's men out of the canyon and pick them off one by one . . ."

He dozed off while pondering on that, but it

seemed that he had been asleep for only moments when he was jerked awake again by a terrible racket. It sounded like someone pounding a giant hammer against something, very fast—*bam, bam, bam, bam!*

A cold feeling of dread washed through Bo as he realized that he was hearing the Gardner gun in action.

Scratch had been startled out of sleep, too. He exclaimed, "Son of a—" as he started to leap to his feet without thinking. His head cracked against the planks of the floor that formed the trapdoor, and he sat back down. He rubbed his head where he had hit it.

The machine gun continued firing for another minute or so, then fell silent. Somehow the quiet was more ominous than the pounding of the gun had been.

"People of San Ramon!"

That was Davidson yelling. Bo and Scratch looked at each other, a little surprised that the mine owner had come to the village himself instead of just sending his men. Bo figured that someone had found the dead guards. They should have used the ropes to haul the corpses out of the canyon the night before, he thought. If the guards had simply disappeared, Davidson might have suspected that they were dead, but he wouldn't have been able to prove it.

Of course, under the circumstances, proof didn't really matter all that much. More than likely, mere suspicion would have been enough to prompt Davidson to take action.

The Texans heard rapid footsteps on the floor

above them, and then the trapdoor rose to let light flood into the hiding place. Evangelina peered down at them, obviously very frightened.

"Davidson is here with his hired killers and some of his other men," she said. "They brought that machine gun you talked about."

"We heard it," Bo said as he and Scratch climbed out. "We've got these rifles, so we could pick off a few of them, but they can't keep up with that British pepperbox."

Enrique seemed more agitated than usual, and his grin was nowhere in evidence. "I do not like that loud noise," he said as he flapped his hands.

"Settle down, old-timer," Scratch told him. "If it starts up again, maybe we can stop it."

From somewhere outside in the village, Davidson shouted, "Come out of your houses, now! Everyone out!"

Evangelina looked tensely at Bo. "What do we do?"

He thought about it for a second, then said, "Go on outside, but stay close to the door so you can get back in here in a hurry if you need to. Scratch and I will keep an eye on things from the window."

They moved to the window and eased each side of the curtain back just enough to see out as Evangelina opened the door. "Come with me, Enrique," she said to the old man.

He shook his head. "No! I will not go out there where that noisy thing is!"

Evangelina took hold of his arm. "Enrique, you have to. I will not let anything happen to you."

He was trembling so hard, it looked like he might

fall over, but he allowed her to lead him to the door and out into the bright morning sunlight.

At the window, Bo and Scratch could now see that Davidson stood in the plaza in the center of the village with half a dozen men around him. The Gardner gun was set up in the back of a wagon. Lancaster stood behind the gun, gripping its firing handles. A long, thin, sticklike apparatus stuck up from the weapon's breech. A sheaf of several hundred bullets had been slid into a slot on that loading stick. The other men, including Jim Skinner and Douglas, were grouped around the wagon and held Winchesters ready to fire.

Slowly, tentatively, the villagers began to emerge from their huts. They shuffled forward fearfully, and flinched when Lancaster swung the barrel of the machine gun toward them.

"Give me half a second," Scratch said, "and I can put a bullet in that Britisher's head."

"Yeah, and somebody else would take over that gun and put a thousand rounds into this hut in the next few minutes," Bo said. "Those adobe walls are pretty thick, but I don't think they'd stand up to that."

"I could shoot Davidson his own self. Then he wouldn't be around to give orders no more."

"Skinner would," Bo pointed out, "and he's just as lobo mean as Davidson."

"Well, you could shoot him while I shoot Davidson," Scratch said. It was a logical argument.

"That might do it, but Lancaster could squeeze off a hundred rounds into that crowd of villagers and mow them down."

"Blast it, there needs to be three of us! Then we could end this right here and now."

That might well be true. And it was possible that the Texans could shoot fast enough to kill Davidson, Skinner, and Lancaster before the Englishmen could fire the Gardner gun. But if that turned out not to be the case, a heap of innocent people might die here, Bo told himself.

"Let's wait and see what he's going to do," Bo suggested.

Scratch grunted. "Nothin' good, I'll bet."

Davidson climbed into the back of the wagon and stood next to Lancaster. "I know that Creel and Morton are here!" he shouted. "Tell me where they are, and no one will be hurt!"

"'Cept us," Scratch drawled inside the hut. Bo flashed a grin over at him.

The villagers shuffled their feet nervously, but no one said anything.

"They've caused me a great deal of trouble!" Davidson went on. "They killed two of my men last night! I'm convinced they killed two more in El Paso last week! Turn them over to me, and there'll be no more trouble! You know that I'm a man of my word!"

"Yeah, he says he's gonna run roughshod over these poor folks and make their lives a livin' hell, and then he does it," Scratch said. "That's keepin' his word, all right."

Davidson glared at the people of San Ramon from the back of the wagon, but only silence continued to meet his demands.

"I know you're hiding those two Texans!"

Davidson said, his voice growing ragged with anger. "Give them to me, or I'll make this whole village sorry!" He turned to Lancaster and pointed at one of the huts. "Fire into that shack!"

Lancaster said something instead of obeying the order instantly. Bo couldn't make out the words, but evidently they were some sort of objection, because Davidson yelled, "Do what I told you, damn it!"

With a shrug of resignation, Lancaster tightened his grip on the gun's handles and swung the twin barrels, one set above the other, toward the hut Davidson had indicated. He tripped the trigger and the Gardner began to spew lead, alternating so swiftly between the barrels that it appeared flame was pouring constantly from both of them. The weapon quivered a little on its tripod as the long yoke of bullets moved down the stick and the empty brass cartridges went flying out to fall like shining rain.

Bo and Scratch could see the target hut from where they were. Villagers scrambled to get out of the line of fire as the slugs pounded into the adobe. Women and children screamed in fear. The terrific onslaught of lead raised a cloud of dust and threw chunks of the dried mud and straw into the air. Lancaster directed his fire at one area. After only a moment, large pieces of the wall began to collapse as the hail of bullets continued striking sledgehammer blows. Lancaster fired until half the bullets in the stick were gone, then eased off on the triggers and looked over at Davidson to say something. Davidson jerked his head in a curt nod.

Bo felt a twinge of disappointment. If Lancaster had emptied the machine gun, that would have been the time for the Texans to strike. They could have killed Davidson and Skinner without having to worry about Lancaster being able to slaughter the crowd of villagers. As it was, though, the ugly threat remained.

"You've seen what I have the power to do!" Davidson shouted at the huddled citizens of San Ramon. "Look at that hut!"

The machine gun fire had knocked out a large, ragged hole in the wall. If a human being had been caught in that storm of lead, what was left wouldn't even resemble anything that had once been human.

"I can do the same thing to you!" Davidson threatened. "But if you give me what I want . . . if you give me Creel and Morton . . . you'll be safe!" He paused for a second to let that soak in, then went on. "Not only that, but I'll reward whoever tells me where to find them! If you've got a son or a husband or a father working in my mine, he can come back here to the village permanently! But only if you give me those damned Texans!"

Scratch let out a little whistle. "That's gonna be a hard offer to turn down, partner."

"Yeah, I know it. Can't say as I'd really blame anybody who took him up on it."

"There's probably a dozen or more of those folks out there who know that we're in here."

Bo nodded. His mouth was dry as he watched the confrontation between Davidson and the villagers.

A part of him wanted to march out there and spare those poor people the ordeal they were going through. If he and Scratch surrendered, though, it wouldn't mean that the villagers would be out of danger. They wouldn't really be any better off than they were to start with.

Bo didn't think Davidson would bother with torture if he got his hands on them again. He'd just have them both killed as quickly as possible, so there wouldn't be any chance for an escape or a rescue, as there had been the last time.

"Reckon we may have to chance a shootout," Bo said. "You take Skinner, I'll take Lancaster. We'll leave Davidson for last. He's the least dangerous of those three, at least when it comes to gun-handling."

"What about the kid?"

"Take him as soon as you've downed Skinner."

"Keno," Scratch said as he lifted the rifle to his shoulder. "Open the ball any time you want."

Bo brought up the Winchester he held.

Outside in the plaza, Davidson told Skinner, "Go get one of those old men and put him out in the middle by himself. Looks like these stubborn bastards are going to take more convincing."

"Son of a bitch," Scratch said. "He's gonna have Lancaster shoot some poor varmint with that devil gun!"

"Not if we can help it," Bo said. "Get ready—"

Before either of the Texans could fire, though, a scarecrowlike figure burst from the crowd. They heard Evangelina cry, "Enrique, no!" She tried to grab the old man, but he moved with surprising speed and spryness and dashed toward the wagon, flapping his arms and making incoherent gobbling noises.

CHAPTER 23

Lancaster jerked the barrels of the Gardner gun toward Enrique as he weaved toward the wagon, and for a second Bo thought the old man was about to be chopped into pieces.

But then Davidson yelled, "Hold your fire! What's he saying?"

Enrique's cries weren't just gibberish, Bo realized. Although his voice was hoarse and choked with fear, the old man was saying, "Over there! Over there!" He wasn't just aimlessly flapping his hands either, but rather was waving toward Evangelina's hut.

"Take down that shack!" Davidson bellowed at Lancaster. "Everybody open fire!"

Bo snapped the rifle butt to his shoulder as he used the barrel to push aside the curtain. He had time for one shot, and it had to count, he thought as he lined his sights on Lancaster.

His finger froze on the trigger without taking up all the slack, though, as Enrique swerved without warning in front of the Winchester. The danger to the old man didn't make Lancaster hold his fire. The Gardner gun began to spit flame and death.

With a flash of white from her blouse, Evangelina flew through the air, tackled Enrique from behind, and knocked him to the ground just as the Gardner's bullets sliced through the air above them.

Inside the hut, Bo yelled, "Get down!" Slugs chewed the curtain to shreds and pounded into the walls, some of them coming through to whine wickedly around the room. The Texans had to retreat and dive through the trapdoor into the space beneath the floor in Evangelina's bedroom.

The one thing they had going for them was that Davidson and his men didn't know about that underground space. They fired straight at the hut, well above the level where Bo and Scratch crouched, so for the moment, the only real danger the Texans faced was from ricochets.

If they could bide their time, they might have a chance to fight their way out of this after all. It was more than a mite nerve-racking, though, to kneel there with all that lead whipping by only a few feet overhead.

The Gardner gun abruptly fell silent. Either it had overheated, which rapid-fire weapons were prone to do, or else had run out of ammunition and was useless until another yoke of bullets was fed into that loading stick. A few more rifle and pistol shots blasted out, followed by Davidson yelling, "Hold your fire! Hold your fire!"

The trapdoor was still open. In fact, it had been shot to pieces as it leaned against the rear wall of Evangelina's room. From where they were, Bo and

Scratch could see into the other room. It was brighter than ever in there, because the pounding from the machine gun had knocked big chunks out of the wall. All the furnishings were torn up, too. Evangelina's home was ruined.

"Out the back window before they have time to reload that damned thing!" Bo snapped as he lunged up from the underground space. "Go!"

He wasn't sure how they would escape on foot from men on horseback, but they had to give it a try. Staying where they were wasn't an option. Davidson would just have Lancaster blast the hut to small pieces around them. Sooner or later, bullets would find them.

"There they are!" Davidson yelled as Scratch dived through the window in Evangelina's bedroom. "Kill them!"

Bo sprayed bullets toward the gunmen as fast as he could work the Winchester's lever. He didn't particularly care if he hit any of them; he just wanted to make them dive for cover. He succeeded in that, and then as Scratch opened fire from the rear corner of the hut, that gave Bo the cover he needed to scramble out the window himself. They would have to fall back, each covering the other, and try to reach the hills before Davidson's men caught up to them. It was a slim chance, but the only one they had.

Or maybe not, because Bo suddenly heard hoofbeats and looked around to see Teresa and Luz galloping toward them while Pepe rode off to one side, firing a rifle toward Davidson's men. The women hauled back on the reins and slowed their horses as they came even with the Texans.

"Get on!" Teresa cried.

Bo vaulted up behind her, desperation giving him the agility of a much younger man. Scratch grabbed the arm that Luz reached down toward him and swung up behind her. The women jabbed their heels into the horses' flanks and sent the animals leaping into a run again as bullets whined around them.

"Get that damned thing going!" Davidson bellowed, and Bo knew he had to be shouting at Lancaster. That was the problem with contraptions as complicated as the Gardner gun—they had a tendency to jam or get fouled in some other way just when you needed them the most.

The riders tore around a hut, putting the adobe structure between them and the hot lead searching for them. Luz lined out toward the hills, followed by Teresa and Pepe.

But then Bo shouted over the thundering hoofbeats, "We've got to go back!"

Teresa jerked her head around. "Are you loco? They'll kill us!"

"Davidson will kill Evangelina for hiding us out!"

Teresa grimaced, obviously recognizing the truth of what Bo said. "We can't help her!" she said. "It's too late!"

"We can't abandon her!" Bo insisted. "Luz, you and Scratch keep going! Teresa and Pepe and I will circle around and try to get to Evangelina before Davidson can hurt her!"

"The hell with that!" Scratch roared. "You're not gonna have that much fun without me!"

"You're all loco!" Luz cried. But she veered her horse, just like Teresa and Pepe did.

They looked back, saw dust boiling into the sky behind them, and knew that Davidson's men had mounted up and were following them. Charging right back into danger like this *was* a little crazy, Bo thought. More than a little really.

But he wouldn't be able to live with himself if they abandoned Evangelina to her certain fate, and he knew Scratch wouldn't be either.

Circling wide, keeping up a running fight as they went, the riders galloped back into San Ramon. Bo wasn't surprised to see that the wagon was still there in the plaza. Davidson was with it, but Lancaster had joined the chase.

Davidson had Evangelina, too. His left hand was clamped around her arm as he smashed his right fist back and forth across her face. He hadn't noticed yet that the riders coming toward him were the fugitives, not his own men.

Instinct must have warned him before they got there, because he jerked his head around and his eyes widened in shock. He recovered quickly, though, thrusting Evangelina away from him with such force that she tripped and sprawled on the dusty ground. Bo saw Davidson scramble toward the machine gun in the back of the wagon, and loosed a round at him from the Winchester, but the bullet went high.

Davidson dived into the wagon bed and came up behind the Gardner gun, which appeared to be loaded again. As he grabbed the handles, Evangelina struggled to her feet and ran to meet the riders. Behind her, Davidson swung the twin barrels toward her.

Suddenly, Enrique appeared once again, seemingly

out of nowhere, and ran toward the wagon, waving his arms and shouting. Bo heard him cry, "Run, Evangelina, run!" before the machine gun opened up.

Enrique had swerved into the line of fire just as Davidson pulled the trigger. The machine gun's pounding roar rolled out. Davidson knew how to fire the gun, but wasn't experienced in handling it. The barrels jittered back and forth.

That caused the slugs spewing from the gun to stitch several bloody lines across Enrique's body as the bullet storm caught him. The machine gun literally carved him into pieces as Evangelina glanced back, stopped, and screamed, "Enrique!"

Before she could do anything else, Pepe's horse was beside her and the big man reached down to scoop her up in the circle of one long arm. He flung her over the horse's back in front of him and held tight to her as he wheeled the animal around. Bullets kicked up dust just behind the horse's hooves.

Bo could tell that Davidson was starting to get the hang of handling the machine gun. He brought the Winchester to his shoulder and cranked off a couple of rounds. One of them spanged off the upper barrel of the Gardner gun. Davidson went over backward, falling out of the wagon. Bo didn't think the mine owner was hit, but the bullet coming so close to him had caused Davidson to leap backward and then tumble out of the vehicle.

From behind Luz, Scratch gave them covering fire as the pursuit began to catch up. Bo waved Pepe toward the hills. Evangelina's arms and legs were flopping wildly as Pepe held her on the horse.

He didn't seem to be in any danger of letting her go, though.

Through the rolling clouds of dust and powder smoke that clogged the air in and around San Ramon, Bo caught a glimpse of Jim Skinner's skull-like face. The gunman's features were flushed dark with fury. Bo snapped a shot at him, but the dust obscured Skinner again before Bo could tell if his bullet found the killer or not.

Teresa leaned forward, and so did Bo. It was a race to the hills now. They were strung out, Pepe and Evangelina well in front, Luz and Scratch trailing them by a hundred yards or so, and Teresa and Bo about fifty yards behind *them*. If they made it to the hills before the pursuit caught up to them, they stood at least some chance of being able to give Davidson's men the slip in the rugged terrain. Right now, though, that was a big if.

Bo felt as much as heard a bullet sizzle through the air near his head. He looked back over his shoulder, but couldn't see anything because of the dust. If he couldn't see the pursuers, then the pursuers couldn't see him and Teresa. They were just firing blindly.

But a lucky shot could be just as fatal as a well-aimed one, he reminded himself.

Almost before it seemed possible, they found themselves in the hills. Teresa sent the horse plunging into a brush-choked gully. Branches whipped at Bo's face, and brambles clawed his arms and legs.

Teresa turned her head and told Bo, "We're going to rendezvous at the place where Luz and Pepe and I have been hiding out!"

"How'd you show up just in time to pull us out of that tight spot?" Bo asked.

"We saw Davidson and the other men heading toward the village from the canyon and thought it might be a good idea to be close by in case of trouble. Sure enough, by the time we got there—"

"All hell had broken loose," Bo finished for her.

A grim laugh came from her tight-set lips. "That's right. I understand now why people call weapons like that devil guns."

"They're pretty bad, all right," Bo agreed. "At least, they are in the hands of men like Davidson."

He looked behind him again, but couldn't see anything except the brush. He hadn't thought that Teresa would be able to lose the pursuit this quickly, but she knew the country around here a lot better than Davidson's men did. And Bo certainly wasn't going to complain about a stroke of luck, not when a mere twenty minutes ago it looked like he and Scratch were about to be shot full of holes.

Like Enrique had been.

That sobering thought brought a frown to Bo's face. He didn't know what had possessed the old man to jump in front of the machine gun like that, but then, as soon as the thought went through his head, of course he did know. Enrique had sacrificed himself to save Evangelina's life. That went a long way toward evening the score for allowing his panic to make him give away the Texans' hiding place.

But no matter what Enrique had done, Bo wouldn't have wished that fate on him. At least he had died quickly, with what Bo hoped was a minimum of pain. Enrique had faced his fear and gone out like a man, and in the end that was just about all any hombre could hope to do.

The horse emerged from the gully. Teresa guided it on a twisting course that led higher and higher into the mountains that bordered the valley. She was careful to avoid ridges or other places where she and Bo might be skylighted.

"You're pretty good at dodging trouble," Bo told her. "A while back, Scratch and I ran into another gal who packed iron and rode like a man. Name of Rawhide Abbott. She was even a deputy marshal."

Teresa laughed wearily. "I have no wish to be a man, Señor Creel. It's true that I like to ride the high country around the valley, but it would have been fine with me if I had never had to pick up a gun."

"Life doesn't always give us much choice when it comes to that, especially out here on the frontier. Sometimes it's a matter of using a gun . . . or dying."

"Sí. And I don't intend to die." Her lips drew back from her teeth in a grimace of rage. "At least, not until I have seen Señor Porter Davidson die. And if the Blessed Virgin is willing . . . his death will be at my hand."

CHAPTER 24

By midday, Bo was willing to admit that they had lost Davidson's men. He had been watching their back trail all morning, and there was no sign of the pursuers. The varmints must have given up and headed back to San Ramon.

He wouldn't have wanted to be them when they reported their failure to Davidson. That loco hombre was capable of just about anything when rage gripped him.

The twisting trails finally brought Bo and Teresa to an isolated spring tucked away in a pocket formed by sheer, rocky walls. They had to follow a cleft in one of those walls to get there. From the outside, the opening wasn't visible even twenty yards away, but Teresa had known it was there, of course. This was where she and Luz and Pepe had been hiding out for the past several days.

Grass grew around the spring, as well as a couple of scrubby trees. The other two horses were tethered to those trees when Bo and Teresa rode up. The animals looked worn out from carrying double. Their heads hung low, and they barely cropped at the grass, as if they were too tired to graze. The horse Bo and Teresa were riding was played out, too.

Scratch, Evangelina, Luz, and Pepe waited by the spring as well. Evangelina's face was scraped, battered, and bruised from the beating Davidson had been giving her when he was interrupted. One of the barely healed scars had broken open under the punishment, causing a trickle of bright crimson blood to worm its way down her cheek and jaw. She looked a sight, and the fact that her eyes were red and swollen from crying didn't help matters.

"Did you see Enrique?" she called out to Bo as Teresa reined their horse to a stop. "Could you tell how badly he was hurt?"

"Señorita . . ." Bo didn't know what to say. He stopped and sighed. "Evangelina, the old man is dead. Davidson killed him. I'm sorry there's no better way to tell you."

"I figured as much," Scratch said. "But you were closer, and we were holdin' out a little hope . . ."

Evangelina began to cry again as Bo shook his head. "He . . . he should not have done it," she said in a voice choked with grief. "He should not have told Davidson where you were hiding, and he should not have given up his life to save me. I do not deserve it."

"I reckon that was his choice to make," Bo told her.

Luz asked, "What do we do now? Head back to El Paso?"

"No!" Teresa cried. "We have to save the people of the valley from Davidson."

"And how are we going to do that?" Luz wanted to know. "There are only six of us. We have limited supplies and only a few guns. Davidson has more than a dozen men and that . . . that machine gun! In a fight it's worth a hundred men, maybe even two hundred!"

"What about the gold?" Teresa asked. "You came down here in the first place because you wanted a share in the mine."

Luz grimaced and made a slashing motion with her hand. "What good is gold if you are dead? I was willing to help as long as I thought there was a chance we might succeed. Now, after I have seen what we are up against, I realize it's foolish to think we can defeat Davidson. All we're going to do is get ourselves killed!"

"Then run away, if that's what you want!" Teresa blazed back at her. "But you'll never get your hands on any of that gold."

Bo and Scratch left the two women glaring at each other as they walked over to the other side of the spring. Quietly, Scratch said, "You know, Davidson's gonna send Skinner and some of those other boys into the mountains to look for us. He ain't gonna let 'em rest until they bring back our heads in a tow sack."

"You're right about that," Bo agreed. "Unless we go back to El Paso like Luz suggested."

"You mean run away?"

"Yeah."

The Texans looked at each other for a second, then shook their heads in unison.

"When hell freezes over," Scratch said.

"Not even then," Bo said.

"So what's the plan?"

"Let me think on it." Bo tugged at his earlobe. "There's got to be some way to get at Davidson besides trying to steal his ore the way Teresa and her friends were doing."

"Yeah, that was never gonna work in the long run," Scratch said. "And now that he's got that machine gun, he'll send Lancaster along with it the next time the gold wagons head for the border."

"We need to hit him closer to home," Bo said. A smile began to spread slowly across his face. "And I reckon maybe I've got an idea how we can do that."

A rocky pinnacle that thrust up above the spring provided a place where Scratch could keep watch on the approaches to the hideout. He climbed up there, taking one of the Winchesters with him, and settled down on a ledge behind some small boulders where no one could see him.

Meanwhile, Bo talked to Teresa, asking her about the trails around Cutthroat Canyon. He told her what his idea was, and she said, "It would be easier if I went with you. I could show you the best place to carry out your plan, instead of just telling you."

Bo shook his head. "Scratch and I will handle this chore by ourselves. The rest of you stay here and keep an eye out for Davidson's men. He's going to send hunting parties into the mountains after us. Scratch and I are sure of that."

"I hope he does," Teresa said. "That will give us a chance to kill them!"

"That won't be easy. Jim Skinner's a mighty dangerous hombre, and I reckon the kid and Lancaster aren't far behind him. Those other men who work for Davidson aren't much better than hardcases themselves."

Teresa looked stubborn for a moment, but then she sighed and hunkered on her heels. She began drawing lines in the dirt with her finger. "Let me make a map for you," she told Bo. "That way you can be sure to get where you need to be."

Once Bo was certain of the route he and Scratch would follow, he turned to the other preparations that they needed to make. He found a couple of limber branches on one of the trees and hacked them off with a rusty old machete. He shaped their ends properly, then plucked hairs from the horses' tails and began braiding them together. Some sort of animal gut would have worked better, but he had to make do with what was available. Once he had fashioned a couple of thin, strong cords from the horsehair, he strung them on the makeshift bows. Then he found some thinner branches he could shape into arrows.

They didn't have anything he could use for arrowheads, but luckily, he didn't need any. He wrapped the ends of the arrows in strips of fabric torn from a spare shirt instead. Then he daubed them with a paste made from gunpowder, which he took from several cartridges after he pried out the slugs, mixed with water from the spring. When he was done, he had four fairly straight arrows and bows capable of firing them. Almost any Indian could have done a better job of it, but Bo hoped the weapons would be good enough to accomplish their goal.

As dusk began to settle over the rugged landscape, Scratch climbed down from the rock pinnacle and reported that he hadn't seen any of Davidson's men searching for them.

"That don't mean they ain't out there somewhere," he went on. "But they ain't got here yet."

"We will keep watch tonight," Teresa said, "although I doubt that the men will continue looking after dark. They will be too afraid that one of us will sneak up on them in the night and cut their throats."

Bo said, "We can hope they'll be worried about that anyway."

"Are you taking the horses?" Luz asked. For the time being anyway, she seemed willing to stay, rather than heading back to El Paso and the business she had there. Bo knew that one more setback probably would be enough to make her abandon their cause, though.

He answered her question by saying, "No, we'll go on foot. Cutthroat Canyon is only a couple of miles from here, as the crow flies, and Teresa has told me which trails to take where horses can't follow us. Stealth is going to be more important than speed tonight."

"When will you leave?" Evangelina asked.

Bo glanced at the sky. The sun had dropped behind the mountains, but a red glow remained in the heavens. "We'll let it get a little darker," he said. "Then we'll head out, and it ought to be good and dark by the time we get to the canyon."

"You should eat something first."

"You mean like a last meal for the condemned men?" Scratch asked with a grin.

Evangelina made the sign of the cross. "Do not even joke about it, Señor Morton. Without the two of you, we would have no chance to ruin Davidson's plans and get our revenge on him."

Bo said, "I care less about revenge than I do about fixing things so that he can't continue making life miserable for the folks in the valley. We're going to make that more difficult for him anyway."

They ate tortillas and beans for supper, and Bo saw that their supplies were indeed running low. He suggested that if they had to stay hidden out in the mountains for much longer, he and Scratch might need to make some snares in an attempt to catch wild game. Shots would just draw the men who were bound to be searching for them.

As soon as enough of the light had faded from the sky, Bo and Scratch took the crude bows and arrows, along with a Colt and a Winchester apiece, and set out toward Cutthroat Canyon. "Be careful!" Luz called after them.

Scratch turned his head and grinned back at her. "See, Luz, you do care after all," he said. "I'm touched."

She snorted. "Go touch yourself. I just don't want anything happening to those guns. We may need them to get back to civilization."

It wasn't long before the Texans were out of sight of the others. They followed the cleft through the rocks, and when they emerged from the narrow passage, Bo took the lead. He had committed the route to memory as Teresa explained it to him, and believed he could follow it, even in the dark like this.

The two miles to the canyon took more than two hours to cover. The trails twisted and turned, and several times Bo and Scratch had to climb steep slopes, which wasn't easy carrying the weapons. Eventually, though, they came to the rimrock above Cutthroat Canyon. Pausing there, they crouched behind some rocks to study the scene below them.

They were across the canyon from the mine. Lights were visible in the windows of the headquarters building and the barracks used by the supervisors. The long building where the workers lived was dark. After slaving away inside the mine all day, those villagers wouldn't want to do anything except eat their meager supper and then collapse on their bunks to sleep the sleep of exhaustion until early the next morning, when the brutal cycle would start all over again.

Some of the workers were in the mine tunnel right now, Bo knew. In his greed, Davidson kept two shifts going, so that the mine operated twenty-four hours a day. That worried Bo. He hoped that the walls and ceiling of the tunnel had been shored up properly and that the support beams were thick and strong. That seemed likely—Davidson wouldn't want to risk a collapse after all, since such a disaster would cut into his profits—but even so, the supports might not be strong enough to withstand what was coming.

They would have to hope for the best, he told himself. At least there would be a little distance between the tunnel and the blast.

"You want the powder shed or the headquarters?" he asked Scratch in a whisper.

"I'll take the headquarters buildin'," Scratch replied. "You're probably a better shot with a bow than I am . . . but I'm a better hand with a rifle than you."

"By the time they start coming out of there like rats from a sinking ship, I intend to be back down here with you," Bo told him.

Scratch nodded. "Good luck, amigo."

"And to you, too, pard."

With that the Texans split up, Bo heading up the canyon along the rimrock. It didn't take him long to reach a spot directly opposite the shed where Davidson's supply of blasting powder was stored. He had brought only one of the arrows with him, leaving Scratch with the other three, so he would have only one shot at the shed.

Laying the Winchester on the ground beside him, Bo fished a lucifer out of the pocket of his jeans and snapped it into life with his thumbnail. He held it to the rag-wrapped head of the arrow, and the gunpowder paste ignited instantly with a sharp flare. Bo stood up as he nocked the burning arrow onto the bowstring, and as he did so he heard a yell of alarm from inside the canyon. As he had suspected, Davidson had posted guards at the shed, and they had spotted the flames.

But those guards couldn't stop the arrow as Bo sent it flying across the canyon. He dove to the ground as soon as he had loosed the shaft, knowing that the guards would open fire on him. Muzzle flame spurted in the darkness and bullets whined over his head. He snatched up the Winchester as he lay flat at the edge of the rimrock and started blasting away in return.

The arrow landed on the roof of the shed and

continued burning. As Bo paused in his rifle fire, he heard one of the guards shout to the other to climb up there and put it out.

"The hell with that!" the second man shouted in terror. "I'm gettin' out of here!"

They dashed toward the mine. Bo sped them on their way with a couple of shots. As he did so, he saw more streaks of fire in the night as Scratch shot flaming arrows on top of the headquarters building and the supervisors' barracks.

The roof of the powder shed was on fire now. Bo scrambled to his feet and started retreating. He looked back and saw part of the blazing roof collapse among the stacked kegs of blasting powder. One of the falling timbers must have broken the lid of a keg . . .

With an earth-shaking roar, the powder exploded.

CHAPTER 25

Bo felt the vibration from the blast through the soles of the rope sandals he wore, but it wasn't strong enough to knock him off his feet. He knew the force of the explosion would be magnified as it traveled through the earth, but hoped that since a lot of it had gone up into the air, it wouldn't be strong enough to shake down the roof of the mine tunnel.

He broke into a run toward the spot on the rimrock where he had left Scratch. As he approached, he saw that the roof of the headquarters building was burning, as was the roof of the supervisors' barracks. Scratch's Winchester cracked steadily as he peppered the buildings with slugs, concentrating on the doors so he could keep the men inside pinned down as long as he could. They didn't want Davidson's men running outside to fight the fires.

Bo came up beside him, dropped to a knee, and started shooting as well. Scratch paused to grin over at him and say, "Sounded like you made that one arrow of yours count, partner. That shed blowed up real good."

"Davidson won't be using that powder in the mine, that's for sure," Bo said. "The flames have spread enough. Let's hold our fire for a minute and see what happens."

Both Texans sprawled out on their bellies at the edge of the rimrock, where they wouldn't present a target for anyone in the canyon. Down below, the flames had spread all the way across the roofs of both buildings, and the walls were starting to burn as well. No one would be able to extinguish the blazes now.

Predictably, only a few more minutes went by before men began to dash out of the headquarters building and the barracks. No one wanted to be trapped in the sort of inferno that the buildings would soon become. Also predictably, they were shooting as they came, spraying lead into the air from pistols and rifles. They were firing blind, because they couldn't be sure where Bo and Scratch were—or even who was responsible for the havoc that had descended on Cutthroat Canyon.

The Texans thrust the barrels of their Winchesters over the edge of the canyon wall and aimed at the men trying to escape from the burning buildings. As they squeezed off shot after shot, they saw several men tumble to the ground. The leaping flames provided a garish light, but Bo and Scratch couldn't tell who had fallen. They hoped that one of them had brought down Porter Davidson, or maybe Jim Skinner—preferably both of the varmints. The deaths of those two men would go a long way toward ending the troubles in the valley.

They backed away from the edge of the canyon in

a hurry as bullets began slamming into the rimrock. They had done about as much damage as they could hope to do for one night, so Bo said, "Let's head back to camp. We'll try to find out in the morning if we got Davidson."

"Or Skinner," Scratch added. "I ain't sure which of those two snakes is the most dangerous."

"Davidson," Bo declared. "He's got the money. It's a lot harder to pull his fangs."

They stayed low until they were well out of sight of the canyon. An orange sky loomed behind them, lit up by the burning buildings. Chances were, the headquarters and the barracks would burn to the ground. Bo hoped that the blaze would destroy the machine gun as well. He didn't want to have to face it again. Going up against that devil gun once had been enough to last him the rest of his life.

"You reckon Teresa and the others heard the blast?" Scratch asked as they made their way higher in the mountains, retracing the path that had brought them to the canyon.

"I'm sure they must have," Bo said. "They had to have heard it in the village, too." He paused. "Maybe it gave them some hope."

Instincts developed over long years of living on the frontier kept Bo from getting turned around as he and Scratch moved through the rugged terrain toward the hidden camp. When they reached the cleft and started through it, the sound of someone cocking a gun made them pause.

"It's just us, Pepe," Bo said quietly, guessing that it would be the big man standing guard.

He was wrong, though, because it was Teresa's voice that asked, "Are you both all right?"

"We're fine," Bo told her. In the thick shadows that filled the passage he couldn't see her, but he felt her hand brush his arm. "You heard the explosion?"

"We heard it," Teresa said. "That's what I wanted to do a week ago, when I came back down here from El Paso. What about Davidson? Were you able to kill him?"

"Don't know yet," Bo replied honestly. "We downed a few of them when they came running out of the buildings we set on fire, but I couldn't tell if one of them was Davidson."

"Neither could I," Scratch added. "I got my fingers crossed, though."

"I'll stand guard here," Teresa said. "Whistle when you get to the end of the cleft so Pepe will know it's you. He's waiting at the other end with a rifle."

Bo said, "We don't mind taking our turns on watch."

"I think you two have done enough for tonight," Teresa told them with a grim chuckle. "Even if you didn't kill him, you've hurt Davidson more than anyone else has been able to in the past six months."

Bo heard the elation in her voice. He couldn't bring himself to be that excited about what had happened. They might have won this skirmish tonight. They might have even succeeded in killing Davidson or Skinner.

But Bo's gut told him no matter how this battle had gone, the war was far from over.

* * *

The glow in the sky finally faded, and by morning there wasn't even any smoke rising from the ashes of Porter Davidson's headquarters. None that Bo and Scratch could see anyway. Along with Teresa, they worked their way through the mountains to a spot where they could look down into the canyon from several hundred feet above it.

Just as Bo expected, the two buildings Scratch had set on fire with the flaming arrows had burned completely, leaving only blackened piles of rubble. In the place where the powder shed had stood was a crater in the ground and a huge hole gouged out of the canyon wall.

Men moved in and out of the mouth of the mine tunnel, so Bo assumed the operation continued normally there. He pointed that out to Scratch and Teresa and added, "I was worried that the explosion would cause a cave-in. I'm glad to see that it didn't."

"I think the men forced to work in there might have preferred being buried in a cave-in to living as Davidson's slaves," Teresa said. "I know I would have."

The three of them were hunkered behind some rocks, being careful not to let the morning sunlight reflect off the rifles they carried. Scratch suddenly pointed and said, "Look yonder. Men ridin' out of the canyon."

Bo squinted, wishing that he had a good pair of field glasses. He couldn't make out who the men were, but he had a feeling the lean figure who seemed to be leading the group was Jim Skinner. When he said as much, Scratch agreed.

"I was hopin' we'd killed that skull-faced varmint."

"No such luck," Bo said. "Is that the kid with him?"

"I think so. Ain't sure, though."

"Where are they going?" Teresa asked as in the distance the men rode out of Cutthroat Canyon into the valley.

"Hunting," Bo said. "That would be my guess."

"Hunting?" she repeated. "For what sort of game?"

"Us," Scratch said.

Bo nodded. "Davidson knows we got away from the village the other day. He's smart enough to realize that we were behind what happened last night. So he's sending Skinner and some of his other men to track us down. They'll try to pick up our sign on the rimrock where we were when we fired those flaming arrows."

"They will never find our camp," Teresa said with an emphatic shake of her head. "It's too well hidden."

"I hope you're right, Señorita."

"Blast it," Scratch said. "That's Davidson, ain't it? The fella pokin' around the edges of what's left of the headquarters building?"

Bo studied the distant figure for a moment and then nodded. "I think so. And that's Lancaster with him. Maybe they're looking for what's left of that Gardner gun."

After a few minutes, Davidson and Lancaster moved out of sight and didn't come back. Bo, Scratch, and Teresa watched for a while longer. Then Bo said, "We might as well go back to camp. We know now that Davidson's still alive, and so are Skinner, Lancaster, and the kid."

"I thought for sure we must've got at least *one* of 'em last night," Scratch complained. "I never have figured out how come the worst varmints are so danged lucky."

"It just seems that way," Bo said. "Justice catches up to them sooner or later."

"Can't be soon enough to suit me where Davidson's concerned."

The three of them started back toward the hideout. Despite what Teresa had said about the searchers not being able to find their camp, Bo wasn't convinced of that. Skinner had a reputation as a killer and slick-draw artist, but Bo had no idea how good a tracker he was. The same was true of Douglas. Either of them might be able to pick up the trail, even though he and Scratch had been careful to leave as little sign as possible. It helped that so much of the ground around here was rocky and wouldn't take footprints.

Pepe was on guard at the entrance to the cleft this morning. "What did you see?" he asked eagerly when Bo, Scratch, and Teresa arrived. His expression fell when they told him that despite the physical damage to the mine buildings, Davidson was still alive, and so were his three remaining hired gun-wolves.

They went on to the camp, where Evangelina and Luz were just as anxious to hear the news, and just as disappointed when they did.

"What else can we do?" Luz asked. "That's it. Davidson can rebuild the buildings and have more blasting powder brought in. He has won."

"No!" Evangelina said. "There must be some way to lure him out into the open where we can get our hands on him. Once Davidson is dead, the others will leave, and life in the valley can go back to normal."

"I wouldn't count on that," Scratch told her. "The rest of those hombres know how much gold is in that mine, and they ain't gonna give it up without a fight, whether Davidson is alive or not."

"They might fall out among themselves, though, without him around to hold them together," Bo said. "That would make them easier to pick off."

"That's what we're gonna have to do. Injun 'em."

Bo knew exactly what his old friend meant. They were still outnumbered and outgunned, so they would have to whittle down the odds against them by picking off Davidson's men one or two at a time. That meant hunting the hunters. It was a dangerous game, but the only one in which they could draw cards.

He explained what he was planning and said, "The four of you will stay here while Scratch and I see what we can do about evening things up."

"I can help you," Teresa said immediately, which came as no surprise to Bo. The fiery young woman always wanted to be in the middle of whatever was going on, especially if it had anything to do with striking at Davidson.

"And I as well," Pepe added.

Luz snapped, "You work for me, not these Texans."

"Our goals are the same," Pepe pointed out. "We all want Davidson's hold on the valley and the mine broken for good, so that he can no longer enslave these people."

"And so that we can get rich," Luz said.

Pepe's massive shoulders rose and fell in a shrug. "That, too," he conceded.

"Scratch and I are used to working together," Bo

said. "It'll be easier for us if you folks stay here and keep an eye out for Davidson's men."

"You mean so we won't get in your way?" Teresa asked with an angry edge in her voice.

"If you want to put it that way, yes," Bo told her, not pulling any punches himself. "I don't want one of us getting shot because we're worrying about you instead of watching out for trouble."

"Fine," Teresa snapped.

"And that doesn't mean you can wait until we're gone and then sneak off and follow us, like you did before when we left you in El Paso."

She just glared at him and didn't say anything.

Bo went through their ammunition. They had enough so that he and Scratch each loaded fifteen rounds into their Winchesters, filling the magazines. They took fifteen cartridges each for their Colts, too. That left enough ammunition in the camp so that Teresa, Evangelina, Luz, and Pepe could put up a fight if they needed to—but it would be good if they could get their hands on more ammunition somehow, Bo thought.

Of course, there was one good way to do that.

Kill some of Davidson's men and take it from them.

CHAPTER 26

The Texans left the camp a short time later. The temperature rose as the sun climbed toward its zenith, and Bo and Scratch both missed their Stetsons. The shade provided by the broad-brimmed hats would have been welcome.

"Reckon we'll ever get all our gear back?" Scratch asked. "Not that it's really important, I reckon, but . . ."

"I know what you mean," Bo said. "I'd like to have my own guns and boots back. We can always replace whatever we lost later, though."

Scratch grinned. "'Specially if we wind up ownin' a share of a gold mine."

Bo looked over at him with a frown. "What are you talking about?"

"Well, I was just thinkin' . . . Luz intends to claim a share in the mine for helpin' these folks, and it seems to me that we've already done a whole heap more to fight Davidson than she has."

"She helped rescue us when we were about to be massacred by that machine gun."

"That's true," Scratch admitted. "And I don't really care how big the shares are. It just seems to me like we ought to get somethin' for our trouble. Maybe a couple o' saddlebags full of gold ore, or somethin' like that."

"We'll worry about that later," Bo said. "First, we have to get rid of Davidson."

"And live through whatever's comin'."

"Yeah," Bo said. "Being alive would make it a lot easier to spend any gold we might happen to wind up with."

He hadn't given any real thought to the riches to be found in Cutthroat Canyon when he'd decided that Davidson's reign of terror had to be ended. As far as he was concerned, the villagers from San Ramon could have the mine. After all these years of drifting, the last thing Bo wanted was to be tied down to some sort of business, and he'd be willing to wager that Scratch felt the same way. The thought of all that gold might be appealing to Scratch right now, but that appeal would wane in a hurry once the urge to roam came over the silver-haired Texan again, as it was bound to do.

They climbed back to the spot that gave them a good view of the canyon and the surrounding area. Again being careful not to skylight themselves or let the sun glint on their rifle barrels, they searched the landscape with their eyes. After a few minutes, Scratch said, "There's a ridge about five hundred yards west of here. Couple of riders just poked their heads above it for a second."

Bo trusted Scratch's eyes. The silver-haired Texan's vision was as keen as an eagle's, despite his age. Bo said, "It was probably two of Davidson's other men. I don't reckon Skinner would make a mistake like that."

"Nope. Nor the kid either, I'll bet. But that's bound to be the search party. Who else'd be ridin' around this Godforsaken wilderness today?"

"Rurales maybe?" Bo suggested.

"They wear those gray, steeple-crowned sombreros, remember? These fellas had on regular Stetsons."

Bo nodded. The Mexican rural police wore that distinctive headgear, all right, just as Scratch said. And even though, as the name of their force indicated, they were supposed to patrol the frontier areas, the Rurales usually stayed closer to the settlements. Out in the middle of nowhere, there weren't enough people to offer them bribes.

"Which way were they going?" Bo asked.

"Headed yonderways," Scratch replied with a wave of his hand toward the southwest. "Don't I recollect Teresa sayin' something about a natural bridge over there?"

"You do," Bo replied as a grin slowly formed on his face. "There's a big gully, and that bridge is the easiest way over it."

"Once those fellas are out on the bridge, there wouldn't be any place for 'em to go if somebody was to throw down on 'em. Can we get there in time, though?"

"Only one way to find out," Bo said.

Moving quickly now, they headed across country toward the natural bridge Teresa had mentioned. Such formations were fairly common in rocky, mountainous country. Bo had seen a number of them in Utah and Arizona.

The idea of bushwhacking the hunters didn't sit well with him. Time and again, this ruckus with Davidson had forced him to do things he didn't like to do. Bo knew he would do whatever was necessary, though, to break the man's hold on the valley and its people. After the brutality in which Davidson had engaged, Bo wouldn't lose any sleep over ventilating some of the mine owner's hired guns.

And shooting Jim Skinner would be no different than shooting a mad dog, he reminded himself.

Since they didn't know the area as well as Teresa, they had to backtrack a couple of times when the trails they were following wound up in dead ends. Maybe they should have brought her with them after all, Bo thought, although he still believed his reasoning was sound. Once the bullets started to fly, he and Scratch didn't need to be thinking about anything except staying alive and killing their enemies.

The natural bridge was empty when they finally reached it, and Bo didn't see any signs to indicate that anyone had crossed it recently. A horse might kick over a rock so that its damp underside showed, or an iron shoe could nick a stone and leave a mark. Bo didn't see anything like that here, and Scratch confirmed his opinion.

The bridge was an arch of stone that spanned a gully about forty feet deep. It was fifteen or sixteen feet wide, plenty big enough for men to ride over it in single file. Two men could ride over it side by side if they had to, although that would be riskier with the dangerous drop into the gully yawning on either side.

"What do you think?" Scratch asked. "One man at each end of the bridge, so they'll be caught between a rock and a hard place?"

Bo thought about it for a second, and then nodded. "Which end do you want?"

"I'll take the other one. I see some rocks over yonder I can fort up in."

Bo found a good place for himself in the rocks near the eastern end of the bridge, while Scratch trotted to the other side. Within minutes, both Texans were well hidden, waiting for Davidson's men to show up.

They didn't have to wait very long. Bo estimated that less than fifteen minutes had passed when he heard horseshoes clinking against stone not far away. The hoofbeats grew louder, and then four riders came into view.

Bo tensed as he realized that Skinner and Douglas weren't among them. He recognized the four men as some of Davidson's mine supervisors, drafted to be manhunters instead. They were hard-faced men, capable of whatever brutal violence was necessary, but they weren't professional killers like Skinner and the kid. Bo realized that he couldn't cut down on them without warning.

He knew Scratch would wait for him to start the ball and would follow his lead, whatever it was. He stayed hidden until the four riders had moved out onto the natural bridge, then stood up, leveled his rifle at them, and shouted, "Hold it right there!"

The men reined their horses to a halt and jerked around in their saddles, reaching for their guns as they did so. They froze as Scratch called from the other side of the gully, "First man who touches iron, I'll blow him outta the saddle!"

Bo felt the skin on the back of his neck crawling. This had to be a trap. Skinner had set it, using these four men as bait. But the Texans needed the guns and ammunition the men were carrying, so they had to risk it.

"Drop your guns and then get off those horses!" Bo ordered. "You'll be walking back to Cutthroat Canyon!"

"Damn it, Burl, we gonna let them get away with this?" one of the men demanded of a companion.

The man called Burl glared at Bo, but said, "Don't look like we've got much choice. They got the drop on us."

He untied the thong holding the holster to his leg, then unbuckled the gunbelt, dangled it from his hand, and let it fall to the rock bridge. When he reached for the Winchester that stuck up from a saddle boot, Bo warned, "Careful with that rifle. Don't make my trigger finger get touchy."

Burl gripped the Winchester by the breech, slid it from its sheath, and then held it by the barrel as he lowered it to the bridge. The other three men followed suit, carefully disarming themselves.

Bo wanted the horses because he figured the extra ammunition the men had brought with them would be in the saddlebags. "Get down and walk over here," he told them.

"You can't make us walk all the way back to the mine!" one of the men complained. "Hell, it must be more than two miles!"

"Yeah, well, when you get there, maybe your sore

feet will remind you that you shouldn't be working for a skunk like Davidson," Bo said.

"You used to work for him yourself, mister," the man pointed out.

"Only until I found out what sort of man he really is. You already knew, so you don't have that excuse." Bo gestured curtly with the rifle barrel. "Move!"

Grumbling and taking their time about it, the men dismounted. Bo was surprised that Skinner and Douglas hadn't shown up by now. Maybe he and Scratch could get away with the horses and the guns after all, and send these men on a long, painful trek back to Cutthroat Canyon.

He should have known better than to hope for such a stroke of luck, he thought a second later. From the corner of his eye, he caught the faintest wink of reflected light from the rugged slope above him and to the right. He twisted sharply to one side as a gun boomed, the report echoing back from the surrounding mountains.

As he hit the ground, a bullet whipped past his ear and slammed into the rocks, throwing grit and splinters of stone into the air. Bo rolled behind a boulder, and as he did so, he saw the men on the natural bridge grabbing for the guns they had dropped. He snapped a shot at them, the slug whining off the bridge.

On the other side of the gully, Scratch had begun firing as well, but he aimed his shots upward at whoever had just bushwhacked Bo. That had to be Skinner or Douglas or both gunmen, Bo thought. It had taken them that long to get into position while the others were crossing the bridge.

The man called Burl emptied his six-gun toward

Bo, but the bullets all ricocheted harmlessly from the rocks. When Burl tried to leap into the saddle, Bo tracked him with the Winchester and squeezed off a shot.

Burl's back arched as he let out a cry of pain. He hung there like that for a second, poised beside his horse with one foot in the stirrup, before he toppled backward off the bridge. His scream lasted only a second before his body crunched into the rocky bottom of the gully forty feet below.

Another bullet from above came too close to Bo for comfort, forcing him to scramble for better cover. He stretched out under the overhang of a rock that shielded him from the bushwhacker's bullets. From this position, he could also fire through the narrow gap between two other rocks at the men on the bridge.

One of them made it into the saddle, but his mount, spooked by the gunfire, skittishly danced too close to the edge. The horse neighed shrilly in panic as its hooves slid out from under it. The rider tried to throw himself out of the saddle, but he was too late. Man and horse both went over the edge.

Bo fired and saw another man double over in agony as the slug punched into his guts. That left just one man on the bridge. Firing a revolver as he ran, he charged toward the western end where Scratch had hidden in the rocks. Scratch put a round from the Winchester into the man's chest that knocked him backward. He landed with his arms and legs splayed out and didn't move again.

That left the bushwhackers high above the gully. Bo rolled over and tried to find an angle from which he could draw a bead on them, but the effort was futile. They couldn't see him and he couldn't see them.

They could sling plenty of lead in his direction, though, probably in hopes that the slugs would bounce around among the rocks and a ricochet would get him. Bo kept his head low and listened to the spent bullets zinging around him. Across the gully, Scratch tried to provide some covering fire, but he obviously couldn't get a good angle on the bushwhackers either.

Bo could hear two different guns up there, so he was confident the hidden riflemen were Skinner and Douglas. For the moment it was a standoff, and Bo wondered how long they would keep up the siege. He and Scratch had limited ammunition, but Skinner and Douglas might not know that.

After a few minutes, the shooting died away. Bo and Scratch had already stopped firing to conserve bullets. Silence settled down over the gully and the natural stone bridge that spanned it.

The three remaining horses had crossed the bridge and stampeded up the trail on the other side, trying to get as far away from the shooting as they could, so now it was just Bo and Scratch, the bushwhackers hidden above them—and the men in the gully who were dying or already dead.

The one Bo had shot in the belly let out a groan. With a wound like that, it would take a while for him to cross the divide. Bo thought about putting a bullet in his head to end his suffering.

He didn't have to. One of the hidden riflemen fired suddenly, the whipcrack of sound echoing through the gully. The wounded man's head jerked, and blood poured out of the hole that had appeared in his temple. One leg kicked, and then he was still.

Douglas had to be responsible for that, Bo thought. He had sensed that the kid had a few shreds of decency left, even though they weren't enough to make him turn against Davidson. Jim Skinner sure wouldn't have performed such a gesture of mercy. Someone else's suffering meant nothing to him.

Silence reigned once again along the gully. Bo listened intently, thinking that maybe Skinner and Douglas were trying to work their way down to where they could get better shots at the Texans. Instead of rocks clattering down the slope, though, what he heard after several minutes was the swift rataplan of hoofbeats.

Someone was riding away.

Two horses, from the sound of it, Bo told himself—but that didn't mean that both gunmen were leaving. This could be a trick as well. Skinner could have sent Douglas back to the horses with orders to ride off and take the other mount with him. Bo wasn't going to budge from concealment until he was more confident that Skinner and the kid were both gone, and he knew Scratch wouldn't either.

The heat continued to grow more oppressive. Sweat trickled down Bo's forehead and into his eyes. He wiped them with his sleeve. Minutes stretched out until they seemed like hours.

"I'm comin' out, partner," Scratch called at last. "I reckon they've lit a shuck."

Bo was convinced of that by now himself, so he said, "All right. But be ready to dive for cover if you have to."

"I always am," Scratch replied with a chuckle.

He stepped out from the rocks at the far end of the natural bridge. Bo emerged from hiding as well, swinging up the Winchester toward the last place where he had seen the bushwhackers. No shots sounded.

"Well, we whittled down the odds a mite," Scratch said as he started out onto the bridge. He checked the last man he had shot. "This fella's dead. Got a box of forty-fives in his pocket. We can use 'em."

"We'll gather up all the guns and ammunition and take them with us," Bo said as he stood at the eastern end of the bridge, swiveling his head around so that he could watch for trouble. "Those horses that ran off probably didn't go very far either. We'll see if we can find them."

He looked down into the gully at the two men and the horse. They all lay there unmoving, busted up by the fall. Bo saw pools of blood around the heads of the men.

Scratch climbed down there and salvaged what he could, coming back up with two belted Colts and a Winchester, as well as the saddlebags from the dead horse. He had the saddlebags draped over one shoulder, the gunbelts over the other.

"You look like you're armed for bear," Bo commented as his old friend joined him at the eastern end of the bridge.

"More like coyote, or even skunk, since we're talkin' about Davidson," Scratch said. "Don't insult the bears."

Bo grinned, but before he could say anything

else, he lifted his head and his eyes narrowed as he heard the distant popping of gunshots.

"Son of a bitch!" Scratch exclaimed. "I hear 'em, too. Sounds like they're comin' from—"

"The place we left the others," Bo finished.

CHAPTER 27

They were too far away to get back to the hideout in a hurry. And after a few moments, the shooting stopped. The following silence was like a dagger in the hearts of Bo and Scratch.

"Let's see if we can find those horses," Bo said. "If we can, they'll get us back there quicker."

"Yeah. Might make a difference."

Scratch didn't sound convinced of that, however.

They hurried across the bridge, and followed the trail on the other side around several bends before they came across the three surviving mounts that Davidson's men had been riding. The horses had stopped to crop at some tufts of hardy grass that grew in the stony ground alongside the trail.

Bo and Scratch approached the animals carefully, not wanting to spook them again. Both of the Texans had decades of experience at handling horses, so they were able to walk up and take hold of the reins, even though the skittish horses rolled their eyes a little. Bo and Scratch had buckled on the gunbelts Scratch had retrieved from two of the corpses; they slung the extra gunbelts and the saddlebags on the back of the extra horse.

Mounting up, they rode back across the rock bridge over the gully and started toward the hideout. They couldn't take the exact same route they had used to get here, since they had been on foot then. Again, not knowing the area as well as Teresa did, they had to use a process of trial and error to find their way, but managed to keep going in the right general direction most of the time.

Silence still hung ominously over the hot, rugged landscape. They spotted some familiar landscapes, and a few minutes later found themselves approaching the narrow cleft through the rocks that led to the hidden spring and clearing. Bo lifted a hand in a signal to stop.

He and Scratch reined in. Scratch's voice was a whisper as he asked, "You reckon Davidson left gunmen waitin' in there for us?"

"I wouldn't be surprised," Bo replied. "But the only way to find out what happened to Teresa and the others—"

"Is to go in there," Scratch finished. "Yeah, I know. I'll go first. You stay out here until I give you the all clear."

"The hell with that," Bo said in one of his rare uses of profanity. "We'll ride in together."

Scratch thought it over for a second and then shrugged. "The same way we charged ol' Santy Anny's army at San Jacinto, right?"

"Right," Bo said.

They lifted their rifles and hitched their horses into a slow walk forward, entering the cleft through the all-but-invisible opening in the rock wall. Since the passage wasn't wide enough for two men to ride abreast, Scratch edged ahead. The sound of their horses' hooves bounced back and forth hollowly from the passage's walls. They couldn't do anything about that. Anyone waiting at the hideout was bound to know they were coming, but they couldn't help it.

The couple of minutes it took to ride through the passage seemed longer. They reined in before they got to the cleft's end, and studied what they could see of the clearing around the spring. They didn't see any of the horses, nor was there any sign of Teresa, Evangelina, Luz, or Pepe.

"If anybody's in there, they know we're here," Scratch whispered. "Might as well sing out."

Bo nodded. "Hello the camp!" he called.

No answer came back, only the ominous silence punctuated by the faint bubbling of the spring.

The Texans looked at each other, then heeled the horses into motion again. They emerged from the shadows of the cleft into the light that flooded the clearing from the sun almost directly overhead.

"Look out!" a man's voice suddenly bellowed. They swung toward it and saw a couple of David-son's men lunging out from behind the scrubby trees near the spring. Guns in their hands spouted flame.

Bo and Scratch left their saddles in rolling dives, Scratch going right while Bo went left. That put some distance between them. Bo came up on one knee and fired the Winchester twice, levering the weapon as fast as he could between the rounds. Scratch's rifle blasted, too.

The pair of would-be killers went down, one man's throat torn open by Scratch's bullet and fountaining blood, the other with Bo's slugs in his chest. Scratch leaped to his feet and ran over to the fallen men. When he reached them, the first thing he did was kick aside the guns they had dropped. Then, he prodded them with a foot to make sure they were dead.

Meanwhile, Bo hurried over to Pepe. He had spotted the big man lying among the rocks near the spring. Pepe's shout had warned them.

Bo knelt beside Luz's bodyguard, who lay on his side breathing raggedly. Pepe's shirt was soaked with blood and his eyes were closed. Bo thought for a second that he was dead, but Pepe opened his eyes when Bo touched his shoulder.

"S-Señor Bo?" Pepe asked, his voice weak and strained now, not the lusty shout it had been a minute earlier. Giving them that warning must have taken just about all the strength he had left.

"That's right, Pepe," Bo told him. "I'm right here."

"Did . . . did those hombres . . . hurt you?"

"No, I reckon I'm fine."

"What about . . . Señor Scratch?"

Bo looked over his shoulder and saw Scratch gathering up the guns from the men they had killed. "He's all right, too. Neither of us were hit."

"The men left here . . . by Davidson?"

"Both dead." Bo paused. "There were only two of them, right?"

"*Sí,* only two. Davidson knew you would come back here . . . when you heard the shots . . . if you were still alive. He thought Skinner might have . . .

already killed you . . . but he didn't want to . . . take a chance on that . . ."

Bo squeezed the big man's shoulder. "Rest easy now. We'll see about patching you up."

"Too late," Pepe said with a shake of his head. "Too late. I know . . . how bad I'm hurt. They thought . . . I was dead . . . That's why . . . they left me here like this . . . but I wanted to stay alive . . . until I could warn you . . . and tell you what happened."

Scratch carried over one of the canteens that Luz and Pepe had brought with them from El Paso. He knelt on Pepe's other side and held the canteen to his mouth. Pepe drank, then grimaced in pain.

"I feel like . . . the water is just running back out of me. I am . . . shot full of holes, no?"

Bo didn't see any point in keeping the truth from him. "Pretty much, yeah. If there was anything we could do . . ."

Pepe managed to lift a hand. "*De nada.* Just help . . . Luz and . . . the two señoritas . . . Davidson took them . . . back to the canyon. He said . . . if you were still alive . . . you would come for them . . . and he could kill you then. If you were already dead . . . he would make them pay . . . for all the trouble we have caused him."

"That son of a bitch don't know about trouble," Scratch said. "We're just gettin' started."

Pepe laughed softly and smiled. Then he said, "When you see Luz . . . tell her I . . ."

No more words came from him, only a sigh. His eyes stared up sightlessly.

"I'll tell her you loved her, Pepe," Bo promised, even though the big man could no longer hear him.

He gently closed Pepe's eyes. "But I reckon she must've known that already."

Bo and Scratch stood up. "We got plenty of guns and ammunition now," Scratch said. "Too bad we don't have half a dozen good fightin' men to use 'em." He let out a low whistle. "Or even just two, if they were those fellas Bodine and Two Wolves we met a while back. Those boys were like ring-tailed bobcats when it come to fightin'."

"Matt and Sam aren't anywhere around here unfortunately," Bo said. "But at least the odds against us aren't as bad as they were. We've killed six of Davidson's men today, plus we downed a few of them last night. He can't have more than a handful left."

"Not countin' Skinner and Lancaster and the kid," Scratch pointed out.

Bo nodded. "Yeah, and they're probably worth at least two men apiece. But there's no getting around the numbers. Davidson must have closed down the mine for the time being, because he doesn't have enough men to keep those hombres from the village working."

"Then what's he done with 'em? Let 'em go back to San Ramon?"

Bo frowned as he thought about it. "I don't figure he'd do that. He'll want to get the mine operation up and running again as soon as he can after we're dead. My guess is that he had them all herded into their barracks and locked up there. All he'd need in that case is a couple of men to guard the building."

"Too bad they ain't loose," Scratch mused. "With the grudges they've got against Davidson and his men, they might just clean out that canyon if they got the chance."

"I was just thinking the same thing," Bo admitted. "Some of them would be killed in the fighting, no doubt about that . . . but men have lost their lives fighting for their freedom as long as there have been tyrants like Davidson."

"And I reckon that goes way, way back," Scratch said. "We'd need to figure out a way to get to the barracks and turn 'em loose."

"We couldn't do it if Lancaster still has that machine gun. That wouldn't be a fight, no matter how many of the villagers there are. It would be plain murder to send them unarmed against that gun."

Scratch nodded in agreement. "Come nightfall, we're gonna have to slip in there and find out what's goin' on."

"I think you're right. That gives us some time to take care of the chore we need to do here." Bo looked down at Pepe. "We've got a grave to dig."

The hard, rocky ground made the grim task more difficult, but over the next couple of hours Bo and Scratch were able to hack out a big enough hole for Pepe by using knives and machetes and their bare hands. The buzzards and other scavengers would have to take care of Davidson's men. The Texans weren't going to waste the time and sweat on them.

When they had lowered Pepe into the grave and covered it again, they stood beside the mound of dirt and rocks with lowered heads while Bo asked El Señor Dios to have mercy on the big man's soul.

Afterward, as they were sitting in some shade at the base of the rock wall to cool off, Scratch said, "You know Pepe worked in a whorehouse, don't you?"

"Sure. What of it?"

"Most folks would say that he ain't fit to go to heaven."

"When people start looking down on somebody else, they usually forget that they're sinners, too. Pepe looked after the girls who worked for Luz and didn't let anybody hurt them. And he was devoted to Luz, you know that. Nearly every big hombre I've ever met has had a gentle heart, and Pepe was no different."

"The psalm-singers'd call you a heathen for feelin' like that."

"Well," Bo said, "I'm not sure I'd want to be in the same heaven where they are anyway."

Scratch chuckled. "Amen to that." He nodded toward the two dead men. "You know, this'd be a pretty nice place if it wasn't for those hombres."

"Give the *zopilotes* and the coyotes a while to do their work," Bo suggested. "Then Pepe can rest here alone in peace."

They didn't know where the two men had left their horses. Part of the afternoon was spent in finding the animals, because Bo and Scratch didn't want the horses dying of thirst because they were tied up and couldn't get to water. They located the horses outside the cleft, several hundred yards away, and brought them back to the hideout. That gave them five mounts.

"Are we takin' all of 'em with us?" Scratch asked.

Bo nodded. "We may need them before this is

over. If we're able to free Teresa, Evangelina, and Luz, they'll need horses, and we may not be able to find the ones Teresa and Luz and Pepe rode down here from El Paso."

"I never would've thought Luz would put on pants and ride a horse," Scratch said with a grin. "I reckon the lure of gold will make folks do things you'd never expect of 'em."

Along with the horses, they had accumulated a small arsenal by now. Taking all of it with them, along with the small amount of supplies they found in the camp, Bo and Scratch rode out late that afternoon.

Another night was fast approaching, and if it was anything like the night before, it would be filled with fire and violence and death. Bo and Scratch both knew that they might not live to see the sun come up the next morning.

But that uncertainty was one thing that gave life its spice, one reason the Texans had always tried to live each day to the fullest. They strapped on their guns and went out to face whatever fate awaited them with fighting grins on their faces.

Anyway, Bo reflected, they were too damned old to change now.

CHAPTER 28

By the time dusky shadows began to gather in the mountains, Bo and Scratch had reached a point where they could look down into the canyon. This wasn't the same observation spot they had used before, because they had learned over the years that always coming back to the same place to spy on your enemies could be dangerous. It was better to move around a mite.

From here, they could see what was left of the burned buildings, as well as the long adobe barracks where the workers brought at gunpoint from the village were forced to stay. Bo spotted a man with a rifle lounging on a stool beside the heavy door. Even at this distance, Bo could see that a thick bar rested in brackets across the door to keep it from opening outward. That seemed to confirm his theory that Davidson had shut down the mine for the time being and locked up his workers so that they couldn't cause trouble. Bo pointed out the guard to Scratch, who nodded.

"Bad news," Scratch whispered and pointed the

other way. Bo squinted and felt his heart sink as he saw the Gardner gun, still sitting on its tripod in the back of the same wagon where it had been the day before. The fire hadn't destroyed it after all.

That eliminated the possibility of freeing the workers and letting them revolt against Davidson's iron-fisted rule. Even an angry mob wouldn't be any match for that machine gun. Lancaster could just mow them down.

"We'll have to come up with some other plan," Bo whispered.

"Somebody's ridin' out." Scratch studied the man on horseback who started toward the mouth of the canyon and the valley beyond. "Danged if I don't think it's that young fella Alfred."

"If anybody can tell us what's going on in the canyon, it's him," Bo said. "Let's go."

"We gonna grab him?" Scratch asked with a grin.

"That's right. Davidson's got Teresa and Evangelina and Luz to use as hostages against us. Maybe we need a hostage of our own."

"There's one thing wrong with that plan, amigo . . . Davidson ain't gonna give a damn what happens to Alfred. You threaten to kill the boy—which I know you won't, to start with—Davidson would just tell you to go ahead and do it."

Bo shrugged as they started back toward the place where they had left the horses. "You're probably right, but at least he can give us some information if we can get him to talk."

Trailing the extra mounts behind them, they rode down out of the mountains and into the valley, then cut toward San Ramon. If Alfred's destination had been the village—and there was really nowhere else in the valley for him to go—he was probably there by now, but Bo figured they could grab him on his way back to the canyon.

As they approached the village, shots rang out in San Ramon, causing the Texans to rein in sharply. "What the hell?" Scratch muttered. "Who's shootin'? Not Alfred, I'd bet a hat on that."

"No, he's no gunman," Bo agreed. Several more shots blasted. Bo looked toward the tower where Davidson had posted a sharpshooter. It was quiet and dark. Running low on men as he was, Davidson might have decided to withdraw the rifleman and order him back to the canyon.

"Reckon we'd better try to slip into the village and see what's goin' on?" Scratch asked.

"I don't know what else we can— Hold it a minute. I hear a horse."

Sure enough, a rider was coming fast toward them, the drumming hoofbeats growing louder as they approached.

"Just one man," Bo judged. "Let's grab him."

They moved the horses into the shadows under some trees that grew along the creek meandering through the valley. The trail from San Ramon to Cutthroat Canyon ran along here, so Bo and Scratch weren't surprised a minute later when the hurrying rider came into view. The slice of moon and the stars floating in the sky overhead provided enough light for them to recognize him.

"It's Alfred," Bo whispered.

"And he's ridin' like all the devil dogs o' Hades are after him," Scratch added.

It was true. There was something panic-stricken about Alfred's nighttime ride. Bo and Scratch waited until he was almost even with their hiding place, then jabbed their heels into their horses' flanks and made the animals lunge out into the trail.

Alfred let out a startled yell. He hauled hard on the reins and tried to swerve around the Texans, but instead his horse reared up, pawing at the air with its forehooves. Alfred wasn't ready for that, and wasn't a good enough rider to cope with such a problem anyway. Arms flailing, he yelped again as he tumbled backward out of the saddle and fell heavily to the ground.

Scratch grabbed the reins of the now riderless horse while Bo dismounted and hurried over to Alfred. He drew his gun just in case, although he considered the likelihood of needing it very remote.

Alfred confirmed that hunch by trying to shield his head with his arms and moaning, "Don't kill me! Please don't kill me!"

"Take it easy, Alfred," Bo told him. "Nobody's going to hurt you."

Slowly, Alfred lowered his arms and stared up at Bo. "Mr. Creel?" he asked in amazement.

"That's right." Bo extended his left hand to the young man. "Let me help you up."

Alfred hesitated, then clasped Bo's wrist and let the Texan pull him to his feet. Alfred's clothes were disheveled from his fall, and lines of fear had etched themselves into his strained features.

"What in blazes is goin' on around here?" Scratch asked as he came up leading Alfred's horse. "What was that shootin' in the village?"

"Cordoba," Alfred said.

With a frown, Scratch asked, "Who?"

"You don't mean Bartolomeo Cordoba, do you?" Bo said.

Alfred's head bobbed in a weak nod.

Scratch looked over at Bo. "He's talkin' about the bandit Cordoba?"

"Well, he calls himself a revolutionary, but everybody knows he's just an outlaw," Bo said. "From what I hear, he has one of the most vicious gangs in all of Mexico."

Alfred used his hand to wipe sweat from his round face. "I can vouch for that. I saw what they did to Clancy."

"Now who's Clancy?" Scratch said.

"The man Mr. Davidson posted in the bell tower with a rifle."

"So he was still up there," Bo mused.

Alfred nodded. "That's right, he was . . . until Cordoba and his men rode into San Ramon and brought him down. They were in the church before he knew what was going on. He never had a chance."

"They killed him?"

Alfred nodded again. "But not before sending word to Mr. Davidson about what they plan to do."

"And that is?"

Alfred swallowed hard and said, "Take over the mine."

Bo and Scratch glanced at each other. The *bandidos* had heard about the gold in Cutthroat Canyon and wanted it for themselves. In a way, Bo was surprised that something like this hadn't happened before now.

"Go on," he told Alfred.

"Like I said, Cordoba sent word to the mine. He wanted Mr. Davidson to send someone to the village to hear his terms."

"Terms of surrender, you mean?"

"That's right. And . . . and I was the one Mr. Davidson picked for the job." A hollow laugh came from the young man. "I guess he figured I was the one he could most afford to lose if the bandits killed me. Mr. Davidson doesn't have many men left, you know."

"We figured as much," Scratch drawled. "We've done killed most of 'em."

"What about Cordoba?" Bo went on. "What does he want Davidson to do?"

"He told me to tell Mr. Davidson that . . . that if he'll surrender and leave the canyon, he and his men will be allowed to ride away unharmed."

Scratch snorted. "What a load of bull! If Davidson and his bunch come out into the open, those *bandidos*'ll shoot the hell out of 'em."

"That's what I thought, too," Alfred said with a nod. "But Cordoba insisted that I carry the message to Mr. Davidson." A shudder went through the young man. "I've never seen anyone so frightening in all my life. Cordoba's a huge man, with a bushy black beard and the eyes . . . the eyes of a madman! The whole time I was talking to him, I was afraid that he'd pull a gun and kill me without any warning."

Bo nodded. "He might have, if the mood struck him. He had a use for you, though, so he let you live." With a frown, Bo tugged on his earlobe. "Did he say anything about that machine gun of Lancaster's?"

"The Gardner gun?" Alfred shook his head. "He didn't mention it. Why?"

"Because he might not have heard about it. He may not have any idea that Davidson has a weapon like that."

"What difference does it make? Cordoba has fifty or sixty men, all of them killers!"

"Fella could make short work of sixty men with that devil gun," Scratch said. "Probably wouldn't take more'n a minute or two."

"The problem is, whoever's manning the gun would have to stay alive to use it," Bo pointed out. "Cordoba's men would be doing their best to pick him off."

Alfred stared at them. "Are you really trying to figure out a way to beat Cordoba? After all you've done to try to defeat Mr. Davidson? Why don't you just ride away and let Cordoba wipe him out?"

"Because Cordoba wouldn't stop with Davidson," Bo said. "Innocent folks would die in the fighting, too, and Cordoba won't treat the people of the valley any better than Davidson has. Plus Davidson is holding some of our friends prisoner. We don't want to see them in the hands of a man like Cordoba . . . assuming they even live through the ruckus."

"After seeing what they did to Clancy . . ." Alfred shook his head. "I can understand why you feel that way. I . . . I wouldn't want them to get Rosalinda in their power."

"What *did* happen to this fella Clancy?" Bo asked. "That's the second time you've mentioned it."

"They shot him. But I guess Cordoba wanted to impress upon me how dangerous he is, because he had Clancy tied to the well in the plaza." Alfred spread his arms and his legs to demonstrate. "Like this, you know. Then the men stood off at a distance and . . . and tried to see how many times they could shoot him without killing him. They kept just nicking him on his arms or his legs. One man shot off his ears. They . . . they just shot him to pieces, a little bit at a time, until he finally died. And Cordoba made me watch the whole thing."

Alfred's voice sounded like he was staring into some cosmic abyss filled with unnameable horrors as he described what he had witnessed. When he was finished, he shuddered again.

"It takes a plumb hydrophobia skunk to do somethin' like that," Scratch said.

Bo nodded. "I'd say you're right. What are you supposed to do now, Alfred?"

"I have to tell Mr. Davidson what Cordoba said. Cordoba is giving him until dawn to surrender."

"What if Davidson leaves the canyon tonight?"

"He can't," Alfred said. "Cordoba posted men at the mouth of the canyon to keep him bottled up inside. I had to pass under their guns when I rode out. It was terrifying, but I knew they had orders from Cordoba not to kill me . . . yet."

"Do you know how many there are?"

"Half a dozen or so. The rest are in San Ramon, celebrating the riches they're going to have. But if they hear any shooting from the canyon, they can get there in a hurry and finish off Mr. Davidson if he tries to escape."

Bo thought the situation over for a long moment. While he was thinking, Scratch said, "Seems to me like the only chance is to hit Cordoba before he expects it."

"That's right," Bo agreed. "We'll have to use the element of surprise . . . and that machine gun will be the biggest surprise of all."

Alfred said, "I can't believe that after everything that's happened, you're going to fight on Mr. Davidson's side again."

"You've heard of the lesser of two evils?"

Alfred nodded.

"Well, I'm not sure there is such a thing here," Bo said, "but Cordoba is the more pressing threat. I want you to ride back into the canyon and tell Davidson that we're offering him a truce. We'll help him take care of Cordoba."

"How in the world are you going to do that?"

"We're going to kill the men Cordoba posted at the mouth of the canyon," Bo said. "Once we've done that, Davidson and his men can attack Cordoba's forces in the village just before dawn. Lancaster will have that Gardner gun, and Scratch is going to be up in the bell tower with a Winchester so he can pick off some of the *bandidos* from there."

Scratch grinned. "So all I have to do is sneak through a whole village of hombres who'd like nothin' better than to kill me?"

"Yeah, that's about the size of it."

"I like it," Scratch said with a nod.

"That's not all, though," Bo went on as he put a hand on Alfred's shoulder. "Even with the machine gun, Davidson is going to be outnumbered. I'm sure he has plenty of extra guns in there. You'll have to convince him to turn loose the men who have been working in the mine and arm them so that they can fight against Cordoba, too."

Alfred started shaking his head even before Bo was finished. "He'll never do that. He won't let the villagers go. He can't trust them, after the way he's treated them."

"He'll have to, and the men will have to realize that they have a bigger enemy now than Davidson. It'll be up to you, and to Teresa, Rosalinda, and Evangelina, to convince them of that. If he can hit Cordoba with a force of thirty or forty men, plus that machine gun, he's got a chance of winning."

Alfred thought it over and finally began to nod slowly, as if realizing that the plan stood at least a chance of working. Anyway, it was better than surrender and certain death.

"If we win . . . what then?"

"We'll deal with that once the time comes. Maybe after we've been on the same side again, Scratch and I can get Davidson to listen to reason."

Bo knew that wasn't true. If they lived through the fight with Cordoba, Davidson would double-cross him and Scratch without hesitation and do his best to kill them.

But knowing that, maybe the two of them could be ready for it.

"First things first," Bo went on. "Tell us as best you can where Cordoba's men are hidden around the canyon mouth."

Alfred did so, reminding them, "I might not have seen all of them when I rode out. There could be more than I think."

"We'll keep that in mind. Give us about fifteen

minutes to get in position, then you ride through there just like you did before. They'll be expecting you."

"All right. But I'm not sure how you can kill six men without raising an alarm and warning Cordoba that something is going on."

"You leave that to us, young fella," Scratch said. "Bo and me was practically raised by Injuns. Skulkin' around comes natural to us."

"Good," Alfred said, "because Cordoba told me that a lot of his men are half-breed Yaquis . . . and they love to torture their prisoners."

CHAPTER 29

Bo and Scratch knew they were lucky not to have run into some of Cordoba's men when they rode down into the valley earlier that evening. Their horses' hoofbeats could have easily attracted the attention of the invading *bandidos*.

So they dismounted and led the horses into the grove of trees on the creek bank instead. They would leave the animals there for the time being. After the threat of the guards at the canyon mouth had been taken care of, they could retrieve the horses.

Bo had a good sense of time, and had been keeping track of it in his head as he and Scratch approached Cutthroat Canyon on foot. He knew that Alfred would reach the canyon mouth soon. Luckily, Cordoba's men had no way of knowing exactly when Alfred had left San Ramon, or they might wonder why it had taken him so long to get back to the canyon from the village.

The Texans dropped to their hands and knees and began crawling toward the canyon, so that their light-colored clothing wouldn't be as noticeable in the darkness. They stayed behind the sparse brush as much as possible.

Bo heard the clopping hoofbeats of Alfred's horse as the young man rode up. Someone challenged him in Spanish, and Alfred replied, "It . . . it's just me. Alfred. I rode to San Ramon before, remember?"

Several of the guards laughed at the sheer terror that was easy to hear in Alfred's voice. That helped Bo and Scratch locate them. One of the men asked, "You bring Bartolomeo's message for your boss, no?"

"Th-that's right."

"We heard the shots. You got to see our men play their favorite game, gringo?"

More laughter as Alfred nervously bobbed his head.

"Maybe before this is over we play the game with you, eh?"

"Señor Cordoba promised . . . promised that if we surrendered, we would be allowed to leave peacefully," Alfred managed to say.

"Oh, *sí,* sure, that's what I meant."

That provoked some hilarity, too. Another man stood up from behind a rock and waved Alfred on.

"Run on back to your boss, gringo," he commanded.

Alfred hurried, all right, bouncing awkwardly in the saddle as he prodded his horse into a run. As he disappeared into the shadows inside the canyon, Bo reflected that Alfred could have gone around San Ramon and kept riding if he had wanted to, not even pausing to get Cordoba's so-called surrender terms. Obviously, that option had never entered the young man's head. He wasn't going to abandon Rosalinda to whatever fate might await her at the hands of the bandits, which certainly wouldn't be anything good.

Once Alfred was gone, the guards exchanged a few lewd comments among themselves about his manhood, then settled down to keep watch on the canyon mouth again. By this time, Bo and Scratch had a pretty good idea where all of them were. Using hand signals to communicate, the Texans decided that Bo would take the three men to the left of the canyon, while Scratch handled the trio of guards to the right. They had to do it without making any racket, too, because gunshots would bring Cordoba and the rest of the *bandidos* charging out from San Ramon.

The night had to remain as quiet and apparently peaceful as it was now. Death, like fog, would come creeping.

Cordoba had given Davidson until dawn to make up his mind about surrendering, so there was no hurry. Bo took his time crawling toward the outermost guard on his side of the canyon. He planned to work his way in toward the opening, one guard at a time.

When he was close enough to the first man to smell sweat and the greasy buckskins the man wore, he slipped his knife from behind his belt noiselessly. The guard shifted and cleared his throat.

That was the last sound he made. Bo came up behind him, clamped his left hand over the man's mouth and jerked his head back, and used his right hand to draw the blade quickly across the guard's throat. A hot flood gushed over Bo's hand as blood sprayed out from the gaping wound. The guard died almost instantly.

Carefully, Bo lowered the corpse to the ground

and started toward the next man, moving as quietly as a cat or an Indian. Just as Bo came up behind him, the guard turned his head to spit chewing tobacco on the rocks at his feet. He must have seen a flicker of movement from the corner of his eye as Bo closed in on him, because he tried to twist around and bring up the rifle he held.

Bo struck swiftly, swiping the knife across the man's throat in a sweeping blow. More blood splashed on him. The guard's mouth opened as he tried to yell a warning. He wouldn't be able to force a shout through his ruined throat, but he might manage to gurgle loudly enough to be heard. Bo couldn't afford that. His free hand shot out and caught hold of the guard's face, the fingers digging in on either side of the man's mouth, which formed an O under the pressure of Bo's grip. The bandit shivered and shook in his death throes, his eyes wide and staring into Bo's from a distance of less than a foot.

It didn't take long for life to fade from those eyes. Again, Bo lowered the dead man to the ground without a sound.

That left just one man on his side of the canyon mouth, and Bo hoped that Scratch was having equal success on the other side. Judging by the lack of an uproar, that was probably the case. Bo crept closer to the last man, and was about to strike when the guard suddenly whirled around as if someone had shouted a warning in his ear.

Too late, Bo realized what had alerted the guard to the lurking menace behind him. Bo had spilled a lot of blood in the past few minutes, and quite a bit of it had gotten on him. The sharp, coppery scent of the stuff filled his nostrils—and the guard must have smelled it, too, and recognized it for what it was. He had known that someone coming up behind him covered with fresh blood couldn't be a good thing.

Bo saw the rifle barrel coming toward him, and lunged at the guard. He didn't try to grab the weapon and force the barrel skyward or toward the ground. Instead he slapped his left hand down on top of the breech so that when the guard jerked the trigger and the hammer fell, it caught the web of skin and flesh between his thumb and first finger instead of the firing pin striking the cartridge in the chamber. The rifle didn't go off.

Bo crashed into the guard and knocked him over backward. As the man fell he howled, "Paco! Jorge!"

The two names were all he got out before Bo landed on top of him, drove the knife into his belly, and ripped the blade to the side as hard as he could, first one way and then the other. The wound was so big that Bo's whole hand plunged into it, and he felt the bandit's guts writhing around his fingers like snakes.

Bo jerked his hand out of the man's belly and smashed the handle of the knife into the man's mouth, feeling teeth shatter under the blow. The guard might not have felt it, though, because he was already close to dying. He shuddered and went the rest of the way over the divide.

Bo didn't think it was likely that anyone back in San Ramon had heard the shout, although he couldn't rule it out. He rolled off the body. The rifle's hammer still pinched the skin of his other hand. He got hold of it and eared the hammer back, freeing his hand. It hurt like blazes where the hammer had dug into it. He shook the hand, trying to ease the pain.

"Bo!" The urgent whisper came from Scratch. "You all right?"

"Yeah," Bo told his old friend as Scratch loomed up out of the shadows. "No real harm done. What about your three?"

"Dead as they can be. I had a little trouble with the last one, but he didn't raise too much of a ruckus."

Bo grunted. "Same here. Did you see any more?"

"Nope. I'd say ol' Alfred was right about there only bein' six of 'em."

"Then as long as nobody comes to relieve them before morning, we're all right," Bo said.

"As long as Davidson goes along with the plan," Scratch pointed out.

"I don't reckon he's got much choice about that," Bo said. "Not if he wants even a chance to live."

To the Texans' surprise, about a half hour later, a soft call sounded from just inside the canyon mouth as they waited there. "Creel! Morton! Are you out there?"

Bo straightened from the rock where he had been sitting. "Davidson? Is that you?"

"Yeah. We need to parley. Are Cordoba's men dead?"

"They are," Bo said. "Come on out here if you want to . . . alone."

Davidson stepped out of the shadows into the

fading moonlight. He carried a rifle, and even in the dim light Bo could tell that his once-handsome face was haggard from strain.

"You took a chance coming out here," Bo commented. "Those bandits could have still been lurking."

"Not that much of a chance," Davidson said, and from the shadows a grim chuckle confirmed it.

"We'd have had it out right here and now if we'd had to," Jim Skinner said. "I'll still do it. You don't know how much I want to kill you, Creel."

"That's enough," Davidson snapped. "I hate these two bastards as much as you do, Skinner, but it appears that we need them at the moment."

"I'd say you need all the fightin' men you can get," Scratch drawled. He hadn't started for the bell tower yet, but he would be leaving soon in order to give himself time to infiltrate the village and climb to the top of the tower before dawn.

"Fightin' men is one thing," Skinner said. "Traitorous, murderin' sons o' bitches are another."

"There's an old sayin' about the pot and the kettle," Scratch shot back.

Davidson said, "Take it easy, both of you. If we're going to deal with Cordoba, we need to work out the plan we're going to use."

"Didn't Alfred tell you what we have in mind?" Bo asked.

"He told me, but he's so scared I can't be sure that he's got all of it right. If we're going to be fighting side by side, I want to hear it from your own mouth, Creel."

"Fair enough." Quickly, Bo sketched in the same plan he had told Alfred to pass along to Davidson.

Skinner objected when Bo came to the part about freeing and arming the men locked up in the barracks. "Boss, you can't turn those damn dirty greasers loose. They won't fight for you."

"They won't be fighting for Davidson," Bo said. "They'll be fighting for themselves. They don't want to live under Cordoba's thumb. Let Teresa and Rosalinda and Evangelina talk to them. They'll make the rest of them see that they've got to go along."

For a moment, Davidson didn't respond. Then he sighed and said bitterly, "I had things under control here, except for those holdups, until you and Morton came to Cutthroat Canyon. I didn't realize you'd ruin everything."

"That's what happens to little tin-plated dictators," Scratch said. "Sooner or later, justice comes callin'."

Back in the shadows, Skinner grunted disdainfully. "Justice! There's no such thing. Only money and power . . . and death. Justice belongs to the man with the fastest gun."

"We'll see about that one of these days," Bo promised. "For now, let's concentrate on Cordoba."

"All right," Davidson said, his voice abrupt as if he had just reached a decision. "We'll go along with what you say, Creel. We'll even turn those peasants loose. But remember, I've got Lancaster and his machine gun. If they don't follow orders, I might as well go ahead and slaughter all of them. They won't be doing me any good."

"It won't come to that," Bo said—but in the back of his mind, he knew it might. It would all depend on what happened in the battle with Cordoba and the rest of the *bandidos*.

He went on. "We'll approach the town quietly, on foot. Men will have to carry the machine gun, because we can't use the wagon. The bandits are celebrating in the village, so most of them will be getting drunk and sleepy by now. Cordoba plans to ride out to the canyon with his men at dawn to get your decision. If we hit them a half hour *before* dawn, they won't be expecting it."

Bo glanced at the stars. "That gives us a couple of hours to get ready. Gather your forces here at the canyon mouth. I'll be waiting for you. By then, Scratch will be up in the bell tower at the church with a rifle."

"I'm obliged for the vote of confidence," Scratch said with a grin. "Hope I don't get killed on the way and let you down."

"You won't," Bo said.

"What about when it's over?" Davidson asked.

"You mean if we win and we're still alive?"

"Exactly."

Bo had thought about that possibility quite a bit, and he knew what he wanted to say to Davidson. "Then you take whatever gold you've got on hand and go. The mine belongs to the people of the valley now."

"What?" Skinner exclaimed. "Hell, no!"

Davidson raised a hand to forestall any more protests from the skull-faced gunman. "Hold on." He turned back to Bo. "We ride out free and clear? You don't try to set the Mexican law on us?"

"That's right," Bo said. "You must have made quite a bit of money off that mine already. You'll come out all right, Davidson. You'll still be a rich man. More than that, you'll still be alive."

"There's still a fortune in that canyon. I could be a lot richer man."

"You could also be a lot deader man," Bo said.

Davidson laughed. "Well, that's true. All right. You've got a deal. You keep those greasers from mobbing us, and we'll ride away."

"Boss!" Skinner said. "All that gold!"

"My mind is made up," Davidson said in a hard tone that brooked no argument. "Of course, we still have to live through the fight with Cordoba."

Skinner continued muttering to himself. Bo ignored the gunman and said, "Be here an hour before dawn. It'll take us at least thirty minutes to get everybody in position for the attack."

"We'll be here," Davidson promised. He lifted a hand in farewell and faded back into the shadows.

When Davidson and Skinner were gone, Scratch said quietly to Bo, "That varmint ain't gonna keep the bargain he made. You know that, don't you, Bo?"

"I know it," Bo said. "Once we're finished with Cordoba, we'll have another fight on our hands."

Scratch grinned. "No rest for the wicked, eh?"

"Well, there hasn't been much in more than forty years since San Jacinto, has there?" Bo asked with a chuckle.

CHAPTER 30

Scratch headed off into the dark night a short time later, after the moon had set, leaving Bo to wait for Porter Davidson and the makeshift army the man was going to put together. He hoped that he was right and the three young women from the village would be able to persuade the men to fight on behalf of their former oppressor. Otherwise, even the machine gun might not be enough to tip the odds in their favor.

Bo couldn't help but reflect on everything that had happened. If he and Scratch hadn't run into Davidson in El Paso and agreed to come down here in the first place, no one would have challenged the man's iron-fisted rule of the valley, at least not effectively.

On the other hand, if he and Scratch hadn't killed so many of Davidson's men, Davidson would have been better equipped to handle the threat of Bartolomeo Cordoba's *bandidos*. But in the long run, whether Davidson or Cordoba emerged victorious from that battle, things would not have changed for the people of San Ramon. Giving them the chance for freedom made it all worthwhile.

Fighting the good fight was always worth the risk.

The stars continued their stately, almost indiscernible progression across the heavens, and about an hour before dawn, as the faintest tinge of gray began to appear in the eastern sky, Bo heard movement in the canyon. He tightened his grip on the rifle he held, just in case Davidson planned to try some sort of double cross.

That wasn't the case, however. Instead, Davidson called softly, "Creel!"

"Right here," Bo replied.

Davidson stepped out of the canyon. Jim Skinner, Douglas, and Lancaster followed him. Behind them came Wallace and the few remaining supervisors from the mine.

Then, to Bo's surprise, he saw Alfred step out into the starlight. The young man clutched a rifle and looked very uncomfortable about doing so—but he was there, willing to fight, if not all that ready or able.

Rosalinda, Teresa, Evangelina, and Luz followed Alfred out of the canyon, and with them came two dozen grim-faced men in peasant clothing—the workers from the mine. A few of them carried rifles, more had pistols, and a few were armed only with machetes or pickaxes. A pickax wielded by a strong man could be a fearsome weapon in close combat, if it came to that.

Evangelina spotted Bo and ran over to him. She threw her arms around him and said, "Señor Bo! Alfred told us you were alive, but I still feared it was not so."

Feeling a little uncomfortable about having a nubile young woman embracing him like that, Bo said, "Yeah, I'm fine, and so is Scratch. Shouldn't you ladies stay in the canyon until the fighting is over, though?"

Teresa gave that familiar defiant toss of her head. "You can say that after everything you have seen? We have as big a stake in this fight as anyone, Señor Creel."

"This is true," Luz added. She hefted the pistol in her hand. "All I ask is the chance to get one of those bandits in my sights."

Bo knew Luz well enough to know that wasn't strictly true. She was still interested in the gold, too. But he said, "You'll have the chance." He looked the group over and then turned to Davidson. "Where's the machine gun?"

"It's coming," Lancaster answered instead. "Several of the lads are bringing it."

Sure enough, four of the men from the village came into sight a moment later. Two of them carried a crate each, probably full of ammunition, while the other two carried the gun itself, one at each end. The Gardner was still mounted on its tripod.

"You'll need to set up so that you can cover the plaza," Bo told Lancaster. "Some of Cordoba's men will already be there, and when the others hear the shooting, that's probably where they'll head when they come out of the buildings." Bo raised his voice a little as he turned to the other men and went on. "The rest of us will work our way through the village, cleaning out the bandits as we come to them. It's going to be bloody, dangerous work, and not all of us will survive. But if we can wipe out Cordoba and his men, the people of San Ramon can live in peace once again."

Judging from the sullen looks on the faces of the men, not all of them believed him. They had lived under the brutal oppression of Davidson and his supervisors for months, and now here they were, fighting to save the lives of the men they hated most. It was odd how things worked out sometimes, Bo thought. But he could also tell from the grim determination he saw that the men realized Cordoba was the greater danger—for the moment.

He turned to the Englishman and said, "Lancaster, you and the men with the machine gun go on ahead. Be mighty careful about it, though. You can't afford to make any noise and warn Cordoba's men that something is about to happen."

Lancaster nodded. "Understood." He held out his hand. "We've fought together, and we've battled against each other, Creel. I'm glad that for now we're on the same side again."

Bo shook his hand and said, "So am I." He didn't harbor any illusions about what might happen after the battle with Cordoba's men was over, though. At that point, Lancaster would be working for Davidson again—assuming that either of them was still alive.

Lancaster and the men with the machine gun set off toward the village. Bo made sure that the others all understood what they were to do, and then they started toward San Ramon, too. The little army moved quietly through the graying darkness.

Bo glanced toward the spot where the bell tower was located, even though he couldn't see it. Scratch ought to be up there by now. Worry for his old friend and trail partner nagged at Bo's mind. He trusted Scratch more than anyone else in the world, and had great confidence in the silver-haired Texan's ability to take care of himself.

But everybody's luck ran out sooner or later. The odds always caught up with a fella.

Not this morning, he thought, sending up a prayer to El Señor Dios. Not today.

Instead of dragging, time now seemed to race by. Almost before Bo knew it, they were right outside the village. He had never been a general—or any other kind of officer—but he lined up his troops, splitting them so that they could attack on the flanks and the machine gun would cover the center. He moved along the ranks, pausing for an encouraging word here and there. He made sure that the women were in the rear, although Teresa argued with him about that. Evangelina and Rosalinda persuaded her to go along with Bo's wishes.

"Don't worry," Bo assured her. "You'll get to fight." He added one of Scratch's favorite sayings. "I'd bet a hat on that."

When he came to Skinner, the skull-faced gunman sneered and said, "When this is over, Creel, we'll settle things. Don't forget."

"I'm not likely to," Bo said.

He moved on and nodded to Douglas. Quietly, the kid said, "If I'm alive in an hour, I'm riding away, Creel. Just thought you'd like to know."

"You're not working for Davidson anymore?"

"I've had enough. I've fought in range wars and railroad wars and just about every sort of war you can think of. But I don't like what he did to the people down here. I'm tired of it stickin' in my craw."

"Does Davidson know about that?"

Douglas shrugged. "I don't work for the man anymore. It's none of his business. And for what it's worth, Lancaster said he's been thinking about it and feels the same way. He told me to tell you, if I got a chance."

"I'm obliged," Bo said with a nod. He believed the kid. Even though they had tried to kill each other on several occasions, he was glad that he wouldn't have to throw down on Douglas and Lancaster again, even though their defection from Davidson's cause took him a little by surprise.

When he reached Alfred, he put a hand on the young man's shoulder and felt the trembling that went through Alfred's body. "You'll be fine," Bo told him. "Just keep your eyes open and your wits about you."

"I . . . I never fought in any battles before."

"Maybe you'll be lucky and you'll never have to again."

That probably wouldn't be the case, though, Bo thought. A man always had battles to fight, even when they didn't involve shooting. The only sure way to avoid trouble was not to live. Bo didn't figure it was worth it.

He came to Porter Davidson, who gave him a curt nod and said, "A lot has happened since that first night in El Paso, hasn't it?"

"Seems like more than a couple of weeks ago."

"It certainly does. You've bested me, Creel. I'm not quite sure how you did it, but you have. I'll be leaving Cutthroat Canyon and this valley a beaten man. I hope you're happy."

Bo didn't believe him any more now than he had earlier. But he just said, "I'll be happy when these folks are free again. That's all."

"You'll understand if I don't wish you good luck?"

Bo laughed. "I'd be shocked if you did."

He glanced at the sky, saw that it had lightened considerably more, and knew the time had come. He moved to the head of the left flank, raised his Winchester over his head so that everyone could see it, and then brought his arm forward in a sweeping signal to attack.

The men on both flanks broke into a run. Bare feet and feet shod in rope sandals or boots pounded against the ground. Cordoba must have posted a few guards, but the men were sleepy or hungover or both, and obviously didn't notice what was happening until the attackers reached the edge of the village. Then, a man in a sombrero with little decorative balls dangling from the brim lurched up from where he had been slumped in a doorway and yelled at the top of his lungs. He started to lift his rifle.

On the dead run, Bo shot him in the chest. The slug knocked the *bandido* back through the doorway.

More of the bandits stumbled out of the buildings. Those who had been curled up in their blankets in the plaza leaped to their feet to see what the commotion was about. Rifles and pistols began to pop, and the machine gun suddenly opened up with a chattering roar. Streams of lead played back and forth across the plaza with lethal results.

Bandits went down, shredded into gory ruin by the pounding bullets.

Cordoba's men weren't going to be defeated without a fight, though. Orange spurts of muzzle flame filled the predawn murkiness. Bullets whined around Bo's head like angry, lethal insects. He emptied the Winchester; then, as one of the bandits rushed him, swinging a big knife, Bo rammed the barrel of the empty rifle into the man's belly. When the bandit doubled over in pain, Bo brought the Winchester's stock down on his head. The blow landed with the satisfying crunch of bone.

Just then, pain lanced into his left calf. He stumbled, and that leg went out from under him. He knew he'd been hit, but he couldn't tell how bad it was. He thought the wound was just a crease, but he couldn't be sure about that and didn't have time to check, because a wild-eyed bandit loomed over him, swinging the muzzle of a revolver toward him.

As Bo looked up at his would-be killer, he saw the church's bell tower behind the man. Just as the gun came even with Bo's head, something flashed in the tower. The bandit's head practically exploded as a .44-40 slug bored through his brain and burst out with a spray of blood and bone splinters. The dead man collapsed, landing next to Bo.

That pretty much answered the question of whether or not Scratch had made it safely into the tower.

Bo tossed the empty rifle aside, grabbed the gun out of the dead bandit's hand, and struggled to his feet. He drew the Colt on his hip, and with an iron in each hand he limped forward, firing to the left and right at the *bandidos* who were running around in a near panic.

A hoarse shout made him look around. He saw Alfred swinging an empty rifle like a club, smashing down the bandits who surrounded him like old Davy Crockett at the Alamo. Alfred stumbled and went down, though, as one of Cordoba's men sunk a knife into his body. The man yanked the blade free, and was about to stab Alfred again when Bo put a .45 round through his brain.

With a flash of skirts, Rosalinda came out of the clouds of powder smoke and dust that had begun to roll over the village. She had a six-gun in her hand, and taking the other bandits by surprise, she blasted them away and then stood protectively over Alfred like a mountain lioness defending her fallen mate.

The machine gun fell silent. Bo didn't know if it had jammed or was out of bullets, or if Lancaster had been hit. When it resumed its stuttering thunder a moment later, he knew that the Englishman had just been reloading.

He heard another sort of roar a second later, and wheeled around to see a tall, massively shouldered man with a bushy black beard laying waste to everyone around him with a pickax he must have picked up where one of the wounded mine workers had dropped it. Based on Alfred's description, that was Bartolomeo Cordoba, Bo decided.

He fired at the bandit leader, but the hammers of both guns clicked on empty chambers. The Colts were empty, and there was no time to reload because Cordoba had spotted him and now charged at him with surprising speed for a man of his bulk, swinging the pickax at Bo's head as he did so.

Bo dropped under the deadly blow and rolled into Cordoba's legs. With another enraged roar, the bandit fell over him and toppled to the ground. Bo tried to roll away, but a huge, hamlike hand grabbed him and slung him back down. Cordoba's crushing weight landed on top of him, pinning him to the ground, and the bandit leader's thick fingers wrapped around Bo's neck and began choking the life out of him.

The empty revolvers had slipped out of Bo's hands, so he couldn't even use them as clubs. He tried heaving his body off the ground and throwing Cordoba to the side, but it was no use. The man was just too big and heavy. A red haze slid over Bo's vision as Cordoba's hands tightened more and more around his neck.

But if Cordoba was using both hands to choke him, Bo suddenly realized, that meant he had dropped the pickax, just as Bo had dropped the guns. Bo began slapping desperately at the ground on both sides of him as his eyes began to bug out from their sockets due to the pressure Cordoba was putting on his throat. Sweat from the massive bandit's face dripped into Bo's face as Cordoba loomed over him.

The fingers of Bo's right hand brushed against something metal. He closed his hand around it, pulled it toward him, shifted his grip so that he held the pickax's shaft just below the head. He swung it up with all the strength he had left, and with a solid *thunk!* the sharp end of the tool sunk for a depth of several inches into Cordoba's brain.

With a bull-like bellow, Cordoba let go of Bo and lurched to his feet. The pickax went with him, buried as it was in his skull. The bandit staggered, turned around in a circle, and then collapsed into a grisly heap. The fall dislodged the pickax. Blood and gray matter oozed thickly from the hole in his head as he spasmed and died.

Gasping as he dragged air through his bruised throat, Bo rolled onto his side and pushed himself to his hands and knees, then to his feet. He realized that the machine gun was silent again, but this time, so were all the other guns. A breeze had sprung up with the dawn, and it eddied the clouds of smoke around the huts in the village.

Bodies lay scattered everywhere. Most of them belonged to Cordoba's men, but Bo saw quite a few of the men from the village as well. He grimaced as he spotted Douglas lying on the ground with half a dozen dead bandits around him. The kid's eyes were open, and he had a single bullet hole in the middle of his forehead. What a damned waste, Bo thought. Douglas might have amounted to something one of these days, if he had lived long enough. But he had made his choice to live by the gun, and he had died by it as well. Chances were, he would have wanted it that way.

"Señor Bo!"

That was Evangelina's voice. Bo turned toward it and saw the young woman hurrying toward him, a pistol in her hand. Teresa was with her, and so was Luz. None of them seemed to be hurt, and he was relieved to see that.

"Are you all right, Señor Bo?" Evangelina asked as she came up to him.

He nodded wearily, then looked down at his left leg. The calf was bloody, but as he had thought, the bullet had just plowed a furrow across the outside of it. "I'll be limping for a while," he said, "but at my age, that's nothing unusual."

He tucked the extra gun behind his belt and began reloading the other gun. As he thumbed the fresh cartridges into the cylinder, he looked toward the bell tower, which was visible again now that the smoke and dust had thinned somewhat. He didn't see anybody moving around up there, and felt a pang of worry. If Cordoba's men had noticed during the battle that someone was firing at them from the tower—

"Still in one piece, I see."

The familiar voice brought a grin to Bo's face. Scratch came out of the smoke as well, Winchester canted over his shoulder. Bo gave him a nod and said, "You hit?"

"Nope. I don't think those varmints ever figured out I was up there. I downed damn near a dozen of 'em before the smoke got too thick for me to see anything. Figured I might as well climb down."

Bo turned to Teresa and said, "Alfred's hurt over there. You might see if you can give your sister a hand with him."

Teresa hurried toward Rosalinda and Alfred, and Evangelina and Luz trailed along behind. The men from the village who had survived the battle began to gather in the plaza.

There were no survivors among Cordoba's men.

"Seen Davidson?" Scratch asked.

Bo shook his head. "Not since the fighting started. I don't know if he made it or not."

That question was answered the next moment, though, when Davidson's voice called out clearly in the early morning air, "They're all together now! Mow them down!"

CHAPTER 31

Bo wasn't surprised by the order. From the start, he had expected Davidson to go back on his word. As he and Scratch turned toward the edge of the village, he knew that everything now depended on Lancaster.

Would the Englishman follow the order—or, as Douglas had told Bo earlier, had he had enough of doing Davidson's killing for him?

Bo and Scratch found themselves facing Davidson, Skinner, Wallace, and two more of Davidson's men. They stood next to the machine gun, behind which Lancaster still crouched, gripping the weapon's handles.

Bo heard movement behind him and glanced back to see the four women coming forward to join the Texans, along with Alfred. Rosalinda was next to him, her arm around his waist to help him. All the women held guns.

Behind them were the villagers, the ones who had been laboring in the mine as well as the women and children and old men who had been trying to eke out a living from the farms that their menfolk could no longer work because Davidson had enslaved them.

Bo lifted his voice and called, "You're outnumbered for a change, Davidson. You can still take that deal I offered you."

A harsh laugh came from Davidson. "And leave all the gold that's still in the ground? The hell with that! It's all mine, Creel, and nobody's going to take it away from me. Certainly not a couple of broken-down old men and a bunch of greasers." He looked past Bo. "Alfred, get clear of them while you've got the chance."

"No, sir," Alfred answered. His voice was weak, but he didn't hesitate. "I quit. I should have quit a long time ago, when I saw what a monster you were turning into."

Davidson's face darkened with anger. "All right then. Have it your own way, you damned fool. You can die along with that whore of yours."

"She's *not* a whore! And nothing you did can turn her into one, you bastard!"

"That's enough." Davidson turned his head. "I told you to shoot them, Lancaster!"

Slowly, the Englishman straightened up, let go of the machine gun's handles, and stepped back. "No, I don't think so," he replied coolly. "Creel, did the kid tell you what I said?"

Bo nodded. "He did."

"It still goes. My honor has been sullied enough. I'm done here."

Davidson wheeled toward him. "You damned traitor! You took my money!"

"Yes, well, we all make mistakes from time to time, old boy," Lancaster said with a smile.

Davidson jerked his gun up and fired at the Englishman. At the same time, Skinner's hand flashed toward his Colt as he yelled, "Time to start the ball, Creel!"

Everything else went away. Bo didn't see anything except Jim Skinner. His hand moved.

When people talked about fast draws, now that Wild Bill Hickok was dead, they mentioned Smoke Jensen, John Wesley Hardin, Falcon McCallister, Ben Thompson, Matt Bodine, and the other famous shootists and pistoleers. Nobody ever said, *That Bo Creel, he's really slick on the draw.*

Because he wasn't. Faster than most maybe, but not in the same league as those others—or as Jim Skinner.

But every man has those moments, those split seconds of shaved time, when he reaches inside himself and finds things that normally aren't there. The courage to stand and fight when he wants to run away, the compassion to reach out to a friend, the strength to lift something that no man should even be able to budge.

The speed and coordination and keenness of eye to outdraw a man who, on any other day, was faster.

This was one of those moments for Bo Creel.

He palmed out the Colt and killed Jim Skinner, putting two bullets in Skinner's chest before the skull-faced gunman could even get off a shot. Skinner rocked back, his eyes filling with pain and surprise in the second before they went glassy in death.

What had seemed like an eternity was really less than the blink of an eye. Davidson's gun roared and Lancaster went down. Wallace and the other men began firing toward Bo, Scratch, and their allies. Shots slammed out from Scratch's rifle and the women's pistols as they returned the fire. Davidson's men tried to scatter, but slugs ripped into them, knocking them off their feet.

Evangelina screamed as she stalked forward, the gun in her hand erupting with flame and smoke as she emptied it into Wallace. He stumbled backward, his own gun sagging as the bullets pounded into him. He collapsed, and Evangelina stood over him and planted her last bullet in the middle of his face. With her chest heaving, she slowly lowered the gun.

That left Davidson as the only enemy still on his feet. He dropped his Colt and lunged toward the machine gun. Bo knew that if Davidson got his hands on the Gardner, he could still wipe them all out. He snapped a shot at Davidson, the revolver bucking in his hand.

Davidson staggered, but stayed on his feet. He reached the machine gun, lunged for the trigger—

Bo and Scratch fired at the same instant. The .45 slug and the .44-40 round from the Winchester smashed into Davidson's chest simultaneously and drove him backward off his feet. He lay there gasping and twitching as blood welled from the holes in his body.

Bo and Scratch approached him cautiously. Davidson stared up at them, his mouth working. "You . . . you damned . . ." he managed to say.

"You should have taken the deal," Bo told him.

Davidson's head fell to the side. He stopped moving.

Scratch looked at Skinner, who lay a few yards away. He nodded toward the skull-faced gunman and said, "That varmint was right about one thing anyway."

"What's that?" Bo asked.

"Today, at least, justice belonged to the man with the fastest gun."

"I don't reckon I ever saw you slap leather like that in all your borned days," Scratch was saying later as he grinned across a table at Bo. The villagers had dragged out the table, along with others, into the plaza, where a fiesta of sorts was now going on. The celebration was tempered by the fact that earlier in the day, in the aftermath of the two battles, they had buried a number of friends and loved ones.

Bo took a sip of tequila and grinned. "Nothing focuses a fella's attention quite so much as some hombre trying to kill him."

"Yeah, well, wait'll folks hear that you outdrew Jim Skinner."

Bo shuddered. "Let's just keep that to ourselves. The last thing I need at my age is a rep as a fast gun."

"Suit yourself," Scratch said with a shrug. "We live such a damn peaceful life anyway, I can see why you wouldn't want to mess it up."

Bo laughed. His wounded leg was stretched out and propped up on a stool. Bandages swathed his bullet-creased calf.

Luz came out of the hut behind them and sat down at the table. She regarded the dancing and laughing and guitar-playing going on in the plaza and then said, "There will be many babies born in this village nine months from now."

"You reckon so?" Scratch asked with a grin.

"Nothing flies in the face of death so much as life," Luz said. "And speaking of life, it appears that Alfred and the Englishman will both pull through. They will need to be nursed back to health, though. Luckily for them, there will be no shortage of volunteers. Rosalinda will take care of Alfred, and Teresa seems taken with the Englishman."

Quietly, Bo said, "I wish Pepe had pulled through, too."

For a moment, a shadow passed over Luz's face. "Some things are not meant to be," she said. "I have a gold mine—well, part of one anyway—but I think I might trade it if only I could . . ."

She didn't finish, but Bo knew what she meant.

They sat in silence for a few moments; then Scratch said, "I reckon I'll ride out to the canyon tomorrow and see if I can find our horses or any of our gear. I'd sure like to get those Remingtons of mine back."

"You can buy whatever you want," Luz pointed out. "Everyone wants to give you and Bo shares in the gold mine, too."

"We might take some of the profits to get ourselves outfitted again," Bo said, "but after that, I'd just as soon see the money go to the folks here in the village."

"Yeah," Scratch agreed. "I've done thought it

over, and bein' a rich man is a blight and a curse. I don't think I ever knew a rich man who was plumb happy. Not that I've knowed all that many rich men, you understand."

Luz put her hands on the table and pushed herself to her feet. "Do what you wish about the gold," she said. "Right now, I think I will go out there in the plaza and dance like the others who are simply glad to be alive."

Scratch stood up and offered her his arm. "I sort of feel the same way myself."

Luz linked her arm with his, and smiling, they went off to join the fiesta.

Bo leaned back in his chair and sighed. The past couple of weeks had been pretty hellacious, but now he and Scratch had the chance to rest up a mite before they drifted on again. He figured it would be a couple more weeks before they started feeling too restless again . . .

Someone sat down beside him. He looked over and saw Evangelina. She smiled at him, and once again he noticed that when she did that, the scars on her face didn't seem to matter near as much.

Bo nodded toward the fiesta going on in the plaza. "Don't you feel like celebrating?" he asked her. "I don't reckon you'd have much trouble finding some young fella to dance with you."

With that serene smile still on her face, she looked out at the plaza and said, "I am where I want to be."

Then she reached over and took hold of his hand.

Bo started to pull away from her. For some reason, he didn't. But he did say, "Dadgum it, Evangelina, I'm old enough to be your grandfather!"

"Perhaps. But you are *not* my grandfather."

"Well . . . no. I reckon I'm not. But if you think you've got to associate with some leathery old coot like me out of gratitude or because . . . because of what happened to you . . ."

He stopped as she shook her head.

"As I told you, I am where I want to be." Her hand tightened on his. "Exactly where I want to be." She turned to look at him again, and he felt the power of her smile even more strongly than before. "What about you, Bo?"

He swallowed. "I don't reckon I can dance with this shot-up leg of mine."

"Then we shall have to find some other way to celebrate the return of freedom to my people."

Scratch was never going to let him hear the end of this, he thought, but then he nodded and returned Evangelina's smile and told her, "I reckon we can do that."

THE LAST GUNFIGHTER SERIES BY
WILLIAM W. JOHNSTONE